# GHOST IN THE GARDEN

## SILVER AND GREY
### BOOK 3

## MARY LANCASTER

DRAGONBLADE PUBLISHING, INC.

Dragonblade Publishing, Inc. is an imprint of Kathryn Le Veque Novels, Inc.
P.O. Box 23
Moreno Valley, CA 92556
ceo@dragonbladepublishing.com

Produced in the United States of America

First Edition May 2025
Trade Paperback Edition

# ARE YOU SIGNED UP FOR DRAGONBLADE'S BLOG?

You'll get the latest news and information on exclusive giveaways, exclusive excerpts, coming releases, sales, free books, cover reveals and more.

Check out our complete list of authors, too!

No spam, no junk. That's a promise!

## Sign Up Here

www.dragonbladepublishing.com

*Dearest Reader;*

*Thank you for your support of a small press. At Dragonblade Publishing, we strive to bring you the highest quality Historical Romance from some of the best authors in the business. Without your support, there is no 'us', so we sincerely hope you adore these stories and find some new favorite authors along the way.*

*Happy Reading!*

*CEO, Dragonblade Publishing*

# ADDITIONAL DRAGONBLADE BOOKS BY AUTHOR MARY LANCASTER

**Silver and Grey Series**
Murder in Moonlight (Book 1)
Evidence of Evil (Book 2)
Ghost in the Garden (Book 3)

**One Night in Blackhaven Series**
The Captain's Old Love (Book 1)
The Earl's Promised Bride (Book 2)
The Soldier's Impossible Love (Book 3)
The Gambler's Last Chance (Book 4)
The Poet's Stern Critic (Book 5)
The Rake's Mistake (Book 6)
The Spinster's Last Dance (Book 7)

**The Duel Series**
Entangled (Book 1)
Captured (Book 2)
Deserted (Book 3)
Beloved (Book 4)
Haunted (Novella)

**Last Flame of Alba Series**
Rebellion's Fire (Book 1)
A Constant Blaze (Book 2)
Burning Embers (Book 3)

**Gentlemen of Pleasure Series**
The Devil and the Viscount (Book 1)
Temptation and the Artist (Book 2)
Sin and the Soldier (Book 3)
Debauchery and the Earl (Book 4)

Blue Skies (Novella)

**Pleasure Garden Series**
Unmasking the Hero (Book 1)
Unmasking Deception (Book 2)
Unmasking Sin (Book 3)
Unmasking the Duke (Book 4)
Unmasking the Thief (Book 5)

**Crime & Passion Series**
Mysterious Lover (Book 1)
Letters to a Lover (Book 2)
Dangerous Lover (Book 3)
Lost Lover (Book 4)
Merry Lover (Novella)
Ghostly Lover (Novella)

**The Husband Dilemma Series**
How to Fool a Duke (Book 1)

**Season of Scandal Series**
Pursued by the Rake (Book 1)
Abandoned to the Prodigal (Book 2)
Married to the Rogue (Book 3)
Unmasked by her Lover (Book 4)
Her Star from the East (Novella)

**Imperial Season Series**
Vienna Waltz (Book 1)
Vienna Woods (Book 2)
Vienna Dawn (Book 3)

**Blackhaven Brides Series**
The Wicked Baron (Book 1)
The Wicked Lady (Book 2)
The Wicked Rebel (Book 3)
The Wicked Husband (Book 4)
The Wicked Marquis (Book 5)
The Wicked Governess (Book 6)

The Wicked Spy (Book 7)
The Wicked Gypsy (Book 8)
The Wicked Wife (Book 9)
Wicked Christmas (Book 10)
The Wicked Waif (Book 11)
The Wicked Heir (Book 12)
The Wicked Captain (Book 13)
The Wicked Sister (Book 14)

**Unmarriageable Series**
The Deserted Heart (Book 1)
The Sinister Heart (Book 2)
The Vulgar Heart (Book 3)
The Broken Heart (Book 4)
The Weary Heart (Book 5)
The Secret Heart (Book 6)
Christmas Heart (Novella)

**The Lyon's Den Series**
Fed to the Lyon

**De Wolfe Pack: The Series**
The Wicked Wolfe
Vienna Wolfe

**Also from Mary Lancaster**
Madeleine (Novella)
The Others of Ochil (Novella)

# CHAPTER ONE

O
N A BRIGHT, cold November morning, Constance Silver left her discreet establishment just off Grosvenor Square and walked smartly through the gracious streets. It was a long enough walk to justify going by carriage, but she preferred the fresh air and exercise to clarify her mind concerning the problems of one business before facing the other.

She was aware as she did so of the eager excitement curling in her stomach. She chose to believe this was due to the possibilities of her new venture into the world of private investigations, and nothing to do with her partner. It could certainly not be the investigations themselves that occupied her, for despite their being open for consultations yesterday and three days the previous week, they had none.

Crossing St. Martin's Lane with the aid of the same sweeper who had cleared her way yesterday, she dropped a generous coin into the boy's chapped fingers and resolved to buy him decent gloves and a scarf for Christmas. She turned into Chandos Street and, at the corner of a narrow lane, paused to admire the polished brass plaque beside a newly painted black door. It bore the legend *Silver & Grey*.

Smiling, she let herself in with a key. The welcoming entrance hall might have been to a home rather than to an office. Constance took off her hat and bonnet and hung them on the coat stand beside a fur-trimmed, heavy wool overcoat. A tall silk hat adorned the shelf.

A small, empty waiting room opened to the right of the hall. To the left were two parlors that doubled as offices, furnished with comfortable chairs as well as desks. In the hope that her partner was with a client, she knocked before she entered the first parlor.

Solomon Grey was alone. He sat at the desk, reading through a pile of papers that she knew had nothing to do with this business, but with one of his many other ventures in the worlds of shipping, industry, and banking. He glanced up and rose as he always did, a dark, elegant man with a presence one could not ignore. Constance, who had been reading men with invariable accuracy for most of her life, had only ever begun to scratch the surface with Solomon, a walking puzzle that she could only enjoy.

"A cup of tea before we are besieged by clients?" she offered.

"Thank you," he said politely.

Already, they had fallen into the habit that he lit the fire and the stove in the morning, and she made the tea. He went out at midday to buy their luncheon, while she completed what little cleaning was necessary. They had talked about taking on one of Constance's girls to do the cleaning and the tea, and showing in clients, but since none of those had been forthcoming, there appeared to be no rush.

Ten minutes later, they sat drinking tea companionably by the fireside and talking about plays they had seen at Drury Lane. She had come to value those times of quiet companionship. It made up for their lack of clients.

A sharp knock brought about a sudden silence. They gazed at each other in surprise and hope.

"It will be the postman," Constance said, trying not to bounce too eagerly to her feet. "Or Mrs. Higgs from the flat upstairs."

While she walked to the door without *too* much hurry, Solomon swept the teacups and saucers from the small table to place them on the desk instead. Along with his pile of papers, it created an impression of industry.

Constance opened the front door to find an expensively dressed lady on the step. She held out a card between her gloved fingers. "Angela Lambert. I would like to see Mr. Silver or Mr. Grey," she said in a surprisingly strong London accent, "if either is available. If not, I'll make an appointment."

"Please come in," Constance said, her heart beating with excitement at this, their first prospective client. "May I take your coat?"

"I can see someone now?" the woman asked eagerly. She must have been around forty years old, a handsome woman who had probably been a beauty in her youth. Inclined now to stoutness, she was nevertheless attractive. Her station in life was harder to fix, since her wide crinoline and expensive garments contradicted her rough accents. She seemed a little shy, a little unsure of herself.

"It so happens we are both in the office at this moment," Constance said, taking the woman's fur-lined coat and hanging it on the third hook. She glanced at the card she had been given: *Mrs. C. Lambert* had been inscribed, above a Westminster address. "Please come this way, Mrs. Lambert, and tell us how we may help you."

She opened the first parlor door, ushering her visitor inside, where, once again, Solomon arose from his desk and walked toward them.

"This is Mrs. Lambert," Constance said. "Ma'am, allow me to introduce my partner, Mr. Grey. I am Mrs. Silver."

Mrs. Lambert inclined her head in response to Solomon's bow and cast a rather sharp look at Constance. However, she sat on the edge of the chair offered to her, her back straight and stiff.

"How might we help you, Mrs. Lambert?" Solomon asked, and sat down beside Constance.

"I don't know if you can," Mrs. Lambert said nervously. "I don't know if you'll even believe me, let alone be able to do anything about it."

"We will tell you honestly if we think it beyond our skills,"

Solomon assured her.

Mrs. Lambert regarded him with a shrewd glance. "You look like a man who has traveled. You must have seen a lot of unlikely things in your life."

"A few," Solomon admitted.

"Ever seen a ghost?"

Constance almost groaned. Just what they didn't need to start off their new venture—a superstitious crank. She hoped she retained her expression of neutral interest. Solomon certainly did.

"Not to my knowledge," he said smoothly.

"Well, I seen one."

"And it troubles you?"

Mrs. Lambert nodded. "Wouldn't have come here otherwise. Saw your flyer on a lamppost and thought, that's who I need. Someone to tell me if it's really a ghost, and either way, what the devil it wants with my house."

Constance set the client's card on the table, where Solomon could see it. At least there actually seemed to be some investigation required. Surely it would be a start, though she could not imagine the outcome of such a case.

"You saw this ghost in your own home?" she asked.

"Well, in my garden."

"What was it doing?"

"Just gliding about," Mrs. Lambert said impatiently. She must have read something in Constance's face, for she frowned and added defensively, "I'm not the only one who's seen it."

"Who else has seen this ghost?" Solomon asked.

"One of the maids and two footmen."

*A substantial home*, Constance noted, judging by the number of servants.

"Tell us what you saw," Solomon said. "What did the ghost look like?"

"Like a girl. A young woman. Veiled and sort of wispy. Like mist. I know what you're going to say! That it *was* mist, but it wasn't. It had too much shape, and it came *through* the mist."

"From where?" Constance asked.

"I don't know. It just seemed to…materialize in the middle of the garden, and moved through it, then vanished into the mist."

"And you just saw it once?"

Mrs. Lambert nodded. "Night before last. Before that, I told the servants to stop being stupid and scaring each other, 'cause there's no such thing as ghosts. Only when I saw it, I weren't so sure."

"So it might have been a real person moving about your garden without your authority," Solomon said.

"It might have been," she said. "It just didn't look like anyone I ever seen before, and the servants don't know her neither."

"When was this ghostly figure first seen?" Constance asked.

"A couple of weeks ago. Goldie—the maid—saw her first through the kitchen window and squealed, but no one believed her until Bert and Pat saw her a week later, and then Goldie saw it again from her bedroom window."

"And where were you when you saw it?" Solomon asked.

"In the back parlor. I'd just come in and went to close the curtains when I saw her clear as day. Well," she amended, "not quite as clear as that. But she was like an apparition, floating through the mist."

"Did she make any threatening gestures?" Solomon asked.

Mrs. Lambert shook her head. "No, she just seemed in a hurry."

Constance met Solomon's gaze briefly. It was not the serious case they had hoped for, but beggars could not be choosers, and they had to start somewhere.

"What exactly is it you want us to do?" Solomon asked.

"I don't expect you to lay a ghost, if that's what you're asking. I just want to know if it *is* a ghost or if it's a person. If the latter…I want to know who she is and what she's doing on my husband's property, because he won't like it."

Constance, who had for some reason imagined Mrs. Lambert was a widow, said quickly, "Is your husband aware of the ghost?"

"He's aware what's been said about it, but he's never seen it and certainly doesn't believe it's a ghost. His footmen, Robin and Pat, are supposed to keep the place secure, and they do, to be fair, which inclines me to the supernatural explanation, though it ain't in my nature."

"If it *is* a person rather than a ghost," Constance said, "who do you think it is?"

Mrs. Lambert shrugged. "Someone trying to scare us, maybe."

"Who would want to do that?" Solomon asked.

Mrs. Lambert's gaze slid down to her hands clasped together in her lap. "I don't know. Someone who don't like my husband, maybe. He's made some enemies over the years, and some of 'em bear grudges. Only I can't see them getting so close as to get caught." She shrugged. "Brings me back to ghosts again."

"Well, we could certainly keep watch on your garden for a few nights," Solomon said.

"No, that wouldn't work," Mrs. Lambert said quickly. "Pat and Robin'd get you, and Caleb—my husband—would know I'd been interfering." She shifted uncomfortably and said, "I thought you might come and pretend to be a servant for a week or so. I'd pay you for that as well as any other fee required for your services. I already told Caleb I wanted another footman." She looked Solomon up and down. "But you wouldn't do."

Solomon raised one eyebrow.

"I don't care what color your skin is," Mrs. Lambert said bluntly. "But no one'd ever believe you're a servant." Her gaze shifted to Constance. "I don't have a proper lady's maid either, but you talk too posh to work for the likes of me."

"I don't have to talk posh," Constance said. "I'll speak any way you like and stick to it."

Mrs. Lambert smiled. "You been on the stage?"

"As good as," Constance said, sustaining a critical inspection.

"You can't wear that kind of dress, neither."

"Of course not. I have a plain back dress I can wear—with an apron, if you like. And pin my hair more suitably."

"Done," said Mrs. Lambert as though closing a deal.

"Here is a list of our charges," Solomon said, placing the relevant piece of paper on the table in front of her.

She barely glanced at it. "Fine. When can you begin?"

"Tomorrow morning?" Constance said. "Mr. Grey can deal with matters here."

"Good," Mrs. Lambert said, standing up. "Don't forget to use the back door."

"I won't," Constance assured her.

"Allow me to see you out," Solomon said politely, conducting her to the door.

Constance paced with excitement until he came back. "Well? What do you think?" she demanded. "Not what I was hoping for, but at least it's *something*."

"I think it's strange," he said. He was frowning as he sat down again. "Why is it something for us? She has a husband, a house full of servants—including at least three manservants. Yet the first thing she thinks of is not to send them to lay hold of this ghost, but to come to us at vast expense."

"She doesn't appear to be short of money," Constance said. "But she does seem afraid of her husband. She doesn't want him to notice she's been interfering, which is why I have to pretend to be a servant. Who is this Caleb Lambert?"

"I have no idea." Solomon picked up Mrs. Lambert's card again. "What's more, I'm not exactly sure where that is. We should go and look this evening. And find out a bit more about the Lamberts. I don't like the idea of your being in there alone."

"I won't be alone. I'll have Mrs. Lambert on my side at the very least."

"Mrs. Lambert, who's afraid of her husband and doesn't trust her servants."

Constance grimaced. "Put like that... You and I will need to be able to communicate. In fact... Why don't we begin this afternoon? I'll get Janey to stay here just in case someone calls with an inquiry."

"Janey?" he said at once. "Of the foul mouth and aggressive manner?"

"That's the one. She'll be polite enough taking messages and making appointments, and if anyone causes trouble, they won't know what hit them. We can send a boy with a note…"

"Write it. I'll find a messenger to send to your house in Grosvenor Square."

ANGELA LAMBERT WALKED smartly along Chandos Street, wondering if she'd done the right thing. Silver and Grey weren't exactly who and what she'd expected them to be. For one thing, one of them was a woman, although now she thought about it, she rather liked the idea. A woman going her own way, making her own decisions.

But both of them were too refined, and too liable to stand out. Mrs. Silver was too pretty not to cause trouble in the house. And Grey… She didn't know if he was dark-skinned European or African, though he talked the Queen's English better than most people Angela had ever met. He wasn't exactly the seedy, unnoticeable type. He wouldn't blend easily into any background. In fact, he was the sort of man people always noticed.

Angela had certainly noticed him. And it had been a long time since she'd noticed men other than her husband. *What would Caleb do if I indulged the attraction?*

*Kill us both, probably.*

No, perhaps Silver was better, on the whole, to have in the house. But Angela would need to be careful now. Damned careful.

JANEY BREEZED IN just over an hour later, bearing hot pies she'd bought from a street seller on the way.

"What d'you want me to do, then?" she asked Constance, who had just let her into the hall. "And where's this gorgeous man of yours?"

Solomon's tall, elegant figure filled the parlor doorway. Janey stared at him with frank appreciation.

"Cor. No wonder she don't talk about you. They'd be fighting over you in our establishment."

"Not if they wanted to remain there," Constance said. "This is Janey, my maid. Janey, Mr. Grey."

"Wotcha, Mr. Grey," Janey said cheerfully. "Want a pie?"

"Thank you," Solomon said gravely, accepting the parcel.

Constance hauled Janey to the office and showed her the appointment book. "Don't make any appointments for me this week or next, and try not to make it sound that Mr. Grey is *too* available, even though he is from tomorrow morning. Don't swear at anyone—unless they deserve it—and help yourself to tea in the kitchen. You can leave when Mr. Grey returns."

"Do I have to?" Janey asked.

"I thought men revolted you these days."

"I ain't touching 'em again, bastards, but I could just look at him for a bit."

"No you couldn't," Constance said firmly. "He's not an exhibit."

"He's a gentleman, ain't he? With an edge."

There was definitely an edge to Solomon. Cool, self-contained, observant, with just that hint of danger that lurked in men who could always take care of themselves.

"Are you clear what you have to do?" Constance asked hastily.

"Of course I am. I ain't stupid. You and him bugger off. I'll be fine."

"Just don't tell clients to bugger off," Constance said as they emerged from the office to find Solomon looking amused.

Already wearing his overcoat, he assisted Constance into hers and picked up his hat.

"Thank you, Miss Janey," he said, and opened the door, quite unaware that he'd made a rare conquest with four words.

THE HACKNEY SET them down in Victoria Street, within sight of the Houses of Parliament and Westminster Abbey. Constance, however, paused to gaze in the other direction.

"Over there," she said, nodding across the road, "is Devil's Acre. A maze of slums built on marshland, all muck, rookeries, poverty, and thieves."

Even Solomon, it seemed, had heard of Devil's Acre. Well, Mr. Dickens had written an alarming article about it a year or so ago, which had raised its level of notoriety.

"You are telling me that the Lamberts live in Devil's Acre?"

"Lord, no," Constance said. "Their address is in the opposite direction. Interesting, though, that they live so close. I wonder if they came from there?" She took Solomon's proffered arm and they began to walk. "I found her an odd mixture, didn't you? Uncertain to the point of shyness one moment, and very sure of herself the next."

"Aren't we all a little like that?"

"Perhaps."

They almost missed the Lamberts' house, for it was set off the road, in one of those unexpectedly quiet corners one occasionally came across in London, where the city's noise and bustle did not seem to reach. The house was tall and dark, its stone grimy with the years. Iron gates at the front guarded a short path with a tree on either side to the front door. It almost looked unoccupied.

A lane led around the side of a walled garden with no obvious way in, until, at the back, they came to a stout wooden door in the wall. Casually, Solomon tried it and found it locked.

They went back the way they had come toward Victoria Street.

Solomon murmured, "Unless you can get a key to that garden door, we'll have to meet at the front, maybe just at the corner of Tothill Street."

"We should certainly do that the first time. Shall we say eight o'clock? You might have to hang around a bit until I can escape."

Solomon was silent for some time. "You'll be too isolated in there. I don't like it."

"Less so once I get in and see the lie of the land. There's nothing much we can do here until tomorrow. The house has an air of secrecy, though, does it not?"

"Yes. While you are inside, I think I need to make urgent inquiries into this Lambert, if only for your safety."

"I've faced worse than him with fewer weapons," Constance said carelessly, her mind on the ghostly sightings. "Let's find another hackney. I can drop you back at the office on my way."

"On your way where?"

"To make my own inquiries."

"Where?" he repeated.

She had to remind herself that they were partners now, that they each had to know what the other was doing and why. Trust was something that had to be constant.

"Seven Dials," she said reluctantly.

He blinked. "Then I will come with you."

She took a deep breath. "Don't be daft. I'm going to see my mother."

# CHAPTER TWO

BEYOND HIS NEED to protect, Solomon was aware of curiosity concerning the mother of Constance Silver. He knew only that she had been a whore when Constance was born, and that therefore Constance had no idea who her father was. In fact, one of the first vulnerabilities he had discovered in her was her longing to belong to a family, from which he had gathered that her mother had never supplied any sense of that.

Constance rarely spoke of her at all, and then it was only ever in passing. Why this sudden yearning for her company?

As though she heard his unspoken question, she regarded him from her own bench in the hackney. "My mother is many things, among them a veritable font of information about people most of us would rather not think about. It would be interesting to know if she had ever heard of the Lamberts."

"Does that mean you are giving me permission to accompany you?"

"You would come anyway."

"I might wait outside the door."

"No one waits in Seven Dials. It's an invitation to be beaten up and robbed. Or worse."

He waited for threats, for excuses, for demands not to judge, but she only gazed out of the window at the impossibly straining traffic on Piccadilly. She had decided to trust him.

Warmed, he said nothing, merely alighted on the edges of Covent Garden where she told the jarvey to stop and handed her down. Immediately, she delved into a warren of side streets and alleys.

"Did you grow up here?" he asked.

"Somewhere very similar. I had my first establishment near here." She liked to shock him with these brazen little announcements, as if to make sure he never forgot who and what she was. Or to be certain *she* didn't.

She entered a doorway and climbed the stairs. "Gerry," she said to the man at the top—a burly young fellow who actually dragged off his cap, his eyes gleaming.

"Miss Connie."

"Is she in?"

"Got someone with her, but just wait in the parlor. She won't be long."

The large youth opened the door, his gaze unfriendly as he subjected Solomon to a thorough visual search.

The hallway was not well lit, but it seemed to be clean. Constance led Solomon left into a gloomy parlor that looked onto a stone wall. But the room itself was packed with things in apparently haphazard order. Little jeweled boxes, elegant statuettes beside others that were clearly cheap junk. Glass and porcelain, silver cutlery, jewelry, and piles of lace and linen covered every available surface.

"What is all this stuff?" he asked, amused.

"Guess," she said dryly. "Just don't spread your answer around."

*Stolen goods…* Was her mother a fence?

It seemed likely as a shady man walked past the door counting the coins in his palm. Beside him, a short, buxom lady dressed in startling purple with improbably blonde hair said playfully, "Don't you trust me?"

"Course I do, Mrs. Jules, else I wouldn't have come," said the man hastily, and vanished along the hall to the door.

Presumably the burly lad at the door had communicated their presence to their hostess, for she sailed in, smiling, shrewd eyes gleaming in her plump, still-pretty face. If he looked hard, Solomon could see where Constance got her looks, though the younger woman was much more refined and slender in appearance.

"Connie, my pet!" the vision in purple exclaimed, opening her arms wide, though it was noticeable she dropped them again well before she came in reach of her daughter.

For her part, Constance said carelessly, "Hello, Juliet."

Brows raised, her mother raked her with her eyes. "Changed your style, Con?" She let out a cackle of laughter. "Never tell me the reformers got you after all!"

"I have merely expanded and diversified my business, as you always taught me. I dress accordingly. This is my new business partner, Mr. Grey. Solomon, my mother, Mrs. Juliet Silver."

"Well!" Juliet Silver exclaimed, looking him up and down as though she had only just noticed him—which was not the case. She had clearly clocked him the instant she entered the room. She offered him one plump, beringed hand. Some of the diamonds were real. "You're lovely, dear, but you don't look much like a pimp to me."

"I daresay you don't look much like a raddled old whore to him, either," Constance said pleasantly.

With an effort, Solomon refrained from blinking. He couldn't recall Constance ever being deliberately rude before. He bowed civilly over Juliet's hand. She hadn't batted an eyelid over her daughter's insult, but her gaze on his was both speculative and admiring—though he doubted he could trust the latter.

"Mr. Grey was never in that kind of business," Constance said.

"What is your business, sir?" Juliet asked.

"Right now, investigations," Solomon replied.

Juliet's eyes widened, though the smile stayed on her lips. "You don't look like a peeler, neither. And if my Connie's gone over to that side, I'll eat my best hat."

"Your headgear is safe, ma'am," Solomon said. "Our investigations are for private clients."

"Still sounds like snooping to me," Juliet said frankly. "Which is just what I don't hold with. I know I told you to get out of the game, Con, but if there's one thing worse—"

"I'm not out of the game. I have added another string to my bow. What do you know of a man called Caleb Lambert, and his wife, Angela? They live in Westminster, behind Tothill Street."

Juliet's eyes flickered. "Enough to keep me out of his way. I'd advise you to do the same, though since you always do the opposite, I'll advise Mr. Grey instead."

"He's a villain, then?" Solomon said with interest, even while he changed plans in his head. Constance would *not* go into that house in any guise. "In what line?"

"Don't know if he's that kind of villain," Juliet said, ambling toward a tray of decanters and glasses on the dresser. "Or not now. More what you might call a ruthless businessman. Like you, I daresay."

Constance snorted. "Then he stays within the law?"

"His business does, most probably," Juliet said, sloshing amber liquid from a decanter into three glasses. "It's what happens to those who cross him that worries me."

"What is his business?" Solomon asked.

"Property," Juliet said. "He owns buildings all over London."

"Devil's Acre?" Constance asked quickly.

Juliet shrugged, carrying the three glasses across to them. "Possibly." Setting the glasses on the nearest table to Solomon, she presented him with one, gave another to Constance, and kept the largest for herself. "Though even he wouldn't want that lot after him. Definitely Cheapside, Whitechapel, and St. Giles, moving into the city and the west. I hear he's trying to get into Prince Albert's good books and build some of his model houses for all those poor people he currently crams into his old places, ten families per leaky room."

"He's a slum landlord," Constance said, frowning as her mother eased herself into the chair beside her drink. "Is there much money in that?"

"Ten families per leaky room," Solomon said wryly, "and the pennies soon mount up."

"Especially with nothing going out on such nonsense as repairs to the leaks, stone, roofs, rot, or anything else." Juliet regarded him with a bit more respect. "In the property business yourself, Mr. Grey?"

"To a small degree. But I've never come across the name of Caleb Lambert."

"Expect you've heard of Huxley Gregg, though."

Solomon's breath caught. "Wasn't he the owner of that building that collapsed in St. Giles a couple of weeks ago? People died."

"Bloody right they did. Well, Gregg was Lambert's partner."

"In that particular building?" Constance asked, sitting down abruptly.

Juliet shrugged. "I'd say so, though they never touched him for it. Gregg must have kept his mouth shut. The parish is leading an inquiry into how it happened, threatening to bring a prosecution against Gregg. But I don't reckon he'll make it that long. There's a lot of bad feeling against him, and someone will take the law into their own hands. He knows it too, keeping least in sight, I hear. He'd probably rather be in prison."

"They'd get to him there too," Constance said. "And not many would cry for him."

"Retribution," Solomon murmured, meeting Constance's gaze. Was that what Angela Lambert truly feared? It would certainly explain her nervousness and her desire to involve outside help to find her "ghost."

Constance took a distracted sip of her drink, looked faintly surprised at herself, and set her glass on the table. "Interesting."

"Unsavory," Solomon added.

Juliet raised her glass in a bitter toast of agreement. Like Constance, she seemed to be an odd mixture of caring and hardness. Yet when he tried to visualize Constance being brought up by this woman, his imagination failed.

"What do you know of the wife?" Constance asked abruptly. "Angela."

"Nothing. Didn't know he was married. Don't like to think of a bastard like that with kids, do you?"

"No," Constance said bleakly.

Even through the closed door of the parlor, Solomon heard the front door opening to let in a raised voice. It sounded like the young man who'd let them in, answered by another, deeper voice.

Juliet knocked back the rest of her brandy as though it was water and struggled to her feet. "Excuse me one moment."

She moved with surprising speed toward the parlor door, which was thrown open from the other side to reveal a stocky man in a fur-collared coat that hung open to show long gold fobs and a loud tartan waistcoat.

Beside Solomon, Constance stiffened.

"Mrs. Jules," purred this vision fondly. "I knew you were at home. The whole place feels different when it basks in the glow of your presence."

"It certainly feels different in yours," Juliet murmured. "You must excuse me, Mr. Boggie, when I am privately engaged."

"I excused you last time," Boggie said unpleasantly. He was a florid man, prosperous and oily looking, which might have had something to do with his neat, waxed moustache. His eyes lacked the hard, mean look of many bullies, but to Solomon they also lacked any humanity, as if there was no one at home.

Until they flickered over him without interest and strayed to Constance, where they lingered. "And what friends they are." He swept off his hat and bowed, not without elegance. "How do you do, madam?"

Solomon's hackles rose. There was something obscene about this man even looking at Constance.

Constance said coolly, "I'd do better in private, sir, as Mrs. Silver requests." Something odd had happened to her accent—neither the unmitigated Cockney she could put on when she chose, nor the refined voice she had cultivated, it was something in between, enough to give an impression of lowborn respectability. She was playing a part, and he knew instinctively that it was not that of Juliet's daughter. There was acute tension in her stillness, as though she recognized the intruder and did not like him.

Boggie looked surprised to be told off.

"Oh, we're finished here, ain't we?" Juliet said to Solomon. "A pleasure doing business with you, sir. I'm quite exhausted now and need a lie-down."

"I *thought* you had something for me, Mrs. Jules," Boggie said, his mouth curling as he dragged his eyes off Constance to impale her mother instead.

"Oh, I got nothing for you, Mr. Boggie," Juliet said with apparent regret. "Gerrald there will show you all out together, and let an old lady have her nap."

"I believe I'll wait," Boggie said.

"I believe you won't," Solomon said gently. "Let us do the gentlemanly thing and leave the lady to rest as she desires. Anything else would be unforgivably rude."

"Would it?" said Boggie, staring at him in mingled astonishment and derision.

"It would," Solomon assured the man, picking up his hat. "Mrs. Silver, my thanks for your hospitality. Good day."

"Good day, sir. Ma'am," Juliet said.

Constance inclined her head as though her mother were the merest acquaintance and sailed toward the door beside Solomon. Boggie fell back before them and found Gerry still holding open the front door. Another, large male figure had appeared from the depths of the house, but it was Solomon that Boggie kept his wary gaze on.

Solomon had learned long ago how to sweep unwanted people out of his way without actually touching them or giving undue offense. Boggie seemed quite bewildered to discover himself on the other side of the closed door to the street.

"Good day," Solomon said amiably, inclining his head before he strolled off with Constance's tense hand on his arm. "He won't go back in now," he murmured. "He'd lose his dignity."

"His what?" Constance said with a hint of savagery. She exhaled slowly. "Thank you for that."

"You know him," Solomon said. "Who is he?"

"Someone I wouldn't let near my girls. I had cause to keep him out of my last establishment."

"Then he knows you?" Solomon said quickly.

"Oh. No, we never met. Even then, I had people to keep out those I wished to. He wasn't quite so full of his own importance then. What I want to know is, what is he doing with my mother?"

"She wasn't exactly welcoming," Solomon pointed out.

"She isn't a fool," Constance said shortly. "But what does he want with her?"

He regarded her curiously. After their greeting to each other and the casual parting, he hadn't expected her to care. "What is Boggie's business?"

Constance wrinkled her nose. "He was a fence. Someone who sells stolen goods. I wonder if he's trying to move in on my mother's business?"

Solomon blinked. Despite his own suspicion, he hadn't expected Constance to admit it. "Your mother is a fence?"

"A trader in antiquities and rare goods. And a pawnbroker," she said in tones that told him her mother was indeed a fence, even if only on the side of her more lawful business. "It was, you know, a step up from prostitution. Or so she told me."

"You don't agree?"

Constance shrugged with unusual irritability. "It's safer and she drinks less. It's her business, nothing to do with me."

"And yet..." Solomon murmured.

Constance sighed. "And yet the habit of protection is hard to break. I don't like Boggie hanging around her."

"She probably doesn't like me hanging around you."

"Oh, she doesn't mind that at all," Constance said. "She'll like it even more now you got rid of Boggie for her with such ease."

Solomon said nothing.

"He'll be back," Constance said restlessly.

"Perhaps we should look into that instead of the Lambert ghost. You will be too unprotected in that house in any case."

"I'm as protected as I ever was. Besides," she said, gazing up at him challengingly, "it's not just about the ghost anymore, is it? It's making Lambert pay if he had anything to do with that building collapsing."

"We can do that without your being in his house."

"We'll do better with his wife around to answer questions."

Solomon swore beneath his breath. "Constance, if you ask questions like that..."

"Don't be silly. I shan't ask. We'll just talk. What do you know about the collapse?"

"The roof caved in, crashed through rotted floorboards, bringing masonry with it. The whole place was riddled with damp, rot, and neglect. The pointing was gone; bricks were loose and damaged. It should have been pulled down, not housing all those people. Only, of course, those tenants had nowhere else to go for shelter."

Curiosity replaced the determination in her eyes. "How do you know all this?"

"I'm on the board of a housing charity. We encouraged the parish inquiry into Gregg's negligence."

"Then you know him?"

"Not personally, but I know he collected the rent with threats, even put it up a month before the building came down and killed at least eighteen tenants, maiming several others who'll never work again." With an effort, he controlled the surging anger. "I never heard the whisper of a partner. Could your mother be wrong?"

"It's possible," Constance said, "but I would doubt it. She hears things no one else does. Always did. People like her, talk to her."

"You don't."

"We've got no illusions about each other, that's all."

But still Constance worried for her. He wondered if that went both ways.

# CHAPTER THREE

"I DON'T WANT you to go," Solomon said bluntly the following morning, when she had rejected all his subtler arguments. "It isn't worth the risk."

"Don't go soft on me, Solomon," she mocked. "I might start thinking you care. I brought you Janey to make the tea and guard the office while you're out asking questions, and I'll meet you at the corner of Tothill at eight tonight."

"I don't like it," he said, his determined, dark eyes holding hers.

Constance was not unmoved by his care, though she would never show it. "We agreed to be partners running this business. If I'm good at anything, it's avoiding risk, and we can't turn down our first commission just because someone possibly unsavory is involved."

She could see from his face that he knew she was right. Though she couldn't help being glad he didn't like it. He was a chivalrous soul at heart, was Solomon Grey.

"You will be careful," he said, glaring at her.

"As will you, poking into matters that annoy dangerous people. Take my footmen if you need them. Janey will—"

"I have my own dangerous people," he interrupted. "You come out of that house at the first sign of trouble."

"Of course," she said, pulling on her gloves. As she closed the parlor door, she wasn't sure if she was annoyed or amused. She certainly felt unusually on edge, but that was more to do with her mother than with the Lambert case.

"I'd love to see you doing the slaving for a change," Janey said, grinning in the hallway. "Don't pull her hair with the comb, and don't forget to polish her shoes till she can see her face in 'em."

"I won't, if you do your job here. Do exactly what Mr. Grey tells you." Constance paused, her hand on the door latch. "Janey?"

"Yes?"

*Damn my mother...* "When you finish here, ask around the girls about a fence called Boggie. See if they know what he's up to."

"All right."

Constance picked up the small, battered bag she had found in her attic, left the premises, and went in search of a hackney.

Half an hour later, she alighted at Westminster Abbey, where no one from the Lamberts' house could see her traveling at such expense, and walked the rest of the way.

The front gates were not locked, though the back door was. She knocked, then turned to survey the garden. It was a decent-sized plot for this part of London, enough for a kitchen garden of herbs and vegetables and a prettier area beyond, with a well-kept lawn bordered by shrubs and roses, and climbing greenery around the three walls. There were a couple of fruit trees, and a small pond beneath a young willow, but nothing that stretched conveniently over any of the high walls to make it easy for someone to climb in that way. Or out.

As gardens went, it looked secure. When filled with thick mist, how easy would it be for a fanciful mind to conjure up ghostly shapes? Especially once someone else had seen them. Angela Lambert had not struck Constance as particularly fanciful, but then, she was very reserved...

The back door opened and a large young man stared at her.

"I'm Silver," Constance said, "Mrs. Lambert's maid, just engaged. I was told to report here this morning."

"Right enough, you're expected," the man said, opening the door wide. "I'm Bert."

Constance walked in, trying to combine the haughtiness of a lady's maid—a very upper servant—with the normal nervous curiosity of taking up a new position.

A group of servants were gathered around a big table in the middle of the kitchen. A well-dressed, middle-aged man with granite-hard eyes sat at the head. He didn't rise as Constance entered.

"This is Mr. Duggin," Bert said. "Butler and guv'nor. Mrs. Feathers is the cook."

"Hello, dearie—name's Ida," Mrs. Feathers said, pouring the contents of a flask into her tea.

"And these two are Marigold and Denise. You'll meet Robin and Pat later—they're out with his nibs."

"With Mr. Lambert?" Constance asked.

"That's what I said," Bert replied, smirking. "Come on, I'd best take you up or she'll be down here looking for you."

Bert did not offer to carry her bag, though he took several not-very-surreptitious glances at Constance as they walked up to the main part of the house and crossed a decent-sized, wainscoted hall. Bert didn't bother knocking, just walked in.

"Your new maid, ma'am. Says her name is Silver." He grinned. "Goes pretty well with Goldie, doesn't it?"

"Away you go, Bert. I'll show Silver around upstairs. When she comes back down, you and Mrs. Feathers can show her where everything is down there. Close the door behind you."

Bert obeyed. However informal his manner, there was nothing disrespectful in it. Not to his mistress, anyway.

"You found us without difficulty, then? Take off your coat and hat."

Constance obeyed.

Angela Lambert sighed. "The dress will do, and there's no reason why you should wear a cap, but you're too damned pretty. Please try not to cause any fights in the kitchen."

"I'll keep 'em all at a safe distance," Constance assured her, adopting an accent with traces of her old one, like a lowborn maid eager to prove she'd come up in the world.

Angela nodded. "You'll do. This is my parlor," she said. "If I'm not in the sitting room—which we're to call the drawing room—I'm generally here."

"Is this where you saw the ghost?" Constance asked, walking to the window.

Angela followed her. "Yes. You wouldn't think it, would you? Not with the sun shining and everything clear and bright."

"Fog changes everything. Where exactly in the garden did you see it?"

Angela pointed toward the apple tree. "There, and then it glided on across the garden." She made sort of round, S-shaped gestures.

"In no particular direction?"

"Seemed to be random kind of movements."

"But definitely toward the house?"

Angela thought. "Yes."

"What was its position when you last saw it?"

"By the willow, there. It seemed to glide over the pond, and then it sort of…broke up and vanished."

"Is it possible the fog swirled more thickly over the figure, hiding it from your view?"

"Yes," Angela said again. "That's what I tell myself. But then I need to know, who was in my garden and why?"

"Yes, I can see that," Constance murmured. "May I go out and look around?"

"Of course. I'll show you the herb garden properly too. I like mint and chamomile tea at bedtime. First, I'll show you your room." Mechanically, Angela picked up Constance's bag and went to the door.

Constance hurried after her. "Mrs. Lambert, I should take it."

The woman flushed slightly, looking flustered and vulnerable for a moment. It endeared her just a little to Constance, who was a good judge of most people but couldn't quite grasp her client.

Carrying the bag, Constance followed her across the hall to a staircase, lit from a tall stained-glass window stretching up from the half-landing.

"I've put you in the room just off mine," Angela said. "It's meant to be a dressing room, but I never use it. And besides, it makes sense in terms of nearness to me, and your own privacy from the other servants. They sleep in the attic rooms. Apart from Mrs. Feathers, who has her own little cupboard bedroom in the kitchen."

Whatever her background, it seemed Angela had exacting standards. Her home was spotlessly clean and well maintained. It was all a little cluttered and over-opulent for Constance's taste—her own much-less-respectable establishment was less vulgar and considerably more soothing to the senses—but her new employer was clearly proud of it in a quiet, almost shy way.

"My husband has come up in the world," Angela said. "We need to be able to entertain gentlemen—and ladies—in style."

"What does your husband do, ma'am?"

"He owns property. Like the aristocracy."

"Is it all like this?" Constance asked, allowing a little awe into her voice. In truth, it wasn't hard, for Angela had just led her into her own bedchamber, a large and luxurious apartment that, apart from the quality of the furnishings, resembled the brothel in which Constance had spent her early years. Red velvet predominated, with lavish cushions and gold embroidery.

"All sorts," Angela said vaguely. She cast an unexpectedly anxious glance at Constance as though seeking approval. "His ambition is to have it all like this or better, but you got to start somewhere. What do you think?"

"Magnificent," Constance said, hoping her own accommodations were plainer, or she would never sleep.

"My husband has the connecting bedchamber. It makes sense when he works so late and goes out early."

"Most considerate of him."

Angela walked in the other direction. "This is your room." She opened the door to a slightly cramped room containing a narrow bed, a small chest of drawers with a mirror, and a washstand, then opened the door to a cupboard. "There's hanging space for dresses in here. Will it do?"

"Of course." Constance laid her bag on the bed, then hung up her plain coat and hat and the two spare gowns she had brought with her. "You had better tell me what I need to do as your lady's maid, and when I'll have free time to investigate in my own way."

They discussed this for a little. Angela had clearly never had a lady's maid before and didn't need one now. But, for show, Constance would be summoned at certain times and be required to carry out duties like pressing clothes and bringing morning tea.

"The other servants used to do those things, but I've told them that from now on, only you are allowed in this room—though when my bed is changed, you'll need one of the maids to help. When you're here with me pretending to help me dress, we can discuss anything you are or aren't finding out."

"Tell me about the household," Constance said, sitting down on one of the two armchairs indicated by Angela. "Is it just yourself and your husband? And the servants, of course."

"Yes. We were never blessed with children."

"Do you mind?" Constance asked impulsively. She herself would never have children, and yet just occasionally, the thought of them slipped into her mind, with the ache of regret.

Angela blinked rapidly but didn't appear to be angry about the intrusion.

"Sometimes," she admitted. "More for Caleb than for myself. He'd have loved a son to leave all this to. To work for. Instead, he's always in such a hurry for more and more success, as if he's afraid time will run out before he's done everything. If we'd had a son, he might have left something for him to do. As it is…" She trailed off, shrugging.

"Your husband is an ambitious man, then?"

"Oh, he's very ambitious, is Caleb," Angela said ruefully. "That's men for you, though, isn't it?"

"Tell me about the servants. How long have they worked for you?"

"Duggin's worked for Caleb forever. He came with us when we moved here, keeps the rest of them in line."

"He's the butler, yes?"

Angela's lips twitched, as though with some secret amusement. "I suppose you could call him that. He's got the right kind of imposing face for it, ain't he? I brought Mrs. Feathers in five or more years ago so I didn't need to cook. She's a bit of a sot, but it don't interfere with her none. Even in a stupor she can whip up something delicious."

"And the man who brought me to you? Bert. Is he a footman?"

"I suppose so. Caleb don't hold with livery. He likes the servants to blend more. He hired Bert a couple of years ago to look after me, run errands for me, take me out when I need to go somewhere. Pat and Robin do much the same for Caleb."

*Bodyguards*, Constance thought. Footmen often were, to a greater or lesser degree, so that wasn't necessarily significant. "What about the maids?"

"They do the cleaning. Goldie—Marigold—is Duggin's daughter."

"So you can count on her loyalty, too?"

"Oh, yes. She came a couple of years ago when we moved here. Brought her friend Denise, the other maid."

"Do you trust her?"

"I trust them all."

"Then none of the servants have cause to upset you by making up stories about ghosts, or even dressing up as one to scare you or your husband?"

Angela regarded her pityingly. "No one'd try to scare Caleb. Or me, by association."

So Caleb Lambert *was* someone to be afraid of. Which made

sense of Angela's reluctance to tell her husband about the investigation.

"A successful man like Mr. Lambert," Constance said tactfully, "must have made a few enemies on the way."

"I told you he has," Angela said. "But this ain't exactly cornering him in a dark alley, is it? What sort of revenge is it to creep about his garden pretending to be a ghost? Which he hasn't ever seen anyway!"

"Fair point. Though I suppose it depends exactly what this person is doing in the garden."

"That's what I don't understand. She don't *do* anything. Do you think… Do you think it really *could* be a ghost? Haunting the house or haunting us?"

"Is that what you believe?" Constance asked, mostly to avoid answering. She always felt the atmosphere of a house, which some of her friends called sensitivity to spirits, though she had never seen one. It was another odd contradiction in the down-to-earth, practical Angela Lambert, though.

"Sometimes," Angela said bleakly. "Nothing we can do if it is, except move! But I need to know."

Constance stood up. "Then why don't you show me the kitchen and the garden to start with?"

It quickly became clear why the Lamberts employed no housekeeper—the lady of the house undertook that task herself. On the way down to the kitchen, Angela looked in on the drawing room where the two maids were busy chattering and cleaning.

"You can do the dining room next and the upstairs landing," she said, with a nod of approval that seemed to please both the maids.

In the kitchen, Ida Feathers was busy pounding dough for bread, surrounded by other bowls and pots and a miasma of delicious smells. She didn't curtsey to her mistress, but she did glance up and nod with an oddly sweet smile.

"She likes to cook," Angela said. "Here's the kettle and the pot and the mint and chamomile for my tea. China tea is here. The laundry room is through here." She lowered her voice again. "Starch is here, and you can heat the irons there. You do know how to use a flat iron, don't you?"

"Yes."

"Good. The washing is sent out, but the pressing is done here. Goldie and Denise were doing that, but you might as well do mine while you're here. Let's go out."

She unlocked the back door, through which Constance had first entered the house, and they went out into the cold garden.

With more leisure to concentrate, Constance looked very carefully at the back of the house, which was largely covered in ivy and other creepers. It had a few low, barred windows, through which no one could get in or out. A path led down the right hand side of the house to the front.

"Are the front gates locked at night?" Constance asked while she looked at the herbs Angela was pointing out.

"Yes. From about six o'clock in the evening. It wouldn't be easy to climb over them—or the walls—but I suppose it could be done."

"Same at the back," Constance observed. "I suppose the door in the far wall is kept locked too?" Since she already knew it was, she was not surprised when Angela nodded. "It would be helpful to have the key. To communicate with my partner when necessary."

Angela frowned. "Why would you need to do that? You're the one that's here."

"I might need him to find out about people or events he doesn't yet know about. Things I can't easily do from here while I'm being your maid. We work together."

"I see." Angela appeared to regard this as something of a novelty. "I suppose I could give you mine."

"Who else has keys to all these doors?"

"My husband, of course. And Duggin. Pat and Robin need keys too, to keep a proper eye on the place."

"Are valuables kept here?" Constance asked. "Beyond the usual, I mean. Or a lot of money?"

Angela shrugged. "Not really. I suppose when the rent's collected, some of it might sit in the house till next morning. Caleb uses banks."

There appeared to be some pride in that revelation. Constance supposed it was more refined than stuffing it in a stocking under the mattress, though she had done that in her time too.

"How often is the rent collected?" she asked.

"Some every week, some each month or even every quarter. Depends on the tenant and their ability to pay. Why?"

"I was wondering if those nights when there was a lot of money in the house coincided with any of the ghost's appearances."

Angela's jaw dropped. "You think someone's pretending to be a ghost in order to get into our house and steal the rents?"

"It's a possibility, isn't it? If Mr. Lambert's habits are known."

"I suppose. We collect weekly rent on a Saturday—which is the day I saw the ghost." Angela still looked doubtful, though she did seem to be thinking it over while they walked toward the apple tree. "But I don't think it was a Saturday when Goldie saw it."

It would have been too simple, Constance thought as they followed roughly the erratic pattern of the ghost's movements to the pond and the willow. There was no obvious place for a person to hide except among the mist-laden branches of the willow, or deep in the mist itself.

"It's not far from here to the door in the wall," Constance mused. "With some nice, swirling mist, someone might get away without being seen."

"Raises the question who. And why."

"True."

"Come on back inside. It's cold out here. I'll be going out this afternoon. You don't need to come with me. Bert will. You can just settle in till I get back, and look around all you want—only not in Caleb's office. He wouldn't like that."

Constance was sure he wouldn't. But she had every intention of getting in there as soon as she safely could.

IDA FEATHERS, THE cook, finished cutting her vegetables while she watched Angela take the new girl back upstairs with her. Wiping her hands on her apron, she felt the outline of the flask in her pocket and mechanically took a little nip.

Ida didn't care for change. For one thing, the new girl would make Goldie and Denise jealous by being superior in rank and in looks. And the lads would fight over her. Robin would win, of course, and that would be bad for Denise's hopes of him. Unless Caleb himself wanted her. For a moment she even wondered if Caleb had foisted the girl on Angela. But no—Caleb was no saint, but he never publicly humiliated his wife with his infidelities. Everyone could pretend she didn't know.

Maybe she didn't, though Ida doubted it. A very knowing woman, was Angela Lambert. Plus, she was kind at heart, which Ida had cause to know. Who else would have found a place for a gin-sodden old woman in their home, let alone given her a wage and something to do all day?

Ida liked to cook. She had always cooked the best meals and sweet treats for her little ones, bless their poor, lost hearts. The ache never went away. But with the gin and the cooking and Angela, she didn't mind the living so much now.

And she could still take care of the new girl, Silver, if she proved to be a problem for Angela. Probably she wouldn't. She had a good face and a good smile. Yet there was something *wrong* about her being here. She bore watching. And Angela need never know if Ida had to remove her.

# CHAPTER FOUR

Leaving Janey in charge of the office once more, Solomon walked round to the site of the collapsed building in St. Giles. Unsure what he expected to learn, he found only rubble. The rest had already been picked over by the desperate and the vultures who always descended on disaster areas.

Gazing at the devastation, he felt the resurgence of anger. This had been a wholly preventable disaster. Negligence by Gregg and his predecessors going back decades was to blame. Along with the overcrowding that had made the building so hard to escape from.

"Going to build a palace out of that, guv?" asked an old woman with a cackle.

Solomon turned to face her. She was carrying a large sack of washing over her bent back. "What on earth happened here?" he asked, in the hope of learning more from local opinion.

She shrugged. "Roof collapsed, didn't it? Everything was rotten, including the bloody landlord." She spat on the ground. "Eighteen dead, more crippled. Some reckon they'll try Huxley Gregg, but he'll get off—his sort always do. Even if they bang him up, won't bring the dead back, will it? Won't stop it happening again, neither. Bad enough dying of cholera without the roof falling in on you to make sure."

"What happened to those who survived? Where did they go?"

She nodded at the next tenement along. "Some squashed in there. Same landlord. Some didn't risk it and went elsewhere if they could."

"Thank you," Solomon said politely.

"Coo!" She cackled again. "Ain't you posh." She went off on her way, and Solomon risked going on to the next doorway. The building looked curiously vulnerable, as if it too might slide to the ground in a heap now that it didn't have its neighbor to lean against.

A bunch of small, ragged children rushed inside in front of him. One shouted, "Sorry, mister!"

"Here," Solomon called after them. "You got a caretaker here?"

Either they didn't hear him or didn't know or care. Certainly, no one answered. He sighed and turned toward the first door off the passage, where he found a young woman with a shawl over her straw-like hair, regarding him with sardonic amusement in her otherwise dull eyes.

He smiled at her. "Silly question?"

"He don't take no care, if that's what you mean. He's more of a rent collector, but he does live here. Him and his wife."

"Where can I find him?"

"Lena!" yelled a voice from within. "Where's my dinner? I got to die of hunger in this dump?"

"Coming, Granddad," the girl said. She nodded to the door directly opposite and went inside her own place, though not before Solomon had seen the number of people, mattresses, and beds slung all over the floor, some with makeshift curtains strung up to give privacy. How many families were living in that one room?

He walked across the grimy passage, trying not to think what might be crunching under his shoes.

His knock was answered rather abruptly by a youngish, scowling man in his shirt sleeves with yesterday's stubble darkening his jaw and his hair uncombed. He might have been thirty years old.

Though his mouth was already open to speak, he shut it again in apparent surprise at the sight of Solomon. "Yes?"

"I understand you are the caretaker of the building? Or at least the rent collector."

"I am," the man said, bridling as though he expected criticism. "What's it to you?" He looked Solomon up and down with growing unease. Solomon wore secondhand clothes he had bought specially to blend in with most societies, but judging by the man's expression, that wasn't really working. "Who are you, anyway?"

"I'm interested," Solomon said, giving up on subtlety, "in the accident next door." He stuck his hand in his coat pocket and jingled the coins there.

The rent collector's gaze dropped to the pocket and rose quickly to Solomon's face. There was calculation in his eyes now, nervous calculation as he glanced over Solomon's shoulder toward the stairs, from where strident voices and footsteps could be heard.

"Come in," he said, all but grabbing Solomon's arm to drag him inside and close the door.

The room was clean, and it was warm enough for its occupant to be comfortable in shirt sleeves in winter. The heat source was a stove burning merrily in the corner. Clearly, there were no leaks or drafts in this room, which was a good size and well proportioned, furnished with a proper kitchen next to the stove, a couple of upholstered armchairs. A table and two hard chairs occupied the middle of the room, with a large bed and chest at the other end.

"You live here alone?" Solomon asked in surprise.

"With my wife," the man said. "What is it you want to know?"

"Begin with your name and your position here," Solomon said.

"Fraser," the man said reluctantly. "Frank Fraser. I pass on problems to the landlord and make sure the rents are in on time."

"Are they?" Solomon asked mildly.

"Not so bad here. Next door…" He trailed off, biting his lip.

"You performed the same service for the building that collapsed."

"Yes," Fraser said. "Not my fault it fell. I told Mr. Gregg all the problems. Up to him to do something about it, isn't it? I ain't got the money or the authority. I just live here cheap for collecting all the rents." His face twisted into a grimace. "You'd think I pulled the bloody building down myself for all the abuse I get now."

"I suppose you're the face of the landlord they never see. Or do they?"

"Not now, they don't. Nobody sees Mr. Gregg anymore."

"Then how do you deliver the rents? Or haven't you had to yet?"

"Weekly ones, I have. They were all weekly next door. One or two here are monthly. I take them to Mr. Gregg's office."

"To Mr. Lambert?" Solomon asked.

A shadow passed over Fraser's face. He looked away toward the window as though something had caught his attention. "Don't know any Lambert."

Solomon sighed. "Please. I don't pay for lies."

Fraser swore. "If he knew I talked to you or to anyone else, I'd be dead. What'll my wife do then?"

"What do the wives of all those injured men from next door do now?"

"That ain't my fault!"

"I gather it's Mr. Gregg's fault, and the law will punish him for it. Maybe. Who'll be your landlord then?"

Fraser shrugged. "How should I know?"

"Isn't it Lambert? In fact, isn't he your joint landlord now?"

"I only ever dealt with Gregg," Fraser said.

Solomon took a guess. "But Lambert's promised you can stay on here doing what you do if you keep your mouth shut."

"A man's got to live. I got a wife."

"And you're to keep taking the rents to Gregg's old office."

Fraser nodded sullenly.

Solomon took some coins from his pocket, but didn't yet pass them on. Fraser's eyes were glued to them. "I understand some of the surviving tenants from next door live here now."

"Reduced rent for a couple of weeks."

"Mr. Gregg is all compassion," Solomon murmured.

"Rooms are bigger, less leaks," Fraser said. "Bit of a squash, maybe, but these people got nowhere else to go."

"Where will I find these survivors?"

Fraser pointed at the ceiling. "Upstairs. First room on the left, or the one across the hall. Some of 'em ain't well. Don't go getting them in trouble with—" He broke off abruptly.

"With Mr. Lambert?" Solomon suggested.

"Don't put words in my mouth. Who'd you say you were again?"

"I didn't," Solomon said, holding out the coins.

Fraser snatched them on his way to the door, which he blocked until footsteps had passed and the outside door closed. Then he stood aside without a word and Solomon left.

He had no real need to speak to the survivors upstairs. Neither pity nor charity would solve their problems in the short term. And yet he went.

He found them easily enough. A woman with four children whose husband lay dying of his injuries. A young girl who couldn't move. Despair and grief and sheer hopelessness were everywhere.

"Has she seen a doctor?" Solomon asked the mother of the girl.

The woman looked at him as if he'd grown horns. Despite the nation's outrage, no one had paid for medical attention. And no one, it seemed, had offered any, perhaps because they all assumed someone else was dealing with such an infamous case.

Solomon slid a handful of coins under the girl's pillow. She didn't stir.

"Thank you, sir," her mother said tonelessly, mechanically.

Money would not cure her daughter.

"I know a good doctor who gives his services free," Solomon said. "I'll send him to you. If you can find out everyone who needs his help, that will make his job quicker."

A tiny spark lit her eye and faded. "Thank you," she said again in the same mechanical voice. All her attention was on her daughter.

Solomon moved toward the door. A young man sitting on the floor, staring at nothing, caught his eye, even among the rest of the desperate cases. He did not appear to be injured, though his shoulders were hunched and pain dulled his lost eyes.

"Were you hurt in the accident?" Solomon asked. He had to repeat the question before the man looked up, regarding him without interest.

"No."

"But you were there," Solomon said.

The man shook his head. "Working."

"His wife and babe were there," a woman said aggressively, thrusting a mug of thin, unappetizing soup into the young man's hand. "They died."

"I'm sorry," Solomon said, appalled by the sheer uselessness of the words. He could not even give money to this man. It would be an insult.

"Finally shut him up, didn't it?" the woman said bitterly.

"What do you mean?" Solomon asked.

"You mean you don't know?" she said in disbelief. "He's Lenny Knox, what kicked up the fuss for your bosses, telling everyone what was going on, threatening to withhold rent till the building was fixed. And now he don't care for nothing. He was doing it for them, wasn't he? For Cath and little Kitty."

Knox was staring unseeingly into his soup. The middle-aged woman, as angry as she should be—as *everyone* should be—gently pushed the mug toward his mouth.

Solomon walked away. Everyone walked away. But he would not leave it.

FRANK FRASER, THE caretaker, knew exactly when the stranger left the tenement. He'd opened his door a crack and was listening. The man made him uneasy, though he'd paid well enough for information anyone else could have told him.

Fraser did not believe he was a greedy man at heart, although he liked his ease as well as anyone else. But he had a decent room here and an expensive wife, and if he were to have any hope of keeping her and moving away from Gregg and Lambert, he needed all the money he could get.

Maybe he could tell the stranger a bit more, get more money, though that was a risk… Part of him wanted to land Lambert in the muck, be responsible for taking him down. The bastard deserved it, mostly for Iris, but also for the poor sods who'd died next door.

The stranger walked past Fraser's net-curtained window. He walked and dressed like a toff—not of the first order, perhaps, but the man had money and no lack of confidence, even in these mean streets, among the kids who'd probably already picked his pockets.

Fraser jangled the coins in his own pocket. He could take Iris to the theatre with that money. Or he could save it to get out of St. Giles, get a similar situation with a better landlord—one who wasn't liable to land him in gaol. Perhaps he should wait and see what mood Iris was in when she got back. Where in hell was she, anyway? Spending the rest of the money he'd given her on more bloody clothes, probably. Trying to pretend she was rich, or making herself beautiful for Fraser?

Or for Lambert?

Discontentedly, he threw himself into the chair and tried to plan beyond his jealousy. He needed to get her away from here.

A thought struck him. How much would Lambert pay to know about the stranger sniffing around? How much would

Gregg pay? If he wasn't dead.

If he were honest, Fraser didn't really want to face Lambert. And yet there was a certain justice in getting money from the man in order to leave him.

CONSTANCE WAS TAKING a closer look at the laundry room and the array of irons, considering the possibilities of the small, high window that looked out onto the neighboring building, when Goldie—Duggin the butler's daughter—wandered in.

Goldie was aptly named with her bright yellow curls escaping from her white cap. She could only have been sixteen years old, though she walked like a more mature, sophisticated woman, all conscious grace and femininity. A natural coquette.

"Oh, it's you," she said without enthusiasm. "I hear as you outrank us all except my old dad. So the missus says."

"And what do you say?" Constance asked amiably.

"I say we never paid no attention to rank before and I ain't about to start."

"Good for you," Constance said. "I like a person who can stick to their principles."

This seemed to throw Goldie off her stride. She peered a little suspiciously at Constance, as though suspecting her of some deeper meaning.

"We've all got our jobs to do," Constance added. "And since I'm the new maid and you've all been here some time, I'll need to rely on your help just for a bit."

"Makes sense," Goldie allowed, although the wary look remained. "But we got enough to do without taking on your duties too."

"Of course you have," Constance said in shocked tones. "I wouldn't dream of offloading my jobs on to you. Might ask you where things are for a bit, though, and who to steer clear of."

"Well you don't want to get on the wrong side of his nibs," Goldie said.

"Mr. Lambert?"

"That's him. Or Duggin, me dad, neither, come to that. The others is all right."

"And the mistress is kind?"

"Strict," Goldie said, considering. "But fair."

Constance edged closer. "What about the footmen?"

Goldie blinked, then laughed. "Pat and Robin? They're fine to me 'cause of who my dad is, but you don't want to run into one of them alone in the larder. Ask Denise."

Constance cocked an eyebrow. "Hands?"

"And the rest. Bert's all right, though. More respect, but then, he works for the missus, so he has to. I wouldn't worry, bit of a lark here, and the wages is good. Honest work, too."

"Seems very respectable," Constance said primly, then frowned. "Though I don't like the sound of this ghost. You seen it?"

Goldie's eyes sparkled. "I did—twice!"

Constance gave an exaggerated shiver. "Tell me! Where'd you see it? In the garden, like Mrs. Lambert?"

"Oh yes, it's always in the garden. First time I saw it was from the kitchen window. Just floating through the mist. Scared the life out of me."

"Where was it going?" Constance asked, wide-eyed.

"Gawd knows."

"Toward the house, or away from it?" Constance persisted, emphasizing her unease.

"Toward. That was the first time, anyway. I saw it again from my bedroom window up in the attic, about a week later, and it was gliding away from the house. I still pulled the curtains shut and shook all night."

"You poor thing." Constance peered out at the wall clock in the kitchen. "What time was that? Late at night?"

"When I saw it from my bedroom it was. Must have been

after midnight—I just got up to use the pot and happened to look out to see how near morning it was, and there she was flitting through the fog. By the time I squealed for Denise to look, she'd gone. It wasn't long dark when I saw her from the kitchen door—about six or seven, maybe."

"What day of the week was it?"

"Thursday," Goldie said after a pause. "Actually, both times were a Thursday. That's odd, isn't it?" She giggled. "Maybe that's her day off from heaven."

Constance gave an appreciative smile. "How come it's always foggy when she comes out?"

"Be reasonable. Get a lot of fogs round here. Harder to find a day when there ain't none!"

"True," Constance said.

Goldie was already moving back toward the main kitchen. "Here's Pat and Robin," she said cheerfully. "His nibs must be home."

Constance followed her to find two burly men had filled up the kitchen, declaring they'd murder for a cup of tea and the best of the leftovers from luncheon. Goldie introduced them, and they each favored Constance with long glances of mingled curiosity and derision.

"Lady's maid, eh?" Pat mocked. He was brown haired and bearded, with thick lips and scars vanishing into his facial hair. His knuckles, when he took off his gloves, were scarred too. "Is that a maid what's too fine to make tea for a working man?"

"Why not?" said Constance. "You can't deny you're too fine to make tea for me."

Robin, clean-shaven and fair, but no less brutal about the face, laughed. "She got you there, Patty. How'd the mistress find you, then?"

"By good luck," Constance said.

A bell rang above the door.

"That's the missus," Goldie said to Constance. "She'll be wanting you to help her change for the evening. His nibs insists on it."

"Here," said Pat as Constance brushed past. "What's your name?"

"Miss Silver to you," Constance said with exaggerated grandeur. Goldie and Ida laughed. The men didn't, but nor did they look angry. She suspected she'd got their notice and had no idea if it was a good thing or not.

She found Angela in her bedchamber, brushing out her hair, an evening gown of burgundy silk already laid out on the bed with a wide crinoline beside it.

"Ah, Silver. Finding your way around?" Angela asked, meeting her gaze in the glass with a frown.

Interpreting the scowl to mean they could not speak freely on account of her husband being in the next room, Constance said, "Yes, thank you, ma'am. Everyone's been most helpful. Shall I unfasten your gown now?"

The day gown was duly removed, the crinoline tied in place, and the evening gown placed carefully over Angela's head. The skirts fell elegantly over the petticoat. The style contrasted rather attractively with Angela's severe look, so Constance didn't try to change the style of her hair by much, merely softened it a little by raising her braid higher and looser.

"Very good, Silver," Angela said, while Constance brushed the odd loose hair off her neck and shoulders.

"Do you require a shawl, ma'am?"

Angela looked uncertain. "Should I?"

It was not a question about warmth—it was a question about etiquette. She was trying to be the kind of wife her ambitious husband needed. Constance felt a pang of pity—and understanding, for she too had studied the ways of her betters and aped them so that nowadays she could pass for a lady in most situations.

"It's a cold evening," she said, going to the drawer that she had already discovered to be full of unworn shawls of all kinds. She pulled out three to suggest, and was actually heartened when Angela chose her own favorite of fine cream wool with burgundy embroidery. Draping it first over Angela's shoulders, Constance then let it fall to her elbows to show how good it looked either way.

Angela nodded emphatically and sailed out.

Mindful of her duties, Constance folded the scarves and put them away. Then she hung up the discarded day gown, inspecting it for stains. Only the hem needed brushing. She was tidying the dressing table when the door opened and a man sauntered in.

It could only be Caleb Lambert. Of no more than medium height, he was powerfully built and handsome in a kind of prosperous, sensual way, although his eyes were hard and his lips thin.

"So you're the new maid, are you?" he said.

Constance straightened then dropped a curtsey while he looked her up and down unhurriedly with apparent enjoyment. "Yes, sir. I'm Silver."

He strolled toward her. "Has Mrs. Lambert already gone down?"

"Yes, sir, just a few minutes ago." She turned away in a bustling manner and walked up to wardrobe door where she had hung the day dress. She reached up for it and started when another larger hand got there first. Lambert stood behind her and much too close. Her flesh crawled with old memory and fresh alarm.

She had to force herself to turn to face him, to pretend she didn't notice his nearness or his entitled and appreciative gaze, which she met directly, masking her cold fear with a small, polite smile.

"Thank you, sir. Will you excuse me? I have to clean the hem in case madam wants the gown again in the morning."

He waited deliberately, long enough to make sure she knew he was thinking about it but didn't have to move if he didn't want to. And then he stepped back, and she twitched the dress and hanger from his hand and walked briskly to the door.

On the back stairs she paused, breathing deeply and waiting until she stopped shaking. She wished Solomon were here.

# CHAPTER FIVE

B EFORE HIS APPOINTMENT with Constance, Solomon called on two of the most interesting acquaintances he had made since coming to England. In fact, it was their fault he had met Constance that first time, in a foggy alleyway behind Coal Yard Lane, when a body had hurtled from the roof and almost landed on top of her. His quick reflexes had saved her life when he yanked her out of the way.

Neither of them had had any idea who the other was then. But there had been a moment between them, a strange recognition, both exciting and sensual. At the time, he put it down to mere physical closeness and the relief of such a near brush with death. But it had been more than that. It was one of the few times he had seen her vulnerability. She had looked understandably startled and almost…scared. And later, with the matter in Coal Yard Lane resolved, they had all gone to this almost-hidden house off Half Moon Street to celebrate. They had not spoken to each other, and yet he had been disturbingly aware of her the whole time, even when he discovered she was the notorious courtesan Constance Silver.

When they met again, it had been unexpectedly at Greenforth Manor when she had been pretending to be a respectable widow for reasons of her own. That had been their first mystery…

He walked up the path to the home of Dr. Dragan and Lady Grizelda Tizsa and knocked on the door. This oddly matched and yet strangely suited couple were addicted to mysteries. Coming in on the edges of one of them had been something of an eye-opener for Solomon.

The door was opened not by a servant—although they had at least three—but by Dragan himself, looking supremely casual in shirt sleeves, unbuttoned waistcoat, and no necktie. He was an almost ridiculously handsome man, a refugee from the heroic struggle for Hungarian independence and democracy. Yet his looks were the least of his charms. They covered a quick mind, a staggering amount of knowledge, and a passionate idealism only slightly dented by the failure of his revolution.

"Grey," he said in surprise, instantly opening the door wide in welcome. "Come in."

"I hope I have not called at a bad time," Solomon said, handing his hat to Dragan and taking off his coat.

"Not if you don't mind the continual chaos. We're just back from Scotland and the baby is fractious. Griz will be glad of the company, as am I." Dragan led the way to the drawing room, which looked more like a study, dominated by a huge desk, loaded on both sides with books and notebooks and piles of paper. A guitar was propped up against a comfortable armchair. "Griz is upstairs with Alexander, but she won't be long. Drink?"

Dragan spoke perfect English with only a slight, rather attractive accent. Solomon accepted a glass of brandy.

"I'm afraid I've come to ask a favor," he said.

"Ask," Dragan said.

"Did you read about the tenement building in St. Giles that collapsed a couple of weeks ago?"

Dragan's lips tightened. "I did." He waved Solomon to an armchair by the fire and sat in the one opposite.

"I have just seen some of the survivors, crammed into the building next door. Some of them have received no medical attention, and they're in a bad way."

Dragan frowned, his mouth twisting. "One should be able to expect more of the richest country in the world. Do you have the precise address?"

Solomon described it as best he could, adding, "I don't know what, if anything, you can do for them, but I feel someone should at least try. I thought of you, but there may be other doctors able and willing. I will pay, but I don't want you tell your patients that."

"We'll come to an arrangement after I've seen them," Dragan said vaguely. "How did you get involved in the business? Through one of your charities?"

"Not really, though perhaps I should have. You may not have heard that a partner and I have set up an agency of private inquiry."

Dragan blinked. "That is a bit of a stretch for you, is it not? How do you fit it in?"

"Oh, my other businesses more or less run themselves. I have taken a step back from them and followed my own interests."

"Good for you," Dragan said, smiling. "Who is your partner?"

Solomon wondered if he was blushing like a schoolboy. "Constance Silver."

Dragan, however, did not even look surprised. "Of course. You had that murder in Norfolk to deal with together."

"Did Constance tell you that?"

"She said something to Griz, though only when Griz asked. Actually, Inspector Harris told us."

Dragan's wife came in at that point, smiling delightedly at seeing Solomon. Lady Grizelda was a duke's youngest daughter, apparently considered eccentric and plain by Society. No one could understand how she came to marry such a dazzlingly handsome man as Dragan, although they had no doubt attributed his motives to her birth and fortune and the influence of her father and brothers. In fact, Solomon thought her beautiful, in an unusual if careless and slightly untidy way. She wore unfashionable spectacles, of course, being extremely short-sighted. Like her husband, she had a quick and ravenous mind, with many unexpected talents and interests. So the revolutionary refugee, who disapproved of aristocracy, and the duke's daughter were kindred spirits.

"Mr. Grey!" she greeted Solomon, throwing out her hand. "How lovely to see you!"

When she sat down on the sofa, Dragan quickly told her Solomon's reasons for calling.

"What a wonderful idea," she exclaimed of their inquiry firm. "Perhaps Dragan and I can help occasionally."

"I shouldn't be surprised," Solomon said. "I don't suppose either of you have come across a man called Caleb Lambert? He seems to have grown rich by means of property, both respectable and slum dwellings. In fact, we believe he may be the business partner of Huxley Gregg, the landlord of the collapsed tenement in St. Giles."

"But they'll never get to charging or trying him, will they?" Lady Griz said. "I heard nothing about a partner. Is one of them your client?"

"Neither," Solomon said. "Our client is Lambert's wife, who is concerned about a ghost seen several times in her garden by different people, including her. We're trying to find the logical explanation behind the sightings."

Lady Griz and Dragan exchanged glances.

"There may, of course, *be* a logical explanation," Griz said slowly. "But don't rule out the supernatural either. *There are more things in heaven and earth…* You should keep an open mind."

Solomon blinked. "I am surprised to hear you say so."

"We had an odd experience in Scotland. It opened our minds to situations that might be rare but that do occur."

Solomon thought back to some of the strange beliefs he'd encountered in Jamaica and shivered. Hastily he dragged his mind back to the matter in hand and turned to Dragan. "You move in radical circles, do you not?"

"More social than political these days, but yes."

"Have you ever come across a young man called Knox? Lenny Knox? He lived in the building that collapsed. Apparently he'd been agitating to get repairs done and rent lowered. It's largely because of him that Gregg can't argue he didn't know about the state of the building."

Dragan thought about it, then shook his head. "I don't believe I have."

"His wife and child died in the collapse. It seems to have destroyed him. You might see him among the more physically injured."

Dragan nodded. It was the best Solomon could do for Knox at this stage.

"I'm going to meet Constance now and see what she has discovered." Solomon finished his brandy and stood up to take his leave.

"I'll come with you," Dragan said, rising, and to Griz, "I'm afraid I have patients to see."

"The morning would do, I'm sure," Solomon said with unusual awkwardness.

"For some, it might not," Dragan replied.

Griz got up and passed her husband his tie and coat. If she was disappointed to spend her evening alone, she didn't show it. Probably, as a doctor's wife, she had grown used to it.

Solomon and Dragan took a hackney together part of the way.

"If you wait until I've spoken to Constance, I'll come with you," Solomon said. "Going into St. Giles alone after dark is not wise."

"I have learned the worst places to avoid," Dragan said. "The rest have grown used to me. Just drop me at Long Acre."

"Be careful," Solomon said uneasily, though Dragan had been a soldier and could presumably look after himself.

"You too. You are a little close to the Devil's Acre, are you not?"

"I don't like her being there," Solomon blurted.

"You have to trust in her good sense."

"As you do with your wife's?" Solomon retorted, although

the cases were, of course, far different.

"Yes," Dragan said unexpectedly. He knocked on the carriage ceiling for the driver to halt. "It can be hard, but she would not be Griz if she didn't try."

He was right, Solomon realized as the hackney rolled on. Constance wouldn't be who she was if she didn't throw her heart and soul into things. And she had survived a dreadful past that had at least provided her with good instincts and the means to recognize and escape from problematic situations. He knew that.

He wasn't sure it helped.

He alighted at Westminster Bridge and walked briskly toward the Lamberts' house. Having worried about being late, he found now he was too early, and so, after peering along the street at the front of the house, he moved along the curving lane and around the back of the house, where smaller, meaner dwellings stood. They might once have been mews buildings for stables and carriage houses, though now they were mostly somewhat run-down cottages.

There were no street lamps here, only the faint glimmer from the street beyond and whatever light escaped the closed curtains and shutters of the surrounding windows. At least the sky was clear, revealing the moon and glittering stars.

A dog barked at his passing. A door closed in the distance, but otherwise he saw no one. Before he reached the door to the Lamberts' garden, it opened silently, causing him to press back into the shadows of the wall.

A slender figure slipped through the door, silver in the beam of the moon, and apparently veiled. For an instant, he imagined he was looking at the ghost itself, and his mouth went dry. Clearly, he had paid too much attention to the Tizsas, for the ghostly figure turned, inserted a key, and turned it in the lock.

No ghost ever made a noise like that. Besides, it moved like Constance, quick, graceful, and sensual. He stepped out of the shadows, and her breath caught as she jerked to a halt.

"It's me," he said wryly.

A small, inarticulate noise spilled from her. She threw herself at him, clutching his arm with both hands, painfully tight. "Sol."

He closed his free arm about her, but already she was hurrying him on as though ashamed of the weakness.

"I don't have long. I don't know when she'll ring for me. Seven o'clock would be better tomorrow, while they're dining."

She said nothing else as they sped out of the lane and onto the street, where she pulled him away from the house.

"What happened?" he asked, trying to keep the fear out of his voice.

"Oh, nothing. I don't like Lambert."

"Is he a threat?" Solomon asked calmly while curling his fingers, itching to damage the man just for frightening her.

She drew in a breath. "No. I've faced worse and I can deal with it. I don't have to like it."

"Neither do I. Come out. We'll investigate some other way."

"We'll never get in some other way. The footmen are more like bodyguards, one for her, two for him. They patrol the garden regularly—I only just made it unseen—and watch the street too."

"For what? Ghosts?"

"I suspect the threats are more substantial. He's a villain, Solomon, the sort you can feel without evidence. A nasty piece of work."

"You wouldn't let him near your girls?"

She cast a quick glance up at him, as though she suspected him of making fun of her. In fact, he was perfectly serious. She was an excellent judge of character, and whether she would permit men near her girls was a better guide than most.

"Is Angela frightened of him?" he asked.

"Yes, I think so, but it's as if she's used to it. I get the impression she's not scared into doing what he wants. She's just being a good wife to him. But she doesn't want him to know about me, and now that I've met him, I'm in full agreement."

"Where do you sleep?"

"A dressing room off their bedchamber. There's a key in the

lock."

With his most immediate worries addressed, if not exactly resolved, he tried to concentrate on the case. "What signs of our ghost?"

"None so far. Angela saw it moving erratically away from the house toward the back wall around five or six o'clock. So did Goldie the maid, who also saw it in the middle of the night—after midnight, she thinks. I haven't spoken to the footmen yet. What have you found out?"

"Nothing helpful, though I'm fairly sure Lambert *is* involved with Gregg in the ownership of the collapsed building. There's a greedy rent collector and so-called caretaker by the name of Fraser who's too frightened to say much. And a lot of injured people crammed next door with no help or medical attention except what they can offer each other. Dragan Tizsa has gone to help. I find…"

"You find what?"

"I don't really care about the damned ghost," Solomon said frankly. "I want Gregg and Lambert to pay for what they did. And didn't do."

"Whoever the ghost is might well shed some light on that…"

"Ask Angela about a troublemaker called Lenny Knox," he said impulsively. "He was organizing the tenants into some kind of revolt against their conditions. His wife and baby daughter died in the collapse and now he would appear to have lost heart. In fact, ask her about Fraser the caretaker too." He frowned. "Fraser hasn't seen Gregg since the collapse, but he still takes the weekly rents to the office. There, they claim to have no idea where Gregg is, and they've never, apparently, had anything to do with any Lambert. But the rent money's going into *someone's* pocket."

"Is this what Angela really wants us to find out about?" Constance wondered aloud. "Is the ghost just an excuse because her conscience bothers her?" She shivered. "I have to go back. Can you come at seven tomorrow?"

"I can." She drew her arm free of his, but he held it a moment longer. "Constance."

She raised a perfectly arched eyebrow. Her eyes were once more clear and damnably lovely. Quite suddenly he was plagued, as he often was, by the memory of lying in bed beside her, untouching, aroused and damnably frustrated. And one precious night when he had simply held her…

He swallowed. "Take no chances. Leave if there is any threat to your safety whatsoever."

"I will, but there won't be," she said, slipping away with a quick, cocky smile that was pure Constance.

As HAD BECOME their habit since moving to this house, Caleb Lambert escorted his wife from the dining room to the drawing room, where they sat by the fire and talked about business.

Caleb had always been in the habit of discussing such matters with her. She was a useful sounding board and, besides, she had a good brain behind her once-lovely face. Not so beautiful now, of course, but she was still a handsome woman and important to him in a way his many affairs were not. She knew that. She was, in fact, the perfect wife for him… If only she weren't so damned common.

So was he, of course, but he had mixed for a long time with the upper echelons of Society as well as the lowest of the low, and he could adjust enough not to be despised. Angela, however, carried her origins in her voice. She could never mix with the wives of the people he was cultivating now. Unless she kept her mouth shut. Perhaps she could just smile…

In a quiet moment, he said, "How do you like your new maid, then?"

"She's very polite and willing," Angela said. "And I like how she talks."

"So do I," Lambert said, pleased. "Maybe you can copy her.

Then I can take you to Sir Nicholas Swan's charity ball."

"Maybe," Angela said. "When were you talking to her?"

Was that suspicion in her eyes? Jealousy? "Just for a moment before dinner," he said easily. "I knocked on your door to see if you were ready and she told me you'd just gone down. Pretty little thing. The lads will be fighting over her."

"I don't fancy any of their chances," Angela said with a curl of her lip. "She's stepping out with a much classier gent."

"Then what's she working for you for?"

"Saving up for marriage? How do I know? I took a shine to her."

"Then you don't want a proper footman after all?"

"Not right now," Angela said, much to his relief.

Another man in the house who owed nothing to Lambert, and yet was liable to hear and see what he wasn't meant to, would have been a dangerous thing. Lambert didn't want strangers so close to him.

"Did you see anything of Gregg today?" she asked.

He shifted uneasily. "No, and I don't want to. If he's keeping his distance, that suits me fine."

"What if he talks to the inquiry, like he said? Lands you in it along with him?"

"Gregg'd never do that, whatever he said to me the other day. Too much the gentleman."

She cast him a look that was almost derisive. "And when all the rents start coming direct to you?"

"By then, the law won't be looking."

"No, but Lenny Knox might. And all those other angry sods who lost family."

"Give it a rest, Angie," he growled. "It's all sorted. None of them will come after me."

"Pride goes before a fall, Caleb."

"I ain't proud. And neither you nor me will fall."

"Muck always rises," she said bitterly.

"We ain't muck," he snarled. "Never think it. We're just

ambitious. Backbone of this country."

Sometimes, he even believed that.

HOW TO EXPLAIN the sheer emotion that flooded Constance when Solomon had stepped out of the shadows? Relief that he was no threat was in there, but swamped by all the rest, chief of which was fierce happiness and the reasonless belief that now all was right with the world.

Solomon had become *necessary* to her. It was a dangerous weakness, for she had not relied on anyone since early childhood. And yet she had to stop herself from seizing him and hugging him close. As it was, she had nearly broken his arm with the ferocity of her grip. And his instant response, while embarrassing her, warmed her from her toes.

If she were honest with herself, that was what made it so much easier to return to the Lamberts' house. She was not alone again among scary, alien enemies. Solomon was within reach. And she could take care of herself.

She had to knock at the back door to get back into the house. Even facing Duggin did not trouble her. "Where've you been?" he asked coldly as she breezed inside and he closed and locked the door behind her.

"Just getting some fresh air before I have to attend the mistress. She hasn't rung, has she?"

He didn't blink often enough, which made him appear oddly menacing. "As well for you she hasn't. You don't leave the premises without permission."

"Without the mistress's permission," she said, as though agreeing. "Or instruction. I'll just go up and make sure her night things are laid out ready."

"She'll be a while yet," said the maid Denise, carrying a tray of dirty crockery into the kitchen. "They're in the drawing room.

After that she always goes back to her parlor for a bit before bed. We'll take their tea up in a bit, then we can have ours and get to bed."

"Except you." Duggin smirked at Constance. "You'll have to wait for the mistress."

"Doesn't Mr. Lambert have a valet?" she asked as though surprised.

"Mr. Lambert is quite capable of dressing himself."

Constance went upstairs and prepared Angela's night things as best she could. She found her skin prickling, every sense alert for the intrusion of Lambert. She put another coal on the fire before she left and returned to the kitchen.

Tea and a light supper were laid out on the table. All the servants were there, though after ten minutes, Pat and Robin went out on their usual patrol of the garden. Conversation was desultory—everyone, presumably, was tired. Constance, used to late nights, was not.

When Pat and Robin returned, they nodded to Duggin and sat down again. A minute later, Duggin rose.

"Get your heads down," he said curtly, and went out.

"Come on, girls," Ida urged the maids, while she got out her flask. "Let's have this washed up and then we're done." She took a healthy swig and stood. "Night, all. Don't let me hear you much longer."

Constance felt the gaze of the "footmen" upon her. She looked directly back at each in turn. There was curiosity and varying degrees of avid lust, so open that it had to come from a sense of power. And that, in servants, had to come from the power of their master. Lambert had power in their underworld, so no one crossed his nearest underlings either. Or refused their advances, no doubt.

Constance, however, was a master of such rejection.

After a considering look at each, she let her bored gaze slide to the curtained window and sat up straighter. "See any signs of Mrs. Lambert's ghost when you were out there?"

"Don't be daft," scoffed Robin. "That's women's rubbish."

"No it ain't," Bert argued. "Me and Pat both saw it."

"Goldie told me," Constance said. "Did you recognize her, then? Is she the ghost of some dead person in a painting or what?"

"You got some imagination," Robin said. "I like that in a girl."

"No you don't," Constance said carelessly. "You just called it rubbish. Well, is she?" she asked, gazing from Bert to Pat and back.

"I never saw anyone like her," Bert said. "Mind you, it weren't that easy to make out her face, what with the dark and the mist and her all veiled and ghostly like…"

"He's right for once," Pat agreed. "Total stranger."

*They're lying.* The realization came with a sweep of excitement that she could neither show nor challenge directly.

"But totally dead," she said.

"None deader," Bert said.

Constance gave a little shiver of anticipation. "Tell me what you saw…"

They were halfway through a story told in the clear hope of impressing her when a ringing bell interrupted them. But at least she'd learned the day, the time, and the direction of the sighting.

"Duty calls," she said brightly. "I'll bid you all goodnight now."

She hurried up the back stairs to the main bedroom and found Angela seated at her dressing table in her nightgown and robe, brushing out her hair.

"Shall I do that?" she asked.

"Don't be daft, I can manage," Angela said shortly. "What have you found out so far?"

"Not a huge amount," Constance admitted, glancing toward the connecting door that led to Lambert's room.

"Don't worry about him. He's still in his office."

What did he do there at this time of night?

Constance said, "I think Pat and Bert might know more about your ghost than they're saying. I think they did recognize her, or at least suspect who she is."

Their eyes met in the looking glass. Angela's fell first.

"Is it possible?" Constance asked steadily.

"Course it is. They give you any names?"

"No. Perhaps you can."

"I didn't hire you to do the work for you," Angela snapped.

"No, but I'm not quite sure why you *did* hire us."

"To find out who she is."

"You already know who she is," Constance said. "Or at least you suspect. Like Bert and Pat."

Angela stood abruptly and paced to the fireplace, where she turned and faced Constance again. "I don't *know*. It's the not knowing that troubles me because that means I can't deal with it. I never believed in ghosts or spirits, never even thought of them until…" She jerked her shoulder, impatient with herself. "Until I suddenly understood that some things are so bad, the dead can't rest. My husband…"

Her gaze flickered away again. She was a woman stuck between the silent loyalty of years and a painful, desperate need to know the truth.

Pity stirred in Constance. "You suspect something your husband did is beyond forgiveness?" she said gently.

Angela nodded. "A building collapsed with people inside it."

Back to that. Although her heart gave a little bump of excitement, Constance kept her voice steady. "I read about that. People died."

"A lot of people," Angela said, pacing again, twisting the belt of her dressing gown in her fingers. "Too many. Among them was a young woman, little more than a girl, with her own baby. A good, clever girl. I met her once."

Was this the family Solomon had wanted her to ask about? "You knew one of the people who died?" Constance said cautiously. "That must be awful for you. But why should she haunt this house? Or this garden?"

"She asked me to speak to my husband, to get the building

repaired before the worst happened. I never did. Never had time."

"But your husband wasn't the landlord," Constance pointed out. "That was Huxley Gregg."

"They're friends," Angela said shortly. "And I'm a woman who used to be like Cathy Knox, young and strong with nothing but ideals and determination to make a better life. I failed her."

"Gregg failed her. Why doesn't she haunt *him*?"

Angela smiled faintly, seeming to relax. "That's what I said to myself. I know it's nothing to do with me, but still, I can't forget her. Guilt's a funny thing, isn't it? Of course, I *know*—in my head—that the ghost isn't Cathy Knox. Can't be. I expect Pat and Bert know that too."

"You think it's a real person with a grudge?"

"Maybe."

"A grudge against you or your husband because of your connection with Gregg?"

"That's what you have to find out."

"What *is* his connection with Gregg?"

Angela shrugged. "They've been friends a long time. Partners in many ventures."

"In ownership of that building?"

"I don't know. He says not."

"But you don't entirely believe him. Where would I find Gregg?"

"Don't know. He ain't been home since the collapse. He doesn't come here anymore, neither. Which at least keeps Caleb out of it."

"But he isn't out of it, is he?"

Angela swung on Constance, seizing her wrist in a grip that hurt. "Don't ever say that. He'll kill you."

# CHAPTER SIX

SOLOMON ARRIVED EARLY at the Silver and Grey office to find Janey already at the door waiting for him. She was dressed as a respectable lady's maid, which it was apparently her ambition to become, but there was no disguising her confident, cheeky grin.

"Wotcha, sir. Sleep in, did you?"

"No," said Solomon, unlocking the door. It was not yet full daylight.

Janey's eyes widened when he ushered her in before him. She opened all the curtains and lit one of the lamps in his main office, while he divested himself of his hat and overcoat. "You seeing herself today?" she demanded as he walked into his office.

"Yes."

"Can you give her a message from me?"

"Certainly."

"Tell her Boggie fancies himself in the higher leagues. Absorbing businesses, legit and other, as he goes. He's got the backing of someone big, and his threats have been working."

Solomon gazed at her, knowing it would be too much of a coincidence. "Who is the backer?"

"Whisper is, it's Caleb Lambert."

"Janey, do you *know* Lambert?"

"Course I don't know him," she said derisively. "Heard of him, though. He owned the brothel I'd have gone to if herself hadn't found me. He don't own it now. Sold it."

"How do you know?"

She shrugged. "Friends."

"Did you tell Mrs. Silver any of this?"

Janey stared at him. "No, she never asked. Why would she care about a bastard like Lambert?"

*Because she's living in his house.* "How do you know he's a bastard?"

"Friends," Janey said again. "Think he was turning respectable like, which is why he sold the brothel."

"Whom did he sell it to?"

Janey thought. "Don't know," she said. "I can find out, though. If you tell her about Boggie."

"I will, of course. One more thing. Do you know about the tenement building collapse that killed people in St. Giles?"

"I heard. Everybody heard."

"Ever hear a whisper that Lambert was involved?"

"No, but I can find out about that too."

"Discreetly, Janey. Lambert's dangerous."

Janey grinned. "So am I. Want some tea, guv?"

DESPITE HER LOCKED door, Constance did not sleep well. Which was why she was already awake when she heard the house stirring, and was able to rise, dress, and go down to the kitchen for a cup of tea before returning to Angela's room to clean out, rebuild, and light the fire. It was Denise who carried the coal for her, not the footmen, none of whom seemed to rise early.

Ida, who was making fresh bread, gave her a slice of yesterday's toasted, with a good slathering of butter and jam. "Mrs. L likes tea and toast in her room at eight."

"Thanks."

There was a pall of fog beyond the window when Constance opened Angela's curtains. *Ghost weather,* she thought with a twinge of excitement.

"Can I ask you something?" Angela asked from the bed, where she was sitting propped up by lacy pillows, a shawl around her shoulders, a tray of tea and buttered toast across her legs.

"Of course." Constance turned to face her.

"You're from my world, aren't you? You're no more a lady than I am."

"Probably not," Constance said. "I suppose it depends on your definition of 'lady.'"

"For these purposes, it's how you sound, and you got that perfect. I could have sworn you were a lady when we first met."

Constance cast her eyes at the connecting door, as she had done last night, and again Angela dismissed her fears.

"He's gone. For the day, most likely. How'd you do it, then?"

"I suppose I'm a natural mimic. And I observed and listened and learned. I was fortunate to have that opportunity."

"I never had it. Would you teach me? When we both have time."

"If you like. Not everyone has a good ear, though."

"I'd like to try." Angela looked embarrassed. "Caleb's come up in the world. He wants a wife who don't sound like she came out of the gutter."

Caleb did not deserve her efforts. He was not faithful to her, judging by the way he'd looked at Constance. She wondered if Angela knew and that was why she tried so hard.

"You don't want to sound like you're putting it on, either," she said.

Angela nodded quite seriously, then changed the subject. "I'll be going out today. I'll take Bert and I won't need you."

"Good. I thought I'd just lurk near the windows or in the garden, looking for ghosts."

"Don't blab if you find out who it is," Angela said sharply. "I want to know first."

"Of course."

Angela nodded. "Then I'll wear that gray gown."

With both the master and mistress of the house out of the way, Constance took the opportunity to look around the place more carefully. She began with Angela's parlor, because Angela was keeping relevant things from her, and that was neither safe nor fair. As she hoped, there was no one in the room, so she went directly to the tidy roll-top desk. Half expecting it to be locked, she lifted the top, and it slid smoothly back.

An appointment book lay in front of her, with a marker at today's date. There were appointments listed, though frustratingly, they were merely initials with times.

*9am – SD*
*11am – W – RG*
*1pm – M*
*3pm – CL – F*

Which meant precisely nothing to her. She could not even make the initials match anyone connected to the case—except, she supposed, the "F" at three p.m. could be Fraser, the caretaker of the buildings at St. Giles. No Huxley Gregg, though. Probably, she was simply meeting friends.

The entries for other days were similar, though the initials were different. Some days displayed very little, an occasional C with a time, which could have referred to Caleb.

Giving up on the book, Constance rifled through the shelves and drawers. On the bottom shelf she found two long, slender ledgers full of figures that again meant nothing to her, although the amounts involved were large.

The smaller drawers and shelves contained only notepaper, envelopes, sealing wax, pens, and ink. It seemed that if Angela received any correspondence, she did not keep it.

The waste basket was empty. The fire in the parlor was not yet lit, presumably because Angela was out for the day, but it had been cleaned and set. The whole room was pristine and somehow clinical. Though furnished like a lady's private sitting room or boudoir, it felt to Constance like an office. Well, Angela was a tidy person.

Emerging cautiously from the room, Constance heard the distant chatter of the maids from the top landing. Presumably they were making beds and tidying bedchambers. Pat and Robin would have gone out with Lambert. It was as good an opportunity as she was likely to have.

She crossed the hall toward the baize door that led to the kitchen. Next to it was Lambert's office, where she had been told never to go. But Angela secretly feared the ghost was the spirit of someone her husband had wronged, probably Cathy Knox. Her more rational belief was that it was some living person he had wronged, who was out for vengeance. If Constance was to truly investigate...

Her heart beating faster, she raised her hand and lifted the latch. It gave a small click, but otherwise, the door opened smoothly. Lambert, clearly, saw no need to lock the door. Because he trusted his household? Ot because none but Angela could read? She realized she didn't even know if Lambert could. Was Angela his clerk?

This room was not so neat and clean. There was dust on some of the shelves and on the carpet and the back of the large desk that dominated the room. But a pile of letters, both opened and unsealed, lay to one side of the desk. Another, half finished, lay in the middle. She was not close enough to judge the handwriting yet.

The fire was not yet lit here either, but on the mantelpiece above it, propped up against the wall, were cards of invitation. Interesting. She was about to move into the room when a sudden, sharp voice made her jump.

"What are you doing there?" Duggin demanded.

He stood holding the baize door to the kitchen, through which he had clearly just emerged with alarming silence. Fortunately, she had her story planned and ready.

"Looking for madam's shawl that she wore last night. Either she mislaid it or I did."

"It's not in there," Duggin said coldly.

Constance sighed. "No, it does not appear to be. Nor is it in the parlor, the dining room, or the drawing room. I wonder if I was foolish enough to pick it up with the laundry by mistake? I'll just nip down and see…"

"Mrs. Lambert is never in this room. No one but Mr. Lambert is allowed in here, apart from on cleaning days."

Constance flared her nostrils. "And there don't appear to be many of those." Closing the door, she ignored Duggin's scowl and brushed past him. He made a fuss about locking the office door. *Damn.*

She pushed open the silently swinging baize door, and for the first time noticed another door on the left, almost hidden in gloom. Duggin came up behind her, making her flesh crawl, although she refused to show it.

"What's in there?" she asked brazenly, nodding toward the newly discovered door.

"The wine cellar," Duggin replied with exaggerated patience. "Mrs. Lambert don't go in there neither. Only Mr. Lambert and me."

Constance sailed on as though she had lost interest. In the kitchen, she made a fuss of looking through the laundry for the missing shawl that was not missing at all, then returned, muttering about nerves, to Angela's bedchamber. And her own.

She closed the door and locked it before extracting paper and pencil from the top drawer of her chest. Sitting on the bed, she began to write down everything they had learned about the ghost sightings, including both rational and supernatural explanations, and Angela's suspicions as well as her own and Solomon's.

It wasn't a memory aid. She remembered everything said to her and everything she read with an accuracy most people found startling. But writing things down sometimes helped her to see patterns and possibilities she hadn't previously thought of.

And there *were* patterns. The ghost was only seen in fog, and only on Thursdays and Saturdays. Moreover, the times and directions of the sightings were consistent, too. Goldie's talk of a day off was actually a possibility, though hardly from heavenly chores.

Everyone who'd seen it agreed the ghost was a female figure. If it was someone from outside—someone working for Lambert's rivals or enemies, or for Gregg—then they faced the problem of the locked door at the foot of the garden. They could have come in via the front, of course—though the gates were apparently locked at night—but no one had ever seen the ghost at the front, only in the back garden. It wouldn't be an easy climb for a woman in skirts, and unless she was very agile—or had help—she would not be able to do so in silence.

Constance tapped the end of the pencil against her teeth.

The likelihood was, then, that the intruder had a key.

Or came from within the house. Angela, Goldie, Bert, and Pat had all claimed to see the ghost. Which, of the females in the household, left only the maid Denise and Ida.

Interesting. What were their backgrounds? Why were they here with the Lamberts?

Constance scrunched the paper in hand and threw the pencil back into its drawer. Then, remembering her own curiosity in the parlor, she took her scrunched notes with her into the main bedroom and fed them into the fire.

SOLOMON, DRESSED IN his normal business attire, went first to the office of Huxley Gregg, a respectable suite of rooms in the city.

He was greeted with courtesy by the clerk nearest the door, who rose, while another two continued to work industriously.

"Good morning, sir. How can we help you today?"

"I'd like to see Mr. Gregg, if you please. Here is my card."

Interestingly, his name clearly meant something to the young clerk, for his eyes widened and began to gleam. "Mr. Grey! An honor to receive you."

"Then Mr. Gregg is available now?" Solomon had hardly dared hope.

"Sadly not, sir. But Mr. Aitken is entirely in his confidence if you'd care to come this way."

*Entirely in Gregg's confidence* might prove useful, Solomon reflected, following the young man the length of the large room to the door at the back. A nameplate read, *W. Aitken, General Manager*.

The clerk knocked and waited to be answered before opening the door and pushing it wide.

"Mr. Solomon Grey, sir," he said in awed tones. "In the absence of Mr. Gregg, I was sure you would be able to help."

Mr. Aitken, a balding, middle-aged man with round spectacles, almost bounced to his feet, walking eagerly forward with one hand already stretched out. "Tea, Jones," he threw at the clerk. "Mr. Grey! I'm Wilfred Aitken. Allow me to take your coat and hat."

Solomon allowed it while the clerk bustled off. Aitken invited him to sit and beamed at him. No wonder. In Gregg's terrible publicity over the building collapse, the manager could never have expected to receive an inquiry from a man of such distinction.

Solomon's gaze strayed around the opulent office, lingering on the portrait of a serious and surprisingly young gentleman above the fireplace. "Is that Mr. Gregg?"

"Indeed it is, sir. I believe it was painted some five years ago. It is a very good likeness, I think, combining as it does Mr. Gregg's gentlemanly origins with his knowledge of business matters."

"It does not seem such a great tactic to allow his investment to collapse," Solomon observed.

Aitken's smile vanished into sadness as he shook his head. "A terrible tragedy, caused by a unique combination of circumstances that have little to do with Mr. Gregg. As you will be aware, our largest concentration of property is in the more affluent areas of the city. For instance, this delightful property, part of our holdings in Belgravia, has just become available. It would be perfect for a man of your standing."

Solomon stretched his lips very slightly. "Would it? I would really need to speak to Mr. Gregg himself before I could consider such an acquisition."

"Sadly, Mr. Gregg has had to make himself unavailable, in order to deal with personal matters."

"Has he? What a shame," Solomon said, rising.

Aitken jumped up with clear alarm.

"Unless..." Solomon paused. "Perhaps you could direct me instead to his partner, Mr. Lambert?"

"Mr. Lambert has offices just around the corner," Aitken said, clearly disappointed, although he opened a drawer in his desk and removed a card, which he passed to Solomon. "But I believe you will find we have more to offer."

"Then this firm is not partnered with Mr. Lambert?"

Aitken licked his lips. "In some ventures. Not in all."

"The house you mention in Belgravia?"

"Certainly," Aitken said eagerly.

"The tenement in St. Giles that collapsed? And the one still standing next to it?"

Aitken's lips tightened. "I believe not."

"Then you alone take charge of the rents from the extant property?"

"It is banked in the usual way," Aitken said stiffly. "If you have an interest in such properties, sir, I believe both Mr. Gregg and Mr. Lambert would be willing to sell."

Solomon tapped his fingers on the desk as though considering. "Is there much money to be made from such lowly investments?"

"There's always money to be made if one knows how."

"That's what I thought," Solomon murmured. "Though a lot to lose if one's investment collapses."

"A once-in-a-lifetime tragedy for us all," Aitken said nervously.

"Of its type, one trusts so, though of course there is always the other ever-present danger of fire, cholera, and other diseases spreading like the wind amidst such overcrowding."

"One is never short of tenants."

"No," Solomon said, eyeing him with dislike. "I don't suppose you are. And you do vouch for Mr. Lambert's reputation?"

"I have every reason to believe in his respectability. He and Mr. Gregg invest together in many ventures."

"And if Mr. Gregg goes to prison," Solomon said, watching Aitken wince, "what will become of those joint ventures?"

"That is so unlikely a contingency that I could not possibly guess. Are you seriously considering the property in Belgravia?"

Out of the blue, a vision flashed into Solomon's mind, of himself walking through a gracious, empty house, inspecting the rooms and making plans. A woman walked by his side, his partner in all things.

*Ludicrous.*

He rose hastily, hoping he didn't look as disconcerted as he felt. "I am always serious, Mr. Aitken. After speaking to Mr. Lambert, I may well be back."

He went immediately to Lambert's office, before any messengers from Aitken could reach him. It was indeed only a short walk around the corner. Here, he was admitted by a large doorman, although a glance at the individual, who wore no livery, caused him to wonder if this was one of Lambert's footmen-bodyguards that Constance had told him about.

"My name is Grey," he said, with more haughtiness than he had employed in Gregg's office. "Mr. Lambert, if you please."

The card he held out in no particular direction was taken not by the large doorman but by a clerk who bustled up to him. His jaw showed a tendency to gape.

"Mr. Grey! Please do sit down for one moment…" The clerk all but fled to one of the two offices opening off the main room. He appeared to be the only occupant of the outer office, if one ignored the muscle.

The clerk obviously knew Solomon's name. He wondered if Lambert did. If not, the clerk clearly enlightened him, for in only moments, he was escorted into a neat, very unbusy office, occupied by another large young man in one corner, and, presumably, Lambert himself.

Unlike Aitken, Lambert did not fawn. He granted audiences in a manner guaranteed to take the self-important down a peg. If he hadn't been born with the gift, it had certainly become natural to him. Solomon disliked him on sight, though whether on the basis of his own instincts or Constance's, he wasn't sure.

The man's hair was dark and oiled, his whiskers well trimmed. His mouth was full, at once sensual and brutal, and his eyes… They were not the eyes of anyone Solomon would ever do business with. Constance's presence in this man's house appalled him.

Only his habitual reserve kept the distaste from his expression. Fortunately, Lambert did not offer to shake hands.

"Mr. Grey," he said genially. "Sit down and tell me how I might assist you."

Solomon sat without gratitude. Lambert resumed his seat on the other side of the desk. The clerk had vanished, although the large man in the corner was still there, lounging on a chair. No pictures or portraits relieved the stark, clean walls of this room, although the carpet underfoot was thick and the curtains opulent. The chair was comfortable, too.

"I have just come," Solomon said, "from the office of Mr. Gregg. I prefer to meet personally anyone I consider doing business with."

"Very wise, Mr. Grey. It's a precaution I always take myself. What sort of business do you have in mind?"

"Property, since I am here," Solomon said in a bored, slightly disappointed voice. "I am always looking for new investment possibilities, and then there is the matter of a suitable residence. Gregg's man, Aitken, was recommending Belgravia."

"It's the new Mayfair," Lambert told him. "We have built

several beautiful homes there that are much admired and sought after." His accent was interesting—less obviously London than his wife's, as though by mixing with the better bred he had sheered the rough edges off it, yet wisely never bothered to pretend to be a gentleman. Presumably that had been Gregg's part in their partnership.

"It is one matter I am considering," Solomon said. "The other is less…expensive properties—such as the one that has landed Mr. Gregg in all sorts of difficulties. You are his partner in that venture?"

Lambert smiled, undisturbed. "You've been misinformed. I don't take such risks."

"Yet your partner does? This does not fill me with confidence."

"Gregg grew careless, which is why I've disembarrassed myself of much of the business we had together. Now we go our own ways."

"Apart from the Belgravia properties."

"For the moment."

"And your St. Giles properties?"

Lambert met his gaze without fear. "Do you have one in mind?"

"To be frank, I'm thinking of the one that fell down, which does give one pause. What will happen to those properties now? Will a new building be constructed on the plot of the old one?"

"Ask Gregg."

"I would if I could find him. He is never at home, and he no longer attends his office."

"Keeping low till the inquiry blows over."

"I daresay that is wise. You, being his partner, wouldn't know where I can reach him?"

"We were never that close," Lambert said.

"Then you could not advise me on the business of…lesser properties?"

Lambert didn't bat an eyelid. "You'd get Gregg's buildings for a song right now. On the other hand, I couldn't advise it."

Clever. Did he know Solomon was not serious about entering the business of slum landlords? Or was he just testing the waters?

"Who could?" Solomon asked. "Whom would I approach about the possibility of purchase?"

"Mr. Gregg, of course. Or his office."

"How odd," Solomon said, holding the man's steady gaze. "I had the impression *you* were the important partner."

Lambert was considering him very carefully, greed no doubt warring with risk. "Perhaps you should come and see me again," he said at last, rising to his feet. "After the inquiry."

"You know, I don't think that will be necessary," Solomon said, standing unhurriedly. "Good day, Mr. Lambert."

"Mr. Grey."

It had been a long time since his neck had prickled in quite such an alarming fashion, or for quite so long. Within five minutes of stepping into the street, he was sure he was being followed.

Lambert was suspicious. Interesting. And it was rather too dangerous to return to the Silver and Grey offices. Instead, Solomon took a hackney to St. Catherine's, where his largest warehouse resided.

# CHAPTER SEVEN

CONSTANCE WENT DOWN to the kitchen about half an hour before a break was due to be decreed. The maids' voices drifted out of the drawing room, so clearly it was not the time to catch Denise alone.

Ida, however, *was* alone, just taking a batch of delicious-smelling scones out of the oven.

"Want a cup of tea, dearie?" she asked amiably.

"I'd love one," Constance admitted, deciding to keep her stories consistent. "I spent all morning chasing my tail, looking for a shawl I'd already put away in its own drawer! I don't know where my mind goes sometimes." She put cups onto a tray by way of helping, and sloshed a little cream into each. She had already noticed how the cook liked hers. "Must be my nerves. I'm always like this when I start a new position."

"Are you, duckie?" Ida poured boiling water from the kettle into the teapot, covered it, and waddled over to the table. Constance brought the tray with the cups. "How many positions you had, then?"

"Just enough to know the signs."

"How'd you learn to be a lady's maid, then? Who taught you?"

"I suppose I followed in my mother's footsteps," Constance said, although those footsteps had nothing of domestic service about them. "Up to a point. I've never been in a house like this before, though. She seems kind, Mrs. Lambert."

"None kinder," Ida said with unexpected fervor.

"Have you been with her a long time?"

"Five years. But I knew her since she was a girl." Ida lifted the lid of the teapot, gave the tea a quick swirl with a spoon, and replaced the lid. "Off and on."

Constance waited for more, but Ida said nothing, merely hefted the pot in an absent kind of a way and poured out the tea.

Constance tried again. "She's not a slave driver, either. Very light on the things she wants me to do for her. She says she hasn't had a lady's maid before."

"Make sure you don't take advantage," Ida said. For once, her eyes were focused and serious.

"I wouldn't," Constance assured her. She sipped her tea. "You're very defensive of her."

"I am," Ida said almost grimly. "Five years ago, I was nothing. I lost my husband and my kids to fever. Had nowhere to live, no job. Had nothing to live for, but she took me in, let me stay for nothing if I just cooked for them. So I did, and then I did it so much that she paid me for it, and brought me here when they moved."

"From the Acre?" Constance said casually. She thought all the more of Angela Lambert for her kindness, her compassion, but she had to pry and poke until she found out something that made sense of the ghost.

"Yes. I ain't sorry to see the back of that place, though it's only a step away. Like another world."

"I heard of this position through someone who worked for Mr. Gregg," Constance lied. "Did he ever come here?"

"Now and again," Ida said with a shrug. "Never came to the old place, and who could blame him? But he were good for Caleb Lambert. Brought connections to the partnership."

"What did Mr. Lambert bring?" Beside muscled ruffians and a knowledge, no doubt, of slums.

Ida tapped her temple. "Brains. Clever sod, is Caleb Lambert."

"You like him?" Constance asked, mostly because it hadn't sounded like a compliment at all.

"Not much. Don't have to, do I? I cook for him and he pays me well. It's the missus I like, and always will."

"Does everyone in the house feel that way?"

A hint of confusion clouded Ida's eyes, a realization, no doubt, that she'd said more than she should. She took out her flask and poured a splash into her tea.

"Don't ask," she said. "But I'd say so. Here come the girls. Duggin won't be far behind."

SOLOMON DID NOT linger for long in his old office. Everything appeared to be working just fine without him. He wasn't sure whether to congratulate himself on that or not.

By the time he left, the mist from the river had risen to connect with outpourings from steam vessels and factory chimneys, clogging the air with thick, stinking fog. It slowed the hackney that carried him into Seven Dials.

In that warren of iniquity, the fog was a mixed blessing. It made his own person harder to see. But then, he could not see attacks coming, either. The footsteps behind him probably only sounded stealthy, and yet someone had followed him from Lambert's office, possibly even before that…

He was concentrating too hard on the footsteps behind. The attack from the right of a narrow alley took him completely by surprise. A paralyzing blow struck his side, and then he was shoved hard up against a wall, the cold steel of a blade at his throat while he gasped for breath.

"You're outside your own world," someone growled into his face, his breath rancid with old beer, fatty meat, and tobacco. "Stay away from the Dials if you want to live."

And then he was free. Without a mark on him. The luckiest

victim in Seven Dials. He hadn't even been robbed. Bizarre.

Solomon started after his attacker so quickly that he bumped into someone else entirely and was roundly sworn at.

"Sorry," he muttered, and barged past. But the fog had grown so thick that it was impossible to tell which of the vague, hurrying figures in front of him had been his attacker. He followed one who looked roughly the right shape, and deliberately jostled him to see the reaction.

But it was a much younger man who glared back at him, slapping his hands defensively over his pockets. "Mind your step."

Solomon gave up. He had been warned off Seven Dials, not the wider area of St. Giles. *Interesting…*

Thoughtfully and with some difficulty, he found his way to the backstreet where Juliet Silver did her business.

The same youth let him in. This time he waited in the hall, on a slightly dusty chair surrounded by curios of silver, gold, and fine porcelain, in between the junk and the tat. But although he was left alone, he knew he was still being watched. In Constance's establishment, it was much more blatant. A blank-eyed footman in livery stood to attention within feet, or directly outside whichever salon he had been abandoned in.

Within a couple of minutes, the boy came back and took him not to the parlor he had seen before but an equally cluttered office where the plump, opulent person that, amazingly, was Constance's mother reached out a hand to him without getting up from the desk.

"What an unexpected pleasure, Mr. Grey. Are you buying or selling, or have you come to ask me for more help?"

"None of these, probably." He took her hand and bowed slightly, which made her eyes dance.

"Connie know you're here?" she asked shrewdly.

"Not yet. How much has Boggie been bothering you?"

She still smiled. "Oh, he don't bother me none, love. I'm much too indolent to get worked about such things."

"What things?"

Juliet regarded him with sleepy eyes that somehow managed to be perfectly sharp. "I'd think you really were a peeler, except you're too well dressed."

"Constance is worried about you."

Juliet raised her brows with polite disbelief. "You just told me she doesn't know you're here."

"She doesn't. But she did ask a"—he broke off at the sheer impossibility of describing Janey—"asked a friend who is working for us to look into Boggie and what he wanted with you."

The disbelief didn't fade, although her eyes remained fixed on him, perhaps with curiosity. "And what did this friend say?"

"That Boggie is trying to buy out your business and that he had the backing of an unsavory man called Lambert."

Juliet frowned. "Is Lambert not *your* unsavory character? Boggie is mine."

"Then you really don't know anything about Lambert?"

"I asked around after you left on Tuesday. Made his money from shares in other people's crimes, and subletting filthy rooms. Rose to being landlord of several such filthy rooms and then tenement buildings. Now he's shedding everything illegal, while spreading further into anything that's only *just* legal. He's a nasty player. And several people do link him to that collapsed building. They seen him there, and his wife. So it wasn't just Gregg."

"I didn't think it was. Yet Gregg's carrying the full blame for it."

"And why do you think that is?" Juliet asked, her lip curling with a hint of contempt for the rich, pampered fellow she thought him.

"Because he's afraid of Lambert," Solomon said. "And no one's going to investigate very far beyond Gregg. A good many of the rich and powerful have fingers in unsavory pies. No one wants to rock a boat full of outwardly respectable slum landlords. Gregg's a scapegoat, but even he will probably be back."

Her lips stretched into a faint smile that might just have been reflected in her eyes. "You ain't just a pretty coat full of bugger all, are you, son? I should've known my Constance wouldn't hook a fool, though she'd have done better to."

"I'm not a fish, madam," he said tartly. "I rarely swallow hooks. Can you fend Boggie off? Do you *want* to?"

She blinked once. "Without being rude, son, what's it to you?"

"Nothing." He shrugged. "It's Constance who cares."

"You got a very odd idea of our family relationship. She don't bother me and I don't bother her."

"She cares," he repeated steadily.

Her eyes dropped. "And you don't understand why, do you? I was the whore who gave her birth and let her follow in my footsteps. Outstripped me for success, and no mistake. And yes, I wasn't much of a mother. Bet you know that too."

"Not from her."

"Obvious, though, isn't it? And you're right. She was all I had, and I wanted to keep her out of it. But I was too fond of the bottle to pay attention, and she was always too damned pretty. She was gone before I realized I was killing myself, and by then she wouldn't listen. She wouldn't get out. She won't do it for you, neither, will she?"

"No," Solomon said.

He hesitated. Constance longed for family, yet largely ignored the mother she had, hoping instead for an unknown father she could admire. Everyone needed a fairytale. And Juliet, like any mother, wanted her child as safe as she could be.

"It's not exactly what you think. That establishment she runs is as much charity as brothel. She helps the desperate out of the trap of prostitution, while those who prefer the profession are made as safe as they can be. She manages the whole thing. No one touches her."

He had no proof of that, just the word of her friend, and yet somehow he knew in his bones that it was true.

He half expected a derogatory remark from Juliet about his naivety. It didn't come. Instead, she spoke of her daughter.

"She's too young and much too pretty to be a true madam… She was never hard enough, neither. I fear for her." Juliet's eyes lifted suddenly to his. "You'd take her out of the whole thing if you could. Wouldn't you?"

"Yes," he admitted. "And yet I've grown to admire her for staying."

A smile lurked on Juliet's lips. "She *would* leave it for you. To be *with* you."

Shock washed over him like a wave. He didn't know what it meant. He didn't even know if she was teasing.

*To be with me.*

*To be with her.*

He couldn't think about that now. In a rush, he said, "I can get you different premises, respectable shop, reasonable rent. And if he follows, I can make life difficult for Boggie's lawful enterprises—rent increases, constant visits from revenue men and the police looking for stolen goods."

She laughed, rich, disconcertingly Constance-like mirth. "That, I would love to see. You almost convince me, love, you do. But it's my goods the police would be all over. 'Cause they know I can't afford a place like that. You don't want my kind of connections."

"You needn't teach me my business, Mrs. Silver," he said.

"Jules will do."

"And I shan't teach you yours. But you could think about it."

"Interesting," she said pensively. "Everyone seems to be trying to move from one side of the law to the other. Boggie, Lambert… I'll be frank with you, Mr. Grey. I can't *afford* to be entirely lawful."

"You could with a more visible business and wealthier customers. But that is up to you." He looked at his watch and rose to his feet. "I must go."

"I asked around about you, too."

He paused, raising his gaze to her face.

"You're a bit of a novelty, a bit of a mystery, and much too wealthy to be out alone in these streets. You'll get lost in the fog. Gerry'll go with you."

Solomon had looked after himself in many of the world's most dangerous ports. But he knew the advantage of accepting favors—or kindnesses. He hadn't made up his mind which this was.

"Thank you," he said, inclining his head. He laid a card on her desk, inclined his head once more, and walked away.

THE FOG WAS swirling thickly outside the kitchen window. Bert was back, so presumably Angela was too, though she had not rung for Constance.

"What does she do out all day?" Constance asked him. "Take tea with friends?"

He regarded her pityingly. "Don't be daft. She ain't that kind. She helps his nibs, don't she? Does the stuff he ain't got time for."

Constance didn't quite like that. Whatever or whoever the ghost turned out to be, she wanted Lambert to pay for the collapsed building. She wasn't sure she wanted Angela to pay too, just for being a good wife. And one who already felt guilty enough to be haunted by the dead victims.

As Bert went off, she stepped closer to the window and peered out into the darkness. The fog was impenetrable now. At least if Solomon managed to get here, no one would see them meet. Great, cloudy globs of it floated and swirled. Easy to imagine ghostly shapes out of it. As a child, she had done much the same in the darkness, when she had been alone and shivering in her cold attic, longing for her mother's presence when she could hear her shrieking with laughter in the street, or in the room below.

She shivered, throwing off the memory. The maid Denise stood beside her.

"Ghost weather," she said derisively. "According to Goldie."

"Don't you believe her?" Constance asked.

"I believe she *thought* she saw something. Trick of the imagination, isn't it?"

"Then you've never seen this ghost?

"Course not."

"But Bert and Pat and even Mrs. Lambert saw it."

"Bert and Pat were scaring each other. Gone soft. Robin and I never saw it, and we got up to look as soon as they shouted."

"You and Robin…?"

Denise looked more defiant than ashamed. "Yes, me and Robin. So don't you go getting ideas." There was a brash warning in her voice.

In most houses, they'd be dismissed for such a relationship. This was not most houses. But the girl was pitiably young.

"I have no such ideas," Constance assured her. "I'm just surprised. Thought you could do better—though I'm sure he's very handsome."

Denise's mouth fell open. Constance meant to leave her with the thought. There was nothing else she could do for her at this stage. Or was there? Not every girl was brought up as wise to the world as Constance had been.

"Here," she said abruptly. "You know how to prevent unwanted consequences?"

"Robin knows," Denise said.

"*Never*," Constance said, "rely on that. Come here."

She felt a little better after their short chat, even though she'd warned Denise that nothing but abstinence was certain. At least Angela was unlikely to throw her out on the streets in the event of an "accident."

Ringing drew Constance's attention to the bell board, and she set off to Angela's room, keeping a wary eye out for Lambert as she went.

She found Angela already in her evening gown, the back fastenings loose as she gazed out into the mist.

"Well?" she asked without turning.

"I don't think it's your staff playing tricks."

"Never imagined it was."

Constance began to fasten the hooks of the gown. "I'll slip out into the garden and keep watch, since it seems to be ghost weather. The dress is lovely, but it needs jewelry."

"It's only Caleb and me," Angela said impatiently.

Constance went to the closed box on her dressing table, opened it, and rummaged. Angela watched her, frowning, and looked surprised when she came up with a single strand of pearls.

"What's the point?" Angela asked.

Constance fastened them about her throat and regarded her in the glass. "Habit. Knowledge. And it works."

It did, subtly softening Angela's severity.

"Dripping in jewels is a mistake for people like us, who'd only be called vulgar. This is tasteful and pretty."

Angela sniffed derisively, though her gaze lingered on the glass. "You be careful in the garden. Keep out of the way of the boys—unless you catch anyone, then you shout blue murder for them."

Constance nodded. Deliberately, she didn't mention Solomon.

As soon as Angela left, Constance hastily tidied up. Then she snatched up her own warm cloak and Angela's discarded morning dress, which was filthy enough around the hems to justify her lurking around the kitchen for most of the evening. Since Angela had spoken openly, she assumed Lambert was not in his dressing room. Certainly, she saw no sign of him.

In the kitchen, everyone was busy carrying things to the dining room and generally preparing for the evening meal. Duggin was absent. In the laundry room, Constance brushed what could be brushed off the disgusting hem and left it soaking. Then she walked through the kitchen with her cloak on. Ida, red-faced and alone for the moment, was dementedly stirring some potion and did not turn from the stove.

Constance went out into the choking mist, moving instinctively to the right, away from the kitchen doors and windows, but keeping her hand on the dank wall of the building to be sure of her bearings.

There was something very eerie about fog as thick as this. She could well understand people interpreting its drifting, sluggish movements as ghostly, soundless figures. Her skin prickled with irrational unease. Mist also muffled and distorted sound so that she would not necessarily hear the click of the latch in the garden door, or if she did, would she even know what the sound was or what direction it truly came from?

She shivered, grasping the cloak more closely around her, and peered into the murk. It was a night like this she had first met Solomon. He had frightened her more than the dead man who so nearly landed on top of her and killed her. She had not been used to that feeling around men. She still wasn't. But she only felt it around Solomon, and she had grown so used to it, in all its varying intensities, that she rather liked it. She would miss that if he left. She would miss him.

*If he left.* What if he didn't? Would they go on like this forever, as friends, partners, companions, until the physical awareness went away?

No, for Solomon would marry one day, and his wife would not tolerate Constance's presence in his life, however chaste that presence was.

She drew out the watch she wore on a chain around her neck and looked at the time. Fifteen minutes until she could expect Solomon. A blacker shred of fog drifted, allowing her a glimpse of the apple tree, and she made her way cautiously toward it, straining her ears for the slightest sound.

Abruptly, she froze. Something had clicked, although she couldn't tell if it came from the house or the garden wall. Someone swore. Someone else sniggered. Pat and Robin. She could locate the sounds now, even make out their shapes moving through the mist toward the garden door. She heard them rattle the latch, to be sure it was still locked, and then they were walking back toward the house, their path erratic, but heading her way.

She was afraid to move or breathe. Though in reality, did it really matter if they found her here? Yes, for they'd probably tell Lambert. Angela had told her not to let herself be seen unless she caught the ghost.

Robin passed within a foot of her. But their attention was all directly ahead, on the misty glow of the kitchen window. When she finally heard the kitchen door close, she moved again toward the back wall, first feeling her way around the apple tree to avoid stepping in the pond, then inching toward the door.

Grasping the key in her pocket, she looked back toward the house. The rooftop was black against the tendrils of mist, the structure mysterious, vanishing into darkness and the occasional faint glow from windows.

She thought about the ghost. Supposing it was a real person, where was it going? Not to the kitchen, for it would be seen. Not to the front of the house, for it had always vanished to the opposite side, to the path. A more thorough check of that side of the building was in order.

She felt rather than heard the movement of the latch, and jerked away from the door. But it didn't move further. She waited, her breath mingling with the mist. Then, slowly, she brought out the key, fitted it as carefully and as quietly as she could, and turned it. Extracting it, she opened the gate, tensing to face any lurking threat.

Fog and darkness. She waited.

"Constance."

With relief, she reached for Solomon's hand and drew him inside, closing and locking the door. She led him back to the apple tree and found him peering down into her face. She stepped closer, standing on tiptoe to reach his ear with her lips.

No one smelled as good as Solomon, all cleanliness and warm spice. "I think we're fine for half an hour at least. The men have just patrolled the garden. The Lamberts will be dining."

He'd moved very slightly when she began to speak, as though at the shock of her breath. But he stood perfectly still now, his head lowered to hers.

"And you?" he said in her ear.

A tingle of pleasure passed through her, because it was sweet, and because he cared and was so preciously close. She had to force herself to remember why they were here.

"I think the ghost will come tonight," she whispered.

"Just because it's foggy?"

"No. It has always been a Saturday or a Thursday. Earlier in the evening, the ghost comes toward the house, even if not directly. When it's later at night, it's going away from the house."

"On the same evenings?" he asked.

"No," she said. "Not that I've found yet, but it makes sense. I don't think it can be anyone in the house—except Angela, and that makes no sense when she sent for us in the first place. Have you found out any more about Lambert?"

"That he's dangerous to tangle with. I think it's him, through Boggie, that's trying to take over your mother's business. And I think he's taking over Gregg's. He's almost certainly responsible for the St. Giles disaster."

"Angela thinks he is too." She paused, resting her strained feet, then reached up once more. "How do you know that about my mother?"

"Janey sent you a warning message about Boggie and Lambert. I went to see your mother to confirm it."

Constance closed her eyes. Her fingers on his shoulder curled, gripping the wool of his coat. "She's in danger, isn't she? And she won't—"

"She might," he murmured. "I've given her a way out, if she'll take it."

"What...?"

"Later."

She shifted her head slightly to look into his face, while he gazed beyond her to the garden. Something in her ached. It often did around him, though she didn't know what it was.

Love, probably, impossible and unrequited.

She rested her forehead against his shoulder, listened to the thud of her own heart, and imagined she could feel his beating in the same rhythm against her. In the circle of his arm, she didn't feel the cold.

Slowly, she turned her head so that she could see the rest of the fog-clogged garden. She was in no hurry to move. They waited.

And then she saw it.

# CHAPTER EIGHT

A T FIRST IT seemed to be just a shifting of the mist, thick and rolling. But then she realized this particular shape wasn't moving. It stood perfectly still while the fog swirled around it. Light and silvery, not quite part of the fog that clung to it, it was undoubtedly the shape of a veiled woman.

With one hand, Constance caught Solomon's face and pushed it to the right angle. She felt his slightest nod against her palm. He saw it too.

The ghostly figure began to glide, perhaps a foot toward the house, and then it vanished into the opaque fog.

Solomon took her hand, and together they crept in the direction they had last seen it. Though her heart beat with excitement and her skin prickled in response to the unworldly thing she had seen, she wasn't afraid. Not with her hand in Solomon's. Chiefly, she was aware of curiosity.

Were they about to solve Silver and Grey's first case?

Not easily, it seemed. No sounds reached her, no further sight of the ghostly figure through the mist. Frustration grew as they reached the wall of the house and peered hopelessly in all directions. The faint glow from the kitchen was marginally brighter from here, but it revealed nothing.

Constance began to feel her way along the wall, remembering her curiosity about that walled-off side of the house. A secret way into the house would surely explain the ghostly vanishing.

She felt occasional patches of brick, but mostly, she touched the damp tendrils of dense ivy and other creepers that covered it. Solomon followed, also running his fingers along the wall but higher up.

The corner of the building almost took her by surprise. She turned to follow the line of the house and bumped her shoulder against the boundary wall that extended from the garden. Constance was not a large person, but she could certainly not walk through that space. She peered down the narrow alley, making out only mist and blank wall. She could probably squeeze in sideways to investigate further, but her clothing would scrape and rustle against the stone.

Solomon's hand on her arm drew her back the way they had come. This time he bent low, feeling along the wall at about her waist height. She could sense his vexation that they had lost the ghost so soon after finding her, but he had not yet given up.

Constance shivered, beginning to wonder if they should seriously consider the alternative explanation—the unquiet ghost vanishing into the ether or through the solid wall into the home of the man responsible for the death of her child. After all, Angela herself couldn't quite shake off that fear...

Constance walked into the solidness that was Solomon. He had come to a halt. She caught her breath, listening intently for whatever threat he had sensed. His fingers, surprisingly warm compared to hers, caught her hand and drew her closer, not with tenderness, but some other excitement.

He placed her hand flat against the wall of the house. As always, there was plant and brick...and a crack in the stone. And beneath it, wood.

Her gaze flew to his. But already he was lifting the creepers. They came so easily that they must have been hanging loose over the hidden door. Excitedly, she crouched down, but she could find no handle to the door. Nor was there space around it to insert more than her fingernails. Then she found the keyhole. Thrusting her little finger into it, she felt something with her nail—surely the end of a key on the other side of the door.

She cast Solomon a quick grin, then shoved her hand into the left pocket of her gown to find the little tool she needed. She had lockpicks in her other pocket, though she was not terribly adept with them. The narrow pliers were simpler.

Inserting them into the lock, she managed to grip the end of the key and turn. They slipped off twice before she got the right hold and turned the key with the faintest click.

Solomon hauled her upright and behind him, wary, no doubt, of some kind of attack from within. But the door did not fly open. No sound came from inside. After several moments, Solomon took a penknife from his pocket and inserted it into the crack around the door. Soundlessly, it opened.

Both lock and hinges were clearly well oiled and smooth. Well used.

Solomon bent low and went in. Constance followed, with a quick glance behind her into the fog. As she drew the door closed behind her, she was sure she heard the whisper of the ivy falling back over it.

Inside was pitch black.

Solomon struck a match, and the light flared, showing a large, cavernous room, and a small wooden barrel just inside the door, the stump of a candle sitting on top. Solomon, who seemed to have thought of everything she hadn't, drew his own candle from his pocket, lit it, and blew out the match. At their feet, a steep wooden ramp led down into a large cellar, surely beneath the kitchen. Various old barrels covered in dust lined the left-hand wall.

As they crept forward and down, still listening intently, she saw that the room was L-shaped. A closed door stood on her right, and around the corner shortly afterward they came upon more barrels, full ones this time, and shelves full of wine bottles. And there, sure enough, were the rough stairs that surely led up behind the kitchen to the door she had asked Duggin about.

This, clearly, was Lambert's wine cellar. But the whole complex of cellars must have stretched at least the length and breadth of the house, with several doors leading to different rooms. Some were closed, others ajar.

A bump on the ceiling above made her start. A faint voice drifted downward, a muffled laugh. The sounds echoed eerily around the stone walls of the cellar, making it impossible to place them.

If the ghost had come in here…why?

The door to the main house above was always locked. Unless the ghost had obtained a key to that one too. Or there were others.

Solomon moved away from her, peering through the doors that were left ajar. Without a word, he took out another candle, lit it from the first, and held it out to Constance.

She took it and moved back the way she had come. That first closed door in the cellar had caught her attention. She took the precaution of putting her ear to the wood first, then, hearing nothing within, she pushed it. It was locked. And this time, when she thrust her finger and then a lockpick into it, there was no key on the other side. Only a faint whiff of dead rat that made her uneasy enough to raise her candle and glance around the walls and the floors for any signs of glaring eyes. Nothing scuttled.

She took the other pick from her pocket, considering that she might as well try. But her hand closed first around the key to the garden door. On impulse, she tried the key in the lock before her, and it turned smoothly.

Catching her breath, she rose to her feet, picked up her candle, and pushed open the door. The smell was strong enough here to make her gag, but no dead rodents were obvious, only a rolled-up carpet.

If the rats were living—or dying—in there, she didn't want to know. She turned her back on the carpet, but there was nothing else to see except an axe propped up in the far corner.

Why keep one rolled-up carpet in a dank cellar behind a locked door?

Her mouth went dry.

Forcing herself, she put one foot in front of the other until she could reach out with the tip of her toe and touch the carpet. Something solid was wrapped in its depths. Most of the way along.

A slight movement in the corner of her eye made her jerk her head around in fright. Solomon stood there, filling the doorway, his nostrils wrinkling. Their eyes met.

He came in and crouched down, grasping the loose end of the carpet before raising his gaze to hers once more. He jerked his head toward the door.

Though she moved out of the way of whatever might roll out, she did not leave. Solomon tugged, hard, and the carpet rolled and unfurled until its innards were revealed.

A man with staring eyes and blood in his hair.

"Dear God," she whispered, her hand over her mouth. It was what she had feared, but the smell… She raised her candle with one shaking hand. "Who is he?"

"Huxley Gregg," Solomon said. "No wonder he's never at home."

He bent and turned the head. Constance did not want to see the wound. She had seen others in the past. Instead, she walked over to the axe in the far corner. Even in the dim candlelight, the brown, dried bloodstains were obvious. Fragments she didn't want to think about clung to the blade.

"Time for you to come out," Solomon said grimly. He no longer troubled to lower his voice. "We have to report this to the police. Inspector Harris?"

She licked her lips, unsure why this seemed wrong. "Not yet. We should tell Angela first. She's our client."

"And her husband probably did this."

"Yes, but… Ten minutes, Sol. I owe her that much."

He straightened, staring at her. "I don't see why."

"Please," she said shakily.

He hesitated, his mouth tightening, and then he took her arm and walked briskly to the door. "You're not going back into that house alone."

"Come with me, then."

She was almost surprised when he agreed. But then, he was determined she should leave in one way or another.

Ida opened the kitchen door to her knock. "What you doing out there?" she demanded. "And who the hell's this?"

A quick glance showed Constance that the kitchen was otherwise empty. The servants must have been upstairs, clearing the dining room. "A friend. We need to speak to Mrs. Lambert. For her sake. Don't tell the others, not yet."

Ida stared at her, then stood back from the door to let them in. "Hurry up. She's in the parlor. He's in his office."

As soon as she pushed back the baize door, Constance could hear the laughter and a certain amount of flirting coming from the dining room. Ignoring it, she hurried straight across the hall, past Lambert's office to Angela's parlor. She entered after only the most cursory of knocks, Solomon directly behind her.

Angela had been busily writing at her desk, but at the interruption, she jerked her head up, frowning sharply.

"We need to talk to you," Constance said when Solomon had closed the door. "We saw your ghost. And we followed it into the cellar—at least, we think we did. But I'm afraid something else is more important. There's a dead body in the cellar. We believe it's Huxley Gregg."

Angela shot to her feet. "What? Nonsense."

"It isn't, ma'am," Solomon said. "And we have to report it to the police."

"I don't believe you," Angela said calmly.

"We'll show you," Constance said. "If you're up to it," she added, for the woman had turned very white.

"Of course I'm up to it," Angela snapped.

She swung away, took a couple of rapid paces, then turned back and strode past them to the door. "Wait here. Give me a few minutes to clear the way, then you can take me there."

"Clear what way?" Solomon said, already grasping the door handle.

"She doesn't want Lambert or his bodyguards to know. She's afraid. Wouldn't you be?" Constance asked.

"She doesn't look afraid to me."

"Neither do I."

"Are you?"

"Not at this moment. I understand her, that's all."

Solomon said nothing, but she could sense his impatience, his frustration. She walked to the window and pulled back the curtains, peering out into the fog. Seeing nothing, she let the curtain fall back.

"This will hit her hard," she said. "She is a good woman, doing her best… She really thought he was leaving the criminal life behind. I think that's the real reason she hired us to find who the ghost is before Lambert caught him and returned to his old ways. I don't believe he ever left them."

"Neither do I."

"Women fool themselves all the time."

Again, he said nothing.

Constance paced some more. The clock ticked loudly on the mantelpiece.

Abruptly, she halted. "What is she *doing*?" She met Solomon's gaze, saw the suspicion there, and felt it seep into her too.

"We need to—"

The parlor door flew open, and they swung together to face it.

Not Lambert, but Angela stood there. "Show me."

There was no sound now in the hallway. Angela led them directly to the baize door and downstairs without even pausing at the wine cellar door. She knew it was locked. She led them downstairs to the empty kitchen. Not even Ida sat there now, and Duggin was nowhere in sight.

Angela unlocked the back door, swiped up a lantern, and sailed out into the dank fog without even a coat on. Solomon strode past her to the cellar door, opened it, and waited until she shined the lantern inside before he bent and walked in. Angela followed, with Constance bringing up the rear. Again, she checked behind her, but she could not see nor hear anything in the dense mist.

She hurried after the others to the left-hand door, which lay open as they'd left it. But as they walked in, Angela's lantern clearly showed them an empty room. No carpet, no body. No bloody axe in the corner.

⫸⫷

FOR AN INSTANT, Solomon met Constance's bewildered gaze.

"There's nothing here," Angela said flatly. "Why do you waste my time?"

Before Solomon could speak, Constance did. "You told him, didn't you? He's already taken the body away."

"I don't know what you mean. The police will not thank you to be called out for nothing."

Solomon regarded her, trying to see her through Constance's eyes. He did not trust Angela, certainly not after what she had just done. But wherever Lambert and his minions had taken the body, they could not be far away. They hadn't had long.

"Constance," he said.

"I believe it's my evening off," Constance said to Angela. "We'll talk later."

As they crossed the garden toward the door in the back wall, they heard Angela locking the cellar door, and a moment later, the sound of the kitchen door closing.

"She's still protecting him," Constance said bitterly. "Even from that. Damn it, Sol, why did she hire us?"

"To find a ghost, not to find evidence of her husband's crimes."

"We haven't even found the damned ghost."

The fog seemed to be lighter, making the door in the wall visible through thick tendrils. Constance shoved the key into the lock too forcefully, and Solomon had to hold her back to make sure Lambert's men were not waiting in the lane.

His mind was racing. What would Lambert do to get rid of a body of a hurry? There hadn't been time to get out a horse and cart, even if the Lamberts kept them in this lane. But he could have slung the carpet over a horse's back, or even a donkey's, and already have vanished out of the lane.

Or would he have hidden it here, in one of the mews buildings?

He stopped dead, his heart leaping into his throat. "It's still in the cellar. In one of the other rooms. She's played us again. There's been no real time for anything else. All she needed to do in the short term was stop us going to the police tonight. By morning, it really will be gone."

Constance gave a frustrated little groan. "You don't *know* that, Sol. Do you really want to go to Harris with this before we're sure? Come on, let's see what's at the end of the lane. Hurry."

He allowed himself to be persuaded, not least because she was right. In the time it would take them to go to Scotland Yard, locate Inspector Harris—or even Inspector Omand—and drag him back here, the body really would vanish. In the meantime, they'd have lost their chance to find it if it really had been removed from the premises already. Why hadn't he thought to look through the other cellars before storming out?

Until they reached the main road, an ambling, empty cart was the only vehicle they saw. Constance hurried up to a crossing sweeper, a small, thin lad who could have been anything between eight and twelve years old.

"Evening," she said, slipping a coin into his grubby mitt. "By chance, have you seen a horse or a donkey pass this way with a rolled-up carpet on its back?"

"Can't see anything in this pea soup," the boy said disgustedly. "Take me life in me hands every time I cross. You going over, missus, or what?"

"We'll both go over, and pay you twice, too, if you answer the question."

"Did I see a donkey? Yes. I like donkeys. They smile at you and like their chins scratched."

"Was it pulling anything?" Constance asked. "Carrying anything?"

The boy thought. "Had something on its back, sticking out on either side. Might have been a carpet rolled up, or a big roll of cloth, I don't know. Didn't look."

"Who was with it?" Solomon asked.

"Old woman," the boy said.

Constance's jaw dropped. She knew who that was. It seemed he was wrong about the cellar. Unless this was a false trail laid to fool them?

"Which way did it go?" Solomon asked.

The boy nodded across the road. "Down into the Acre."

"Good lad," Constance said. "We'll cross now."

The boy took them over, sweeping the muck aside as he went. No vehicles passed them in the still-dense fog.

"No," Solomon said firmly. "We're not going into Devil's Acre at this time of night. If the body's really with that donkey, it'll be to dump it in the river. Well go around the Acre. Who is the old woman? The one who let us into the kitchen?"

Constance nodded. "It might be. Ida Feathers, the cook. She's devoted to Angela. Angela took her in when she was at her lowest, and keeps her on though she drinks like a fish."

"Could she dump a body in the river?"

"She's got strong arms. But she's just as likely to dump it in the Acre. Another body would barely be noticed there, and the police rarely go in. Besides, not many would weep for Huxley Gregg."

It was a fair point, and one that made him uneasy. He had been so determined to keep Constance out of Devil's Acre that he grasped at any excuse. Had he been on his own, without her to worry about and protect, what would he have done?

It was a question he kept coming back to over the next couple of hours. None of the characters they spoke to along the fog-shrouded riverbanks and stairs claimed to have seen an old woman with a donkey and a carpet.

"We've lost her," Constance said, clearly as frustrated as he. "Even if she's already dumped him in Devil's Acre, we'll have no proof it was her. No one there will speak to the police or to strangers. In fact, if the police even go there, it's an excuse for a riot. Let's hope the donkey was a false trail laid for our benefit. Shall we go back and break into the cellar again, as you suggested in the first place?"

Solomon had the feeling that even if the body had still been in the cellar when they left the garden, it would be gone by now. They had given Lambert a decent length of time to remove his evidence.

"Perhaps," he said. "Though I don't fancy running into Lambert's thugs in the cellar."

"I can go back into the house first and find out who is where. If we hurry, we'll catch them before bedtime."

He stared at her. She didn't actually mean to go back there, did she? Not with a recent murder in the house and Angela Lambert making it clear where her first loyalties lay. He supposed Constance still had to collect her things, and bit back his rejection of her idea. She would have to be straight in and out again, though—would it be long enough to gather useful information? And would she be watched? If so, they couldn't break into the cellar.

It was a lowering thought that they had made a mess of this between them. Their trivial ghost case had turned into a murder, and they had lost the evidence of the body, the weapon, and the scene of the crime.

Lambert had walked away from every crime he had ever committed. He must not be allowed to continue.

"Why would he kill Gregg?" Solomon said suddenly as they hurried back toward the Lamberts' house. "Gregg was a useful public scapegoat and clearly hadn't implicated him."

"Maybe Gregg threatened to tell everything to the inquiry. Maybe Lambert was just afraid he would."

"No crime has ever stuck to Lambert. Other people do his dirty work and pay the price while he continues on his way. Yet he killed Gregg on his own premises—or one of his minions did—and left the body there for days. Why would he risk that?"

"It wasn't much of a risk," Constance said. "No one goes into the wine cellar except Lambert and Duggin. And, possibly, our ghost."

In spite of himself, Solomon shivered. "Gregg wasn't married, was he? Did he have a sweetheart, a mistress who met the same fate?"

She turned her head to look at him. The mist was slightly less dense here, and her eyes glittered with both curiosity and doubt. "You're giving serious thought to the supernatural explanation?"

"The Tizsas warned me not to rule it out. Apparently they had some sort of…encounter in Scotland."

"Angela's afraid it's Cathy Knox," Constance said. "She met her at the tenement before it fell, and Cathy begged for her help, to get Lambert to do something about the state of the building."

"Did she?" Solomon said softly. "Then everyone knew how dangerous that place was. And everyone seems to know Lambert was involved. Perhaps I should speak to Knox again."

The crossing sweeper had gone. A few people melted in and out of the mist, some of them the worse for drink. Solomon and Constance negotiated their way back to the mews behind Lambert's house. His unease returned, more intense with every step.

He opened his mouth to say he would go with her, just as a familiar, ghostly figure glided through a high wall and into the lane.

# CHAPTER NINE

F OR AN INSTANT, the blood froze in his veins. It seemed he *was* seriously considering the supernatural explanation.

But of course she hadn't wafted through a solid wall—she had surely walked out of Lambert's garden door, where she paused a moment. Locking it?

Then she glided up the lane away from them, and his paralysis broke. Grabbing Constance's hand, he broke into a run after the silvery figure.

The fog must indeed have been thinner, for they didn't lose sight of her this time. She was slender and wispy and veiled, but she heard them. She glanced over her shoulder, as if with alarm, then broke into a run—much less smooth, much more human.

"Got her," Constance gasped with some glee.

But ahead, just at the end of the lane, a carriage loomed out of the mist. The driver sat inhumanly still on his box. A horse stamped its foot. Solomon swore beneath his breath, and they ran faster. But the ghost wrenched open the carriage door, leapt up, and slammed it behind her as a whip cracked and the horse took off at the gallop.

Solomon and Constance ran around the corner after it, and as far as the main road, where they could no longer even hear it. They had no idea which direction it had taken, and there was no one around to ask.

Constance, still breathing raggedly, grasped his arm and turned back toward the lane. "Well. Whoever heard of a ghost traveling by hackney? At least we've proved she's a real person. The question is, what the devil was she doing there?"

"At least she wasn't carrying Gregg's body," Solomon said dryly.

"Perhaps it was already in the carriage."

"That would certainly match the rest of our luck this evening."

"She must be someone's lover," Constance said. "Only, why is it such a secret? Denise the maid sleeps in Robin the footman's bed. I suppose they don't want strangers in the house."

"They accepted you," Solomon pointed out.

"Angela wants to be more of a lady, to match Lambert's rise in the world. Funny when you think about it that she chose me. I shall inquire about sweethearts." She inserted her key into the garden door's lock and turned. The ghost had indeed locked it behind her.

"How many inquiries do you intend to make in the five minutes it will take you to collect your things?"

She paused, her hand still on the key, and glanced up at him. "What things? I'm going inside to see who is in the house, so we know if it's safe to go into the cellar again. I'll save other questions for tomorrow."

They were speaking very low, so that even someone in the garden would not make out their words. With difficulty, Solomon maintained a mere murmur.

"No. You can't stay there now. The case is over."

"Of course it isn't," she said impatiently. "We don't know who the ghost is."

"Hang the ghost! It's Lambert we want."

"That isn't what we were hired for."

Panic rose in him. "No. You're going home tonight."

Her jaw dropped. Even in the dark and the fog, he could see that. It made her no less beautiful. Or precious.

"I thought you were serious about our agency," she said, a trace of anger in her bewildered hiss.

"I am. Just not to the point of finding *you* in the cellar next time."

"Don't be ridiculous. I can look after myself and have done in worse houses than this. I need to go back, both for the ghost and for Gregg. The ghost will be back on Saturday, if she follows her pattern. We should be ready and waiting in the cellar."

"Saturday is two days away. We'll make plans in the office tomorrow."

She stared at him, nothing friendly in her eyes now. That hurt. "Are you laying down the law, Solomon? I thought this was a partnership."

"It is, and I want to keep my partner, however annoying she is."

A glimmer softened her eyes. "Don't be foolish. You know the only sensible way forward is for me to return. I can guarantee Angela has not given me away to Lambert."

"Are you blind to her? Or just idiotic?" he said disastrously. "Get your things if you must, but I'll only wait five minutes before I come in and get you."

She took the key out of the lock slowly. Just for a moment, he thought he had won.

"All evening," she said, so low that he had to bend nearer to hear her at all, "you have ignored what I say. You have given me orders without discussing anything. Now I am supposed to give up our case? If that is your idea of partnership, Solomon, it is not mine."

He ignored the injustice of that, for danger pressed in on him, an entirely different danger to any he had faced before. He had never cared so much before. He had forgotten how.

"Constance, you can't trust Angela or her protection," he said urgently. *"She betrayed you."*

"Everyone does, in the end."

Pain hit him so hard he stepped back. That was what she thought of him? "Your mother was wrong," he blurted. "You would not cross the street to be with me, would you? Because there is always someone more interesting, more dangerous, just around the next corner. Are you really dissolving our partnership over *this*?"

Her head flew back. Her eyes blazed like a cat's in the darkness. "A partnership involves *partners*. It seems we were never that in the first place." She whisked herself inside the garden door, even as he reached for her, and shut it in his face. He barely even heard the key turn in the lock, only her muffled footsteps marching away from him.

FURY CARRIED CONSTANCE across the garden so fast that she narrowly avoided bumping into the apple tree. Fury and disappointment and hurt and—What the devil had he meant about her mother?

Casting that aside, she concentrated on the partnership argument and on his belief that if she didn't obey him, she was dissolving it. That was not the Solomon she thought she knew. Or had she ever known him? Had she not just been drawn to that beguiling mixture of danger and respectability? To say nothing of his beautiful person. And she thought it was friendship, love… Whatever name she gave it, had she really been so wrong?

She didn't want to be wrong. She wanted this agency, this work, this partnership. She wanted *him*, in whatever capacity she could. And she had just shut the door on him. Literally and metaphorically.

Was that really the end of it? Had something precious been broken between them? Somewhere, she knew he had been looking after her, but that was no excuse for laying down the law as though she were his servant, his tool. Under no circumstances could she ever be those things again. Not to anyone. That he was used to giving orders was no excuse. Not when he spoke to his partner.

And yet…

And yet she had a part to play, and to do so, she needed her wits about her. Knocking firmly on the back door, she thrust the quarrel aside to some small, lonely part of her mind where she refused to dwell.

Duggin opened the door. "Where've you been?"

"Evening off," Constance said breezily, brushing past him into the kitchen. "Courtesy of the mistress. She hasn't rung yet, has she?"

To her surprise, all the servants except the cook were sitting around the kitchen table, drinking a last cup of tea. No one wore outdoor clothing, or clothes spattered with mud or blood…

"Mrs. Feathers gone to bed?" she asked cheerfully.

"Obviously," Duggin said.

Ignoring him, Constance fetched herself a cup. "Any tea left in the pot?"

"Enough for one," Goldie said. "It's yours."

Constance took the long way back to the table, passing the closed door of Ida's bedroom. Snores emanated from within.

*Were we following a false trail? Or did she just beat us back to the house?*

Constance poured herself a cup of tea and sat down. Everyone was looking at her. "What?" she said, as though surprised by their interest.

"You've only been here two days and you've already had an evening off," Denise said resentfully.

"Well, Mrs. Lambert didn't need me. I'm pretty flexible, as long as I get the time I'm owed. Anything happen here while I was gone?"

"Quiet evening," Robin said. "Always is on a Thursday."

"Why's that, then?" Constance asked, quite aware of Duggin's warning glare on the footman, who, however, only grinned derisively.

"His nibs stays in on a Thursday," Robin said.

"He stayed in on Wednesday too," Constance pointed out.

"How do you know?" Robin challenged.

"Because you were here. And because Mrs. Lambert told me."

A bell rang. In the main bedchamber.

Her stomach twisted with nerves, but she took a last swallow of lukewarm tea and stood up. "Duty calls." She had no idea what, if anything, any of them knew about the evening's events, but at least none of them had attacked her.

Lambert, however, was a quite different matter. As she passed the ground-floor landing, she quickly tried the wine cellar door. Locked, of course. It would have to be in the middle of the night now before she could try to get back in…

She half expected Lambert to be lurking in the passage. That he wasn't did not provide much comfort, for he could easily be in his wife's bedchamber. She knocked once, drawing a breath for courage, and walked in.

Not for years had she been quite so prepared to dodge whatever blows came her way. She had already swerved and ducked before she realized only Angela was in the room.

She was fully dressed, still, standing near the window as she turned to face her.

"So you are still here."

"We have an agreement. We have established your ghost is human and female and travels by hackney—both horse and carriage caused far too much noise for spirits, I feel."

"You are angry with me," Angela observed.

"You have made us complicit in obstructing the law. Why should I not be angry with you? Where is the body?"

Angela sighed. "I should have known you would suspect me."

"Whom was I supposed to suspect?"

Angela shrugged. "You already know my husband is not a good man, and he has many minions."

"Minions who appear to have spent the evening at home."

"They are far from his only minions. It doesn't matter. I took the matter into my own hands. I could not have the police here, poking about, arresting Caleb."

"Why? What else would they have found?" Constance asked swiftly.

"I don't know." It sounded like the truth. Certainly, Angela did not try to look away. "Is murder not enough?"

"Why did he kill Gregg?"

"Probably because Gregg was about to expose him."

"As his partner in St. Giles?" Constance asked.

"Yes."

"Then why did Gregg risk coming here?"

"I don't know that either." Angela paced away from the window, crossing to the door and back again, before flinging herself into one of the armchairs. "It seems so foolish that I suspect it might not have been Caleb at all who killed him. It could easily have been one of his professional enemies, or one of the angry tenants. Someone might have followed Gregg here."

"And killed him in your cellar?" Constance asked with blatant disbelief.

"Do you know for certain that he died in the cellar? He could have been put there afterward."

"There was blood. On the cellar floor. The axe was there too."

"Not a huge amounts of blood," Angela argued. "Not enough to prove the matter, either way. Content yourself with the fact Gregg met justice—considerably more than the law would have provided. Forget it. I hired you to find the ghost. You found out she's human. Who is she?"

Angela's swift change of subject was chilling. She had just dismissed a murder committed in her home, most probably by her husband, with the ease of moving down the agenda at a church meeting.

Not that Constance had ever attended one of those.

"I don't know yet," she said. "But if she entered the house when we first saw her, she had been here for more than three hours. Presuming you had no female visitors this evening—"

"We had no visitors at all."

"Someone did. Do any of your male staff have sweethearts or mistresses?"

"None that they would dare entertain while at work." Angela sounded impatient again. "She can't be anything to do with the staff." Almost angrily, she drummed her fingers on the chair arm, frowning at Constance. "Look, I wish it *had* been a ghost. But I still think I'm right about motive. Whoever she is, she means harm to my husband. And I mean to stop her. She's dangerous. Dangerous enough to have killed Gregg. Dangerous enough to draw you to his body and implicate Caleb."

Oddly, those were things Constance had not thought of. She considered them now, doubtfully. The female who had fled up the lane and leapt into the hackney had been young and agile, but she had also given the impression of feminine frailty.

"You mean she killed Gregg with an axe, on your grounds? And then hid him in your cellar?"

"Caleb could have hidden him when he found the body. He can't afford to have corpses around the house. Or she deliberately hid him here. After all, *you* nearly brought the peelers down on us."

Constance stared at her. "Don't you think you should simply ask your husband? Before you start making up fantasies to excuse him? Since you got rid of the body and the weapon, we now have no evidence to help us find out the truth. I should turn you over to them right now."

A faint smile curved Angela's severe lips. "But you won't, will you? I doubt your own past will bear much scrutiny. Or carry much weight with the law."

"I might surprise you there, so please don't wager your life on the possibility."

Angela rubbed her forehead tiredly. "Look, I'll see—" She broke off, her gaze flying to the dressing room door. Sure enough, Constance heard the faint footsteps in the passage and the soft opening and closing of a nearby door.

"Unhook me and go to bed," Angela said, turning her back.

Constance walked over to her. Her fingers felt too large and too clumsy for the job. At any moment, she expected Lambert to walk in.

"Goodnight," Angela said.

"Goodnight, ma'am," Constance replied, and retreated to her own chamber.

She turned the key in the lock. The lamp was not lit, so she just lay down on the narrow bed as she was. After all, she would be going out again in a couple of hours to look around the cellar. On her own. Without Solomon. Providing Lambert did not sleep in his wife's bed.

She meant to listen out for that. But, somehow, she fell asleep.

SOLOMON WAITED FOR rather more than five minutes in the lane behind Lambert's garden, even though he knew she would not let him in.

He had achieved the exact opposite of what he had intended—Constance safely away from that house. Instead, fear for her seemed to have drowned his wits and made him say things guaranteed to drive her back in there and away from him. Shutting the door in his face had been an unmistakable message, yet still he hoped she would see the danger for herself and come out...

While he waited, their words echoed around his mind, bitter and agonizing.

*"She betrayed you,"* he'd told her.

*"Everyone does, in the end."*

*Everyone.* As though she had just been waiting for his betrayal. Even after all they had shared together. She had slept in his arms the night they solved the Maule case. He had thought it was trust.

But she had never trusted him not to betray her, and this, this argument tonight that should have been a discussion, must feel to her like his betrayal—of her and of the partnership they had formed.

Would she walk away from it now? Was that it ended?

They had each put money into the venture, but that was the least of what he would lose if she ended it. A life without Constance in it, without the hope of seeing her…

A void was opening up before him, black and gaping. He remembered that void. It had been there, vast and terrifying, when he lost David, his brother, at the age of ten. But he was no longer a child to panic and disintegrate. He was a man with responsibilities to his staff and his workers, and everyone else who depended on his being there at least somewhere in the background.

Constance was not dependent on him, though it seemed he wanted her to be. That it was the other way around, that he was dependent on *her*, was another shock.

A life without Constance…

She wasn't coming.

And he could not go in there to fetch her, alone or with several policemen, without risking her life. Instead—a novel idea was forming—should *he* not trust *her*? Trust her opinion, her ability to take care of herself? This was her world far more than his, the world she had sprung from and never quite left behind. He was the alien, not just in terms of country and race, but in the privilege he had been born into.

He had never struggled for food or shelter. If he had walked into dangerous situations—which he had, deliberately and otherwise—he always knew that safety lay on the other side, not more of the same struggle to exist. Constance's strength had brought her through that old life to what she was now. Clever, perceptive, compassionate…and still strong.

His admiration for her, like his feeling, had crept up on him. He didn't seem to know how to deal with it except by protecting her. But she was right: they were partners.

Beyond the garden wall, he heard the faint sounds of foot-steps. He couldn't fool himself that they were hers. Someone tried the door. Solomon flattened himself into the shadows, but the door never opened. It was just Lambert's men patrolling the premises before bed. There was no sign of panic or trouble among them, no screaming or shooting from the house.

Constance was not stupid enough to walk into danger she could not deal with in her own way. She knew these people. He did not.

Faintly, through the fog, he heard the sound of the kitchen door opening, closing, and locking. The night was quiet, shrouded. Solomon waited another quarter of an hour, just to be sure. And then he walked away—from Lambert's house, but not from the inquiry, and certainly not from his partnership.

# CHAPTER TEN

SOLOMON WENT FIRST to the office, to change into his more normal garb. He didn't wish to shock his neighbors—or his servant—by being seen in these worn and ill-fitting clothes. But when he got there, he found the lights still on, and Janey in the waiting room, eating sandwiches and drinking tea with a ragged young man who looked vaguely familiar.

They both sprang up as Solomon entered with his key.

"There you are," Janey exclaimed. "We was just about to give up on you. This is Mr. Knox. He wanted to wait."

Solomon's eyes dropped to the plate of sandwiches.

"I bought 'em meself, with me own bleeding money," Janey said aggressively.

"Then you will be reimbursed," Solomon said mildly. "You're not required to stay so late, you know. It's after midnight."

Mollified, Janey said, "Knew you'd be back 'cause you said you would. Mr. Knox here came at six."

Solomon held out his hand to Knox. "I'm sorry to have kept you waiting so long."

The man shrugged. He still looked white and ill, but his eyes had lost something of that terrible dullness Solomon recalled from St. Giles. "Not as if I had an appointment. I'd nowhere else I had to be, and Miss Janey said it was fine to wait."

"Of course. Come through to the office. Perhaps you'd make some tea, Janey? And then take that waiting hackney back home."

"Really?" She brightened. Reaching for the remains of her

sandwich, she stuffed it in her mouth and went off to the kitchen, while Solomon led Knox into his office.

They sat in the comfortable chairs. Janey brought the remains of the sandwiches.

"Dr. Tizsa said I should come and talk to you. He thinks you're investigating Lambert as well as Gregg." Knox paused, rubbing his forehead. "First, though, I meant to thank you for sending him—Dr. Tizsa—to us. He's worked wonders already for some of those poor… Well, he's made a difference."

"He's a good man and a clever doctor."

"He fought for people's rights," Knox said. "In Hungary. Not just protests. Actual war."

"I know."

"I wouldn't like it to come to that here."

"It's a different situation," Solomon said vaguely, trying not think of the atrocities and the slaughter of the slave revolt in Jamaica, which had been put down so mercilessly, only a few years before the law finally granted them freedom.

Knox stirred uncomfortably. "I say that because I don't want you to think I'm just an agitator, a troublemaker. I'm not. I don't want bloodshed. I just want a bit of fairness. I don't want people to die in squalor, just for other people's greed. That's wrong."

"Yes," Solomon agreed. "You speak like an educated man, Mr. Knox."

"I went to school. Apprenticed to a carpenter, found I was good at it. My master kept me on after, while I saved up to get married and start my own business. Got married first. We had a decent room, but I…I got involved in other people's fights. People who couldn't read and write, people who had nothing and no one to stand up for them. I wrote to their landlords for them, tried to get regulations enforced. Worked, too. Word got around, and I helped with some employment issues at a factory. Threat of strikes can work wonders in the right situation. We might not have achieved a *fair* wage, but it was better one."

Janey brought tea and poured it, setting the cups and saucers before each of them. Then, rather to Solomon's surprise, she poured one for herself and sat down on the hard chair, notebook in her lap.

Knox did not appear to mind her presence. Perhaps he had already told her.

"Good for you," Solomon said.

"In one way. Not in another. I got the attention of Caleb Lambert, who owned the factory."

"I see…"

"I lost my job. Suddenly, I wasn't needed. And no one else would take me on, even though I'm a skilled carpenter. It was Lambert's doing. I found out he's a vindictive ba—er, man. Came out of Devil's Acre with grubby money and big plans I'd interfered with. For his own reputation he had to ruin me, show I should be grateful not to get my legs broken or vanish in the Thames.

"We couldn't pay the rent on our pleasant little room. Cathy couldn't get work either. Plus, she was pregnant and didn't keep well. We got a cheaper room, shared with a decent family, curtained off so at least we all had some privacy, but the money still dwindled too fast, especially with doctor's fees for Cathy."

Knox swallowed. "I'm sure you can guess the rest. I picked up casual work when I could, but it was never enough. We ended up in that hellhole that collapsed. I had nothing to lose, or so I thought. I couldn't believe it when I saw Lambert there, conferring with that smug sod, Fraser."

"Lambert owned the building?" Solomon said eagerly.

"Huxley Gregg owns it officially, but he's in Lambert's pocket."

*Not anymore, he isn't.* "Do you have proof of this?"

"Every rent day, Lambert's at Gregg's office. I've seen them—nothing else to do, have I? I wouldn't like to say how they divide the spoils, but I'm sure the lion's share goes to Lambert. It wasn't just our building—it's lots of them, including where they so generously put the survivors when ours fell in on us. They've even got some kind of public subscription going to rebuild it, and a fine place that's going to be. On paper."

Solomon leaned forward. "And Gregg was organizing this public funding?" His own charity must have contributed to it. Why had he not kept a closer eye on that?

"Lambert, though he has other people to speak for him. He's even started ordering materials for the build, and they're far inferior to those proposed on paper."

"They could be for his other projects... But one way or another, he's committing fraud."

"If you can prove it."

"I probably can."

GOLDIE'S HEART BEAT like a rabbit's as she crept up the stairs with the master's morning cup of tea. Normally, her father or one of the lads took it, but they were all arguing about Silver, the new girl, and Goldie took advantage of their distraction.

She knocked and went in, to find the master was already up and partially dressed. Her mouth went dry at the sight of his muscles rippling as he pulled the shirt over his head. Since he didn't acknowledge her presence, she walked up to him, holding the cup and saucer in front of her like a sacred offering.

He noticed her at last, and an amused smile curved his lips.

"Thank you," he said gravely, taking it from her.

She didn't step back. "Are you well, sir?" she asked boldly.

As she had hoped, his attention lingered. It did in the mornings. Denise said it was because he didn't sleep with Mrs. Lambert anymore, and men's urges were always strongest when they woke. But Denise thought she knew everything, because of Robin. Goldie knew the master was better than that, more than that. And she longed to take Mrs. Lambert's place in his heart and his bed.

"Very well, my dear. When did you grow so pretty?"

She tossed her head. "I've always been pretty, sir. And now I'm grown up."

His eyes wandered over her like a caress she could almost feel on her hot skin.

"So you are," he murmured.

She raised her face, very aware she stood too close to him, and that neither had moved back. His gaze lingered on her lips. Did she imagine the infinitesimal move toward her?

*Please! Please...*

A breath of laughter stroked her face. "Does your father know what a minx you are? Scarper before we both pay."

Still, he didn't step back, but he did begin to drink his tea, his eyes warm above it. And he had given her an order, so she smiled pertly and swaggered out, because she had got his attention and his dismissal had been reluctant.

*One day...and soon.* No mere footman for her. She would have the master.

"I WANT YOU to come with me this morning," Angela said abruptly to Constance. She was drinking her morning tea in bed and clearly planning her day.

"Of course. Where are we going?"

Agela wrinkled her nose. "To the dressmaker. She's far too snooty for my taste, but you might get better work out of her. You've certainly got better taste."

"What are you looking for?"

"An evening gown for some charity event of Caleb's. It means a lot to him that I go and we fit in. I suppose he reckons I can if I don't open my mouth."

"Oh, you can manage a polite *good evening*. And a *yes, no, excuse me,* or, when all else fails, *indeed!* Keep smiling and everyone will approve of your good manners and modesty."

Angela laughed, a rare, pleasant sound that made Constance smile in return. "How do you know these things?"

Constance, who'd had little to do with respectable ladies and much to do with their husbands, said vaguely, "Several gentlemen have explained it to me."

Constance had her own, discreet dressmaker, largely unfrequented by the rich and fashionable of Society, but any fears she harbored over accompanying Angela there were quickly laid to rest.

They traveled by coach, an old-fashioned but comfortable affair, with Bert clinging to the back. He waited outside the dressmaker's, leaning against the vehicle, eyeing the passing shop girls and exchanging appreciative remarks with the coachman.

Angela's dressmaker, no doubt chosen by Lambert, was a thoroughly fashionable shop run by a smart, middle-aged woman purporting to be from Paris and clearly used to catering to the rich and powerful women of London.

Lambert was indeed aiming high. And his wife's discomfort in such an establishment was palpable. The assistants, and Madame Bouvier herself, were only too aware that Angela did not belong there.

"*Bonjour, madame,*" Madame Bouvier greeted her, smiling graciously. "May we help you?"

"Yes, I want an evening gown. Something like that one with—"

"When does madame require the gown?"

"Next Tuesday at the latest."

Madame Bouvier shook her sleek head. "But no, madame, that is not possible!"

"It is, if you begin now."

"We cannot possibly! The first appointment I have available is on Monday."

"There are no other customers here now," Angela pointed out.

"But I expect Lady Gilbert and her three daughters any moment, madame. I do not have time to attend you!"

Angela, who no doubt had faced down villains who would have caused madame to faint from terror, turned away chagrinned, but with no idea how to deal with one snobbish dressmaker.

Constance stepped forward. "What a pity," she said. "You cannot truly believe that Lady Gilbert will attend at nine o'clock in the morning! If she has breakfasted by eleven, I shall be surprised. Never mind. Mrs. Lambert will go next door, as everyone advises."

Madame's eyebrows flew up.

Constance smiled and lowered her voice. "Perhaps you have forgotten that Mrs. Lambert pays promptly. Unlike your aristocratic clientele, who are—er…fashionably late. If they pay at all. Goodbye, madame."

"Wait," Madame Bouvier said, brushing past Constance to get at Angela. "It is true that Lady Gilbert is not the most punctual of my customers! I'm sure we have time to choose something suitable…"

Since Angela seemed to draw strength from Constance's presence, she lingered in the shop, bored and anxious on her own account. She really needed to use this time at her own establishment. What she wanted to do was go to the Silver and Grey office and confront Solomon.

Talk to Solomon.

She should not have stormed off, shutting the door in his face. She could not believe he would end their partnership over such a silly quarrel, but he had always been one of the few men she could not read. She had hoped to be able to report any cellar discovery, or lack thereof, when next she saw him—it would at least have been an excuse to meet him before this evening. If he even intended to come this evening. But she had fallen asleep last night and not wakened until dawn. There had been no time and no opportunity to break into the cellar again. Angela was behaving as though last night had never been and that everything was fine between them.

In the meantime, Constance gave her advice on the new gown—fewer flounces and a softer-colored fabric. The dusky-pink silk was perfect, with modest yet exquisite lace trim around the neckline and hem.

"If madame is able to come for a fitting on Monday morning, we will try to finish all by Tuesday."

"Thank you," Angela said, and left the shop with incomparable dignity—an impression she spoiled by casting a wicked grin of triumph at Constance. "I wish I'd had you around last year."

"Where now, ma'am?" Constance asked.

"You can go home," Angela said. "I won't need you. Bert, you come with me."

Constance was disappointed. She had hoped to find out exactly where Angela went during her outings. But at least if she went back to the house, she could ask questions that might lead to the identity of the ghost.

Constance stood back submissively while Angela climbed into the carriage. Bert closed the door and suddenly, beyond him, Constance found herself looking straight at Janey.

She stood at the corner of Bond Street, dressed as a lady's maid and looking bored, as though waiting for her mistress to emerge from one of the other shops.

On impulse, Constance stepped up to the carriage window, and Angela pulled it down.

"Would you mind if I went on some errands of my own before returning to the house?"

Angela, clearly understanding this was on her business, nodded at once. "Just be home before dinner."

"Of course."

"Blimey," Bert said disgustedly. "You get more time off than you spend at work."

"Perks of an upper servant," Constance said grandly, and walked away.

Janey still lurked at the corner shop window. Constance pretended to pause to look in. But Janey's attention seemed to be on a handsome if rather ragged young man leaning against a nearby lamppost. She nodded, and the man ambled off in the same direction as Angela's carriage.

"Sorry, missus," Janey said cheekily. "We're following *your* missus. Mr. Grey's orders. He wants to know where she goes."

"Who is *we*?" Constance managed faintly.

"Me and Lenny Knox," Janey said, and skipped off.

Stunned as Constance was, she now had a reason to speak to Solomon. Instead, she walked westward along Oxford Street to her own establishment. It came as something of a shock to realize that Janey must have followed the carriage from Lambert's house and Constance had not even noticed. So much for observation and detection. No wonder Solomon didn't want her.

SOLOMON HAD THOUGHT of the task of following Angela Lambert last night, mostly from curiosity as to what the woman got up to all day, but partly to give Knox something to do that Solomon could pay him for, and provide distraction from the man's unbearable loss. At the last minute this morning he had sent Janey with him, largely because of his early visitor.

His visitor was Juliet Silver.

She arrived at the Silver and Grey office a bare ten minutes after he did, and almost on Janey's heels. Since Solomon himself opened the door to her, Juliet had no need to announce her name. She merely breezed past him into the hallway, saying appreciatively, "Very nice. Got a moment, duck?"

No one addressed Solomon as *duck*. He was *sir*, or *Mr. Grey*, or, very occasionally, some derogatory epithet he disdained hearing. Constance was the only person in years to call him by his Christian name. He should have resented *duck* for its lack of respect, the affront to his dignity. Bizarrely, he found he didn't mind it. He might even have liked it.

"Perhaps you wouldn't mind waiting in here, ma'am?" He showed her into Constance's office, where he had already lit the fire in determined hope that she would be back. Since Janey didn't bat an eyelid when they passed her, he could tell they were not acquainted, and he felt obliged to keep it that way if it was what Constance wanted.

"I've taken your advice and moved out," Juliet said abruptly. "Where's this new shop of yours?"

*Well, that will teach me to make promises I am not ready to keep immediately.*

"One moment, if you please."

He bade Janey take her a cup of tea and then come straight back to his office. He didn't want her and Juliet chatting and discovering their mutual acquaintance. That was up to Constance. He knew the women she lived with were her friends, yet it was Solomon she had taken to her mother's premises. That inspired both warmth and a sharp regret for last night's behavior. He was threatening everything that had grown up between him and Constance.

Returning to his own office, where Knox had arrived, he came up with the plan to send Janey to watch the Lamberts' house.

"She can go closer than you without the danger of being recognized," he told Knox. "And when it comes to following Mrs. Lambert, you can take it in turns to be nearer her so she's less likely to spot you. She's usually with a bodyguard, remember, and he might well recognize you, too."

He shook out a purse and gave a handful of coins to each of them. "For hackneys and lurking at food stands and tea shops. Don't take chances."

Knox nodded and rose to his feet. Since his clothes were on the ragged side and Solomon's overcoat would have trailed on the ground, Solomon gave him his wool jacket to wear over his own for warmth. They looked an odd couple as they departed, but Solomon was glad to see a brightness about Knox's eyes, a relief to be doing something, a *need* to go after the man he held responsible for the deaths of his wife and child and so many others.

A man needed a purpose. No one knew that better than Solomon. It was only recently he had discovered that making money, even improving the lot of his workforce, was not enough for him.

He took his tea through to the other office and sat down by the fire, opposite Juliet, who was looking around her with interest.

"She always had good taste, my Connie. No vulgar opulence for her. I bet her establishment looks more like a duchess's drawing room."

"Actually, it does, as far as I have seen. Where, Mrs. Silver, are your things?"

"The best of it's at your back door," she said brazenly. "I left more at a friend's and sent some to Connie's establishment. She'll be fizzing mad, but she'll keep it safe for me."

Solomon stood up and went to haul the trunk through the back door and into the office.

"Thanks, duck. Now, you see I've taken you at your word and I'm trusting you, because Con does. You wouldn't take advantage of me, would you? Charge me a fortune now you know I'm desperate?"

"Of course I wouldn't."

"I ain't asking for favors, mind. I'll pay a decent rent."

"If you're paying it to me, I don't want you fencing."

"Mr. Grey," she said, shocked and offended, although her eyes were twinkling. "You already said. I never been respectable before, but I'll try anything once."

"Hmm. I shall need to pay a few calls, see what is available that might suit you."

"You do that, duck. Finish your tea first, though. I ain't in that much of a hurry. Where's Connie?"

*In Lambert's house, where I left her.* Deliberately, he quashed the resurgence of anxiety. If they found a way to make this work, he would have to learn to deal with such worries. "Working," he said. "She may not be into the office, though I will try to speak to her later. Who's the landlord of your old place?"

"Didn't Connie tell you? It's mine. I own it, legal like. Ain't worth much, mind, all squashed up between its neighbors and all them stairs. But it'll do."

Solomon frowned, new ideas springing into his head. "No. No, she didn't tell me that."

"One of my regular gents left it to me when he turned up his toes, bless him. That's when I gave up the old game and took to selling."

"When you say gent," Solomon said, "do you mean a gentleman as the world understands the term?"

"Lord no—common as muck, Charlie Roe, but he were decent."

"Did Constance know him?"

"Met him once or twice, but she wouldn't come with me when I moved there. I thought it might be fun, the two of us."

There was hurt in her voice that she couldn't quite hide, but no blame.

"Was he Constance's father?" Solomon asked bluntly.

Juliet's jaw dropped, her cup suspended just beneath her chin. "Is that what *she* thinks?"

"It might be." It might be what she feared.

Juliet thought about it. "Nah. I didn't know Charlie till later. Tell the truth, duck, I don't know who he was and I don't much care."

"Constance cares."

Her eyelashes, still long and luxurious like Constance's, swept down over the slightly puffy skin beneath her eyes. "I was never enough for her. But I tried to tell her there's no fairytales in real life. Does she hate me?"

"No. She just wants to belong somewhere, with people who make her comfortable."

"In a nobs' brothel?" Juliet said in disbelief.

"The women are her friends, her responsibility."

"Her family," Juliet said, and swallowed. "I never gave her that."

Solomon's breath caught. A tide of longing, warm and exciting and bright with sudden hope, crashed over him, knocking everything else aside.

"Why did you say what you did?" he blurted.

"What, duck?"

"That she would give up what she has, not *for* me but to be *with* me?"

Juliet stared at him, then gave a twisted smile. "'Cause I know my girl, son, whether she wants me to or not. She's always had friends, even men friends who want to be more, but she never looked at any of 'em the way she looks at you. Up to you what you do about it, of course, but whatever the business we do here now, I won't have…" She trailed off, as though scratching around for the right words to describe what she wouldn't have.

"Neither will I," he said hastily, trying to climb free of the glorious, terrifying dream that had overwhelmed him. What in hell had they been talking about? Her old premises. "Boggie," he said with relief. "Does Boggie know you own the building?"

"Course he does."

"He doesn't want your selling business, legal or otherwise," Solomon said with certainty. It *was* Boggie or his minion who had followed him and warned him off in Seven Dials. And now he knew why. "He wants your building to rent out the rooms. No wonder Lambert's behind him."

# CHAPTER ELEVEN

L EAVING JULIET IN possession of Constance's office, under instruction to answer the door in the unlikely event of anyone calling, Solomon went to visit one of his favored business associates.

Sir Nicholas Swan was an aristocratic rebel who had gone his own way and made his own fortune. Like Solomon, he lived in a large, old house near the river, quite outside the fashionable parts of town, and was on several of the same charitable boards. He also had an interest in commercial properties.

"A shop?" Sir Nicholas said in surprise when they sat comfortably in his home study. "This doesn't sound like one of your ventures!"

"It isn't. I'm inquiring for a friend."

"I'll send someone round this afternoon, if you like."

"Thank you. If you could send him here…" Solomon passed over his Silver and Grey card, which made Sir Nicholas blink. "The other thing is…Huxley Gregg. Do you happen to know who his solicitor is?"

"Actually, yes. We had dealings before all this trouble."

"I want to know who falls heir to Gregg's estate."

"Why?"

"I don't believe he was the sole owner of that building or several others, and I need to know who owns them now."

Swan frowned. He had a very alarming scowl when he chose. "Give me two minutes," he said. "I'll come with you. Oh, and you *will* come to our charity ball, won't you? We're raising money to rehouse the surviving victims of the disaster, to build some decent homes with proper plumbing and so on. I know, they need the help now, not in another year, but to be honest, people are more inclined to give after a disaster. My wife is arranging it. She's bound to have sent you a card."

"Of course," said Solomon, who could not recall it. "May I bring a friend?"

Swan grinned. "As many as you like, as long as they—or you—cough up!"

An hour later they entered the offices of Granger, Granger, and Kemp, and were fortunate to discover a harassed-looking Mr. Kemp just arriving.

"Forgive me if I've forgotten our appointment," he said. "I was called away urgently, and my clerk should have canceled everything until this afternoon." He shuddered. "Mortuaries are not my favorite places."

"Mortuaries?" Sir Nicholas repeated, startled.

"Yes, I was called away from the office by the police, who wanted me to identify the body of one of my clients. Come in, gentlemen."

"I don't suppose," Solomon said, obligingly moving a heap of papers from one of the visitor's chairs to a table, "that this dead client's name is Gregg?"

Kemp froze in the act of hanging up his coat, his gaze fixed on Solomon. "Good God, is it in the newspapers already?"

"Not that I know of, but we came in the hope of discussing with you certain matters relating to Mr. Gregg, and no one has seen him for days."

"The police found his body in Devil's Acre," Kemp said, hanging his coat on the hook and gesturing his guests to sit. "Not a pretty sight, I'm afraid. Dead for days, of course."

"How many days?" Solomon asked.

"Four or five, they think."

Solomon nodded thoughtfully. After a moment, he became

aware that the other two were gazing at him, as though waiting for something.

"You didn't ask *how* he died," Kemp said.

"Violently, I would guess."

"You guess correctly. What is your interest in the matter, Mr."—Kemp glanced at the cards before him on the desk—"Mr. Grey?"

"I have been investigating the collapse of the tenement in St. Giles."

"Grey and I represent a charity working for better housing," Sir Nicholas intervened, by way of explanation. "We were eager for Gregg's prosecution, along with anyone else associated with him in the ownership or upkeep of the building."

"Well, you can't prosecute him now," Kemp said. Impossible to know if it was a matter of satisfaction or disappointment to him.

"But we could go after any partners," Solomon said.

"He insisted he acted alone in that and certain other ventures," Kemp said. "And only his name is on the title deeds."

"Other ventures such as the building next door? Mr. Kemp, where do those rents go? Mr. Gregg's people assured me they were paid into a bank account."

"It will all be looked into now. He had several bank accounts, personal and business ones."

"Do you happen to know who is his heir?" Solomon asked.

Kemp hesitated. "I have already told the police, so I suppose it doesn't matter if you know. His brother does, after all."

"His brother is his heir?" Solomon said, disappointed at the disproving of his theory.

"No. His elder brother, Mr. Alfred Gregg, knows he is *not* the heir. Huxley Gregg changed his will a year ago to leave everything to his 'friend and associate of many years,' Mr. Caleb Lambert. I imagine the elder Mr. Gregg is grateful for the distance between them since the scandal of St. Giles. He resides mostly in the country, which is why I was called upon to identify the body."

*Got you*, thought Solomon savagely.

Only he hadn't. The inheritance was an undoubted motive for murder. But it was not proof. The body in the cellar had been that.

Constance had been right last night. They should have followed the donkey into the Devil's Acre.

CONSTANCE DID NOT stay long at home, only enough to sort out a couple of minor squabbles and speak to everyone. They were managing perfectly well without her—they always did, which was somewhat lowering when she liked to think she was necessary to the whole business. She approved a prospective new girl—a very young one given to theft whom they would have to watch carefully, though at the moment she was too sick and too grateful for a bed to give them any trouble.

Besides that, there was the small matter of a load of furniture and boxes that had been delivered to the establishment and which clearly belonged to her mother. At least she had taken the threat of Boggie seriously, which was such a relief that Constance bade her people store it all in the cellar. After all, she had a discreet arrangement with the local police.

"Evenings are good," Maggie reported. "But all the gentlemen are asking after you. You'll have to put in an appearance soon."

"I will," Constance said vaguely, and set off for the Silver and Grey office.

As she opened the front door with her key, her mother emerged into the hall. "Afternoon, Con."

"Good God. What are *you* doing here?"

"Minding your shop. Himself is out, and so's the girl."

Constance closed the door, removed her hat and coat, and walked purposefully into her own office, where she all but fell over a trunk and a carpetbag.

She stared at her mother. "Have you moved in?"

"Nah, moved out. Your Mr. Grey told me he had premises."

"Yes, but you own that house," Constance said. "You said it was your security."

"Well, it's a roof," Juliet said. "But you always told me I'd never get rich in Seven Dials. I'd get bugger all for selling it and all."

"You can't fence on Solomon's turf. He's a law-abiding man."

"He's a good man. Not necessarily the same thing."

"In this case, it is. I mean it, Ma, you'll have to be straight."

Juliet stared at her. "You run a house of ill repute. How is *that* legal?"

"Solomon does not own my house. Are you going to sell the place in Seven Dials?"

"Not to Boggie, I'm not. Solomon thinks your Lambert's behind him. I don't make enough to interest a man like Lambert. If he's going straight as everyone thinks, what's he want with a fence?"

"But you own a building with lots of rooms," Constance said slowly. "Solomon is probably right."

Discontentedly, she threw herself into one of the armchairs. Although relieved to find her mother away from Boggie, she did not want any witness between herself and Solomon when they met again. Her stomach still twisted with anxiety. Had they just argued? Or was their partnership truly broken?

He was looking after her mother…who was indirectly associated with the case. She had nothing to contribute except…

The sound of his key turning in the front door latch had her springing up before she could think. Would he be cold and angry? Or apologetic? Which should she be?

Foolish panic overtook her. Would he assume her presence meant she had left the Lamberts' house? Would they quarrel about her going back? Again? How far should she dig in her heels and how much would he resent it? She had been silly to allow friendship with a man to become so important, and yet if she no longer had it…

The door was pushed open.

"Constance," Solomon said in surprise. He carried a rolled-up newspaper in one hand. "Is everything well?"

His unreadable mask was back in place, but just before it came down, she was sure she glimpsed a storm of emotion.

"Perfectly," she replied, as carelessly as she could. "Angela has given me the afternoon off, while Janey and Lenny Knox, of all people, follow her about her business."

"It seemed a good idea at the time. So long as no one recognizes Knox. Lambert ruined him quite deliberately for fighting for a decent wage. It wasn't even for him."

"People tend to die for opposing Lambert," Juliet remarked. "Looks like we're all in the same boat. If you're right that he's behind Boggie."

"They've found Gregg," Solomon said, spreading his newspaper on Constance's desk. "In Devil's Acre. You were right."

Constance looked at him quickly. It was his only acknowledgement of last night's disagreements, though it was hardly the main one. Because her mother was there, watching them like some curious if overfed bird, she hastily dropped her gaze to the newspaper.

The murder of Gregg, after the outcry of the collapsed building and before the inquiry could apportion blame, was big news. The police had said little, but the reporter's speculation was rife, concluding that some angry survivor, or a family member of someone who died in the disaster, had taken the law into their own hands. The tone of the article was decidedly sympathetic to such a motive, and foretold that the killer would never be found.

"Understandable," Solomon murmured. "But not entirely fair. I've been speaking to his solicitor and to Sir Nicholas Swan, who knew Gregg years ago. He was born a gentleman and did not always associate with the likes of Lambert. Until about a year or so ago, he was just a decent man trying to make an honest living. He cut a few corners, always in pursuit of the quick profit, trying to outdo his brother, who inherited the family's estates. Then he began to invest in slum properties because they cost little and turned a quick profit. The first time he partnered with Lambert, and after that it was on his own, officially, but Kemp—the solicitor—believes Lambert was pointing him toward properties, including the one that collapsed, and kept some sort of unofficial finger in the pie."

"He was just Lambert's tool?" Constance asked.

"Not just. He clearly made no effort to walk away, but Kemp suspects there was an agreement. That Gregg's bank accounts will show that he made comparatively little, considering the flow of rent."

"He was paying a percentage to Lambert?"

"To whom he leaves everything in his will. There is some evidence that Gregg was trying to move out of slums into Belgravia and the like, but so was Lambert. They were partners in those ventures."

"And now Lambert has everything," Constance murmured, "slums and mansions, all respectably inherited, with no blame attached for the disaster. Why would he kill Gregg, though? He was the perfect scapegoat and clearly useful in introducing him to better Society and the business of the wealthy. Which, according to Angela, is his goal."

Solomon shrugged. "Perhaps Gregg had had enough and threatened to tell everything to the inquiry. Perhaps Lambert just needed an influx of money for some other venture."

"Cold," Juliet commented. "And bad for business."

"You're right," Constance said to her. "Anyone moving from one world to another needs to avoid the law or buy it off. Solomon, I think we should speak to the police, at least to Inspector Harris."

Only as she said it did she realize that both of them were talking as if their partnership was still intact, that they were still pursuing this case together.

"I agree," he said.

He didn't point out that he'd wanted to do so last night. They really needed to listen to each other…

Solomon passed a card to Constance's mother. "Mrs. Silver, this man will call to show you around some likely premises for your shop."

"Where?" Juliet asked eagerly.

"Covent Garden, I think. And further west. You might also want to think of selling your old house to me, just to avoid further trouble."

"That just moves the trouble to you," Juliet pointed out. "Besides, what do you want with a house in Seven Dials?"

"I might renovate it, an alternative to building new houses. If you choose to sell." He picked up his hat and transferred his attention to Constance. "Shall we?"

Constance, after a doubtful glance at her innocent-looking mother, preceded him out of the office. Since they appeared to be working together, she was happy to ignore last night's quarrel.

It was Solomon who brought it up.

"I know you are capable," he said, with no warning, without even offering his arm or looking at her. "And I know this is more your world we are dealing with than mine. But I don't have so many friends that I can afford to lose them. I am overprotective, not unappreciative of your talents."

She was not untouched, though she reacted with humor. "Your view of my talents is so different to other men's." She took his arm without invitation. "I said some things I should not, things I did not mean."

"I have never betrayed you and never will," he said quietly.

"I know."

He looked at her at last. "Are you safe in that house?"

"For now, yes. Though I am happier when Lambert is not at home. One of us, if not both of us, needs to be in the cellar when the ghost comes back on Saturday."

"We don't know that she will. She might consider herself

rumbled and stay away."

"What is she doing there?" Constance asked. "Laying gunpowder like Guy Fawkes?"

"We saw no sign of it. Though several of the doors were locked. They are so careful of safety, why does no one patrol down there as they do the grounds?"

"Maybe they think the only way in is through the house," Constance said. "That door is pretty well hidden."

"So how does our ghost know about it?"

"Because she found it for herself?" Constance said. "Or because she has an ally inside. A lover, though I can't think who. None of the servants vanish for long periods of time, unless they're out with Lambert or Angela. Even Duggin is usually in his own pantry and mostly visible."

"Which leaves Lambert himself," Solomon said. "Where was he during our ghost's visit?"

"At dinner with Angela," Constance replied, frowning. "For part of the time. But they didn't sit together in the drawing room last night, as they did the night before. Angela was already in her own parlor by the time we told her about the body. The servants thought he was in his office, but I don't know…"

"It would explain how furtive he is, keeping out of Angela's way, and the servants'."

Constance wrinkled her nose. "Would he bring another woman into his wife's home?"

"Winsom did," Solomon said, reminding her of their first mystery at Greenforth Manor.

"But Lambert relies on her!" Still, he had wandering eyes, if not hands.

"Hence his secrecy," Solomon said. "Is that the real reason Angela hired us? To find out her rival's identity?"

Constance closed her mouth. It made an unpleasant kind of sense. "Perhaps. But she did seem genuinely…*afraid* that it truly was a ghost, in particular the ghost of a St. Giles victim, such as Lenny Knox's wife. There is genuine guilt in her, Solomon."

He did not discount what she said. "I wonder if Lambert feels guilty, too, in his own way. Perhaps the ghost is to do with his making amends somehow? Or trying to. Have you time to come to St. Giles before you go back to Angela?"

"Well, she's not going to dismiss me," Constance said wryly. "Though the other servants are already looking at me askance."

They went directly to Scotland Yard, since they were sure this was where Inspector Harris could be found.

Ten minutes later, he stood glowering at them across his small office. "Are you two going to start plaguing me like the Tizsas?" he demanded.

Solomon presented him with a card. "Our new venture for those who cannot or will not involve the police. We are looking into matters that concern a ghost, Caleb Lambert, and the murder of Huxley Gregg. Are you involved in the case?"

Harris continued to stare at them. Then he sighed, indicated the chairs opposite his chaotic desk, and commanded them, "Cough it up."

Solomon blinked, uncomprehending. So Constance told him about hunting Angela's ghost, the discovery and disappearance of Gregg's body, and how they thought they had pursued it as far as the invisible boundary of Devil's Acre.

"I assumed they were going to dump it in the river," Solomon confessed. "But when we tried to pick up the scent again, we had lost it. Then we saw in the newspaper that Gregg's body had been found in Devil's Acre."

Harris had listened without interrupting, though his sharp, intelligent eyes were gleaming.

"I will enjoy Lambert's face when we arrive with a warrant to search his fine house and arrest him," he said dreamily.

Contance exchanged a glance with Solomon.

"The thing is," she said, "it would be more satisfying yet to prove Lambert was as much to blame for the St. Giles disaster as Gregg, and stop him from inheriting if we can."

Harris's eyes went cold again. His lips tightened. Undoubtedly, he could see the point. "I can't *not* investigate a murder on the strength of your intuition," he snapped.

"No, but there are plenty other avenues to investigate," Solomon argued, "evidence to collect that does not involve raiding his home—for example, Gregg's bank accounts to match against the rents he gathered, and Lambert's also. Find out who sees him on Thursday and Saturday evenings. The ghost is connected somehow. Give us until tomorrow night before you arrest him."

Harris scowled, drumming his fingers on his desk.

"It would be a shame to jump in too quickly when you might be able to tie him into so many other things," Constance wheedled. "You could close down his whole organization with a little patience…"

# CHAPTER TWELVE

"I NSPIRED," SOLOMON SAID wryly as they sat in the hackney taking them to St. Giles.

"True, though." Constance hesitated, then said, "We are acting against our client's interests. She doesn't want her husband arrested or hanged. She didn't hire us for that."

"No. She hired us to find her ghost, and we agreed. Anything else is outside our agreement."

"It's as well we made her pay half her fee in advance. Solomon? Don't let my mother take advantage of you."

His eyes crinkled at the corners, rather beguilingly. "I am not known as a soft mark to anyone else." Their eyes met. "She misses you. And she regrets much, much that you would forgive in any other woman."

"I do forgive her," Constance said. Curiously, it was true. "In fact, there is very little to forgive. I just refuse to be where I am not wanted."

"She does want you. But she knows she has lost you."

Constance dragged her gaze free. She didn't like the clawing of old pain. "Oh, she'll never quite do that." It was meant to be funny, although her voice broke. "Don't think I haven't tried."

She gazed out of the carriage window for a time, at the passing traffic and the street vendors, all yelling their wares so that it was indecipherable above the noise of wheels and horses against the cobbles.

"So which of these women do you think might be the ghost?"

she said at last.

"Any of them who can walk," Solomon said. "They all know Lambert was at least one of their landlords, and most of them would be happy to knife him. She looked young to me, but I suppose she was just spry. I never saw her face."

"Neither did I. Or her hands."

Constance, used to her large house, with her large sitting room and bedchamber all to herself, with the others never sharing more than two to a room, had almost forgotten the sort of overcrowding she found next to the collapsed building. Disease would be rife here, worse during the winter, when whole swaths of them could be carried off, and there would always be other, even more desperate people waiting to take their place. Once she'd thought this the only way to live, and there had always been someone to look after her when her mother was "out." Later, she was so desperate to be alone even for five minutes that she had hidden in cupboards and cellars…

But this was not about her. She walked forward.

Solomon had been here before. So had Dr. Dragan Tizsa, and many of the survivors from the building next door knew Solomon had sent him. There was distracted gratitude from Emmy, the mother of a mostly paralyzed girl of twelve who had begun to eat, grudging nods of respect from a few, hopeful stares from a few others.

"You're doing a good thing," one woman said to him, ignoring Constance. "Dr. Tizsa and you. There's a bit of life about them again. Even Lenny."

Solomon said nothing, merely nodded, but Constance regarded the woman with more interest. She could have been anything between thirty and fifty years old, with a face lined by hard work, hardship, and tragedy. But her eyes were those of a fighter, and she moved with swift economy. Constance wondered if, veiled and in a fog, the woman would appear to glide. She could easily imagine her running up a back lane and jumping into a carriage. Only the hackney fare would have been beyond her.

Solomon obviously had the same idea, for he said suddenly, "This may seem an odd question, but have you ever seen hackney carriages stop here?"

"Don't be daft. Nor omnibuses, neither. No one here can afford them."

"Were you here yesterday evening?" Constance asked.

"Where else would I be? Spending my gold at Covent Garden?"

Constance regarded the woman's contemptuous face and took a chance. "We think someone from here might be visiting Caleb Lambert, for whatever reason. It would at least be good to know who it wasn't."

"I'd stick a knife in him if I could," the woman said at once. "And maybe I will one day. But it weren't no one in this room. There's a will, but not the energy."

"Did you know Huxley Gregg was murdered?"

"Heard it from a patterer at the market. Good riddance to him. Hope the same right-thinking philanthropist does the same for Lambert. Only there'll always be another to take his place."

"You talk like an educated woman, Mrs....?"

"Smith. And I'm not. I just listen."

"Me too," Constance said. "Do you know anyone, from here or anywhere else, who would seriously try to hurt either Gregg or Lambert? Not just talk, but risk everything to do it?"

"Why would they? There isn't much point, is there? The world needs change, not more violence or revenge."

Constance thought she was right. There was hatred and hopelessness in this room and so many like it, but they were too weary for action.

She said as much to Solomon as they descended the filthy stairs.

He nodded, then paused. "Except perhaps for *these* people. The rent collectors." He moved faster and rapped smartly on the first door. From the one opposite and another near the front door, two children's shaggy heads appeared and vanished.

The door in front of them opened to reveal a pert, pretty young woman. She wore a plain, working dress, covered by an apron. But no patches were visible.

"Yes?"

Solomon took off his hat. "Mrs. Fraser?"

"Yes?"

"I thought so. I was talking to your husband the other day. Is he at home?"

"He'll be back directly. Why?"

"I was hoping for another word."

She frowned, suspicion glaring out of her blue eyes. "Here, you're not that journalist bothering us again? We only collect the rents. Someone's got to."

And she shut the door in their faces.

Constance forgot to breathe until they were out in the street again.

"That's her," she said in a rush. "I'll bet you anything that's our ghost."

IRIS FRASER ALMOST fell on her husband Frank as he returned to their room.

"He was here again!" she blurted before the door was even properly closed.

"Who?" Frank demanded.

"That journalist you spoke to the other day. I'm sure it was him. Tall, sallow bloke, speaks like a gent. Had a woman with him."

"What sort of a woman?" Frank asked, scowling.

"I don't know," Iris said impatiently. "Too bloody pretty by half, though her dress was nothing to marvel at. Nosy cow, too."

"Why, what did she ask? Ain't we got any tea?"

"I'll get it later. She didn't ask anything, but she was peering inside, trying to see over my shoulder."

Frank laughed. "Looking for dust?"

"I don't know, but I don't like people coming round here. What if they know?"

"Know what?" Fraser said, throwing himself into the comfortable chair.

"That I go and see *him*."

"Why should anyone know that? You take care, don't you?"

"Yes, but someone chased me down that lane last night, and it weren't bloody Lambert."

Frank curled his lip. "Maybe Mrs. Lambert. You'll need to watch your back, girl."

"Frank, I don't want to do it no more. Ain't we got enough money yet?" She sat in his lap, because he liked that, and traced a pattern on his shirt front with one finger.

Frank sighed. "I suppose we have. Tell the truth, I don't much like you going there either."

"Then why d'you let me? You said you wasn't frightened of him."

"I'm not," Frank bragged. Iris knew he was lying. "I just like that he thinks he's getting one over on me, stealing my wife. And in reality, you're taking his presents and selling them, so *we're* getting one over on *him*."

"You wouldn't feel the need to if I wasn't going to his bed twice a week."

Frank shifted. "Does no harm to keep him sweet."

She flattened her hand on his chest to lever herself up and glare at him.

"All right," he said hastily, "you're right. It ain't worth it. You can't just stop going, though. We don't want to make him mad with us. Go tomorrow as usual, tell him I'm getting suspicious and you're worried and can't come for the next few weeks. Likely he'll move on to some other girl."

Iris didn't quite like that idea, either that Lambert would find it so easy to move on from her, or that Frank would think it so easy. But at least she was winning the argument.

"Can't I just send a message?" she wheedled.

"Don't be daft. Who would you trust that to? Or should I take it to him meself?"

She sighed. "Fair enough. Once more, then, and I ain't ever going back after that. We've got to find another place to stay."

HAVING RELUCTANTLY SEEN Constance into a hackney to return to the Lamberts' house, Solomon drowned his misgivings by questioning all the hackney drivers at the stand, including the new ones as they turned up. It was time consuming but instructive.

It was dark by the time he arrived back at the office to find the lamps lit and both Janey and Knox drinking tea in her tiny office.

"Any callers?" he asked casually, having established that Juliet Silver was no longer on the premises, although her trunk and bags remained in Constance's parlor.

"No," Janey said, "but there's a note on your desk. Cup of tea, guv? I mean sir."

Solomon accepted. "Did you manage to keep Mrs. Lambert in sight? Where did she go?"

"Around a load of buildings and offices. The offices is mostly landlords, Mr. Knox says, and the buildings tenements you wouldn't even want your enemies living in."

"Did she go to Gregg's office?" Solomon asked, perching on a corner of the desk.

"Nah, nothing half so respectable looking."

"What was she doing? Was she buying property for her husband?"

"Maybe, or just seeing what's available. She had that big cove with her most of the time, and also another she picked up at one of those offices. She seemed to be looking over the buildings quite thoroughly."

"Looking for dangerous flaws?" Solomon speculated. Constance seemed to be right that Angela was concerned by the St. Giles disaster.

"Yes," Knox said. "Partly. Pretty sure she was collecting rents too. Fraser does that in the St. Giles properties, but these others were all over the place. Whitechapel, Cheapside."

"Did she go into Devil's Acre?"

Knox shook his head. "Lamberts aren't that daft. They come from there. If one of their buildings collapsed in the Acre, they'd get rough justice right away. I doubt they own anything there. Too risky. I suspect her visits today were to minimize risk as well as collect the rents."

"Is that why she came to your building in St. Giles?"

"Maybe. Or seeing if she could cram in more people. My Cathy spoke to her, said she listened and was sympathetic. But nothing happened."

"Was Lambert there too when your wife spoke to her?"

"No, they never came at the same time. Lambert only came to see Fraser. Then the rent usually went up."

"Although Gregg was your landlord."

"Officially. Lambert's always liked other people to do his dirty work, keep him out of trouble. Especially now he thinks he's respectable."

Which was one of the many things that made Solomon uneasy. Even if Lambert hadn't killed Gregg with his own hands, why would he have had it done in his own house? Why hide the body there so long? Even if one of his staff had overstepped and done the killing without permission, why would they have left Gregg in the wine cellar, where only Lambert went?

Lambert and Duggin, the "butler."

A sudden chill shook Solomon. He really didn't want Constance in that house for another night.

IN THE KITCHEN, Alfie Duggin heard the knock on the door and glanced up from his tea to see Angela's girl, Silver, breeze through the open door.

"Has she rung?" Silver asked, taking off her hat and coat.

"Not yet," Ida said. "She's only just in herself."

"I've got time to put these away, then," Silver said, heading for the stairs.

"Might even have time for a quick cup of tea," Ida said kindly to her back.

"Come on, then, you've all had your tea," Duggin said to the remaining staff. "Jump to it. Here. Pat." Duggin stood to corner the "footman" and lowered his voice. "Keep your eye on her."

"Bert already is. We all watch her when we can."

"Good." Duggin let him go and scowled at the giggling maids as they went about their business.

He wasn't sure that Denise was a good influence on his daughter. Goldie could certainly aim higher than Robin, who had Denise eating out of his hand, but he didn't like the idea of Goldie entertaining men at all. He'd caught her looking at Lambert himself once or twice, and he definitely didn't like that. She was still his little girl, although her mother, may she rest in peace, had been no older when he'd first taken her. Lambert had been a catch once, but he'd never leave Angela—who was worth two of him anyway.

Duggin sat back down beside Ida, who was pouring a splash more gin into her empty teacup. "What's your view on Angela's girl?" he asked abruptly.

Ida shrugged. "No harm in her. Angela likes her."

"Do you?"

"I do, as it happens. I gather you don't."

"She ain't one of us. I don't like strangers in the house. And she must have Angela wrapped around her little finger to get hours off every bleeding day."

"You don't know that she's been off duty," Ida pointed out. "She might be doing stuff for Angela. She don't have to go through you all the time, Alfie. Content yourself with Caleb."

Duggin grunted, and Ida splashed the dregs of her flask into his cup. It was enough for a swallow. "I don't trust her. She talks too hoity-toity and she's too damned nosy."

"Course she's nosy. So would you be in a new house with new master and mistress. You want to know how everything and everyone works. Besides, she ain't so different from you and me."

"How d'you work that out?"

"I can tell. She's had her share of knocks. Dragged herself up by her bootstraps, same as Angela and Caleb and you and me."

"You telling me she lived in the Acre?"

"Maybe not the Acre, but there's other places just as miserable."

Duggin sniffed and got up again. "I hope you're right about her. 'Cause I think she's got Angela just where she wants her. And that ain't good for us."

"You underestimate women, Alfie," she said vaguely. "You always did."

That Ida had no misgivings about the lady's maid was some comfort to Duggin, but he still didn't like her. He watched as she came back down, drank half a cup of tea, then jumped up to answer the bell rung from the bedchamber.

Duggin didn't put it past Lambert to have rung that bell. Which was another worry. Lambert had noticed her. The little Fraser tart from St. Giles wouldn't keep him occupied forever, and if he took up with Silver instead…well, that would hurt Angela more. What was she thinking about, hiring a maid with looks like that? She must have known Lambert would look twice.

Well, who was Duggin to judge? His own marriage hadn't lasted long enough for him to get the hang of wives. There were other important things in life.

Just before the Lamberts went in to dine, Silver slipped out again through the kitchen door.

Duggin caught Pat's eye as he came in from the dining room, and jerked his head toward the door. Pat nodded and went out after her.

CONSTANCE WASN'T SURE that Solomon would come this evening, when they had spent most of the afternoon together. But she wanted to know what Janey had reported about Angela's doings, and if Solomon had learned anything useful from the hackney drivers.

And then she also wanted to discuss how to catch their "ghost," and how much to tell Angela of their plans.

So while everyone was busy preparing the dinner, she simply took her shawl and walked out into the garden.

It looked very different without the mist. The light from windows and stars and the streetlights on the main road all penetrated the darkness so that it took only a few moments for her eyes to adjust and make out the path to the garden door.

"Constance." Solomon stepped out of the shadows beneath the wall, and she took his arm without thought. She could not believe how close they had come to severing their partnership, ending their friendship.

He said at once, "She's up to her neck in Lambert's business, though she might be trying to minimize the chances of any further disasters. That's where she goes all day."

"She does everything to please him," Constance said. "All the time. Even whores have time off. Did you have any luck with the hackney drivers?"

"Yes. A couple had taken her from the stand to Victoria Street, and picked her up at midnight by arrangement at the corner of Tothill Lane."

"It's got to be Iris Fraser," Constance said with some satisfaction. "I looked in the Lamberts' stables, by the way, and they don't have a donkey, only carriage horses, so we might not even have been following Gregg's body last night. If Mrs. Fraser is our ghost, though, why would she kill Gregg?"

"To get his rents?" Solomon suggested. "Or maybe her husband did it in a fit of jealousy."

"And locked his body in Lambert's cellar?"

"We don't really know how cozy Lambert and Gregg were. He might have had a key."

"Like the ghost." Constance sighed, then held her breath, cocking her ear to hear better.

"I heard movement behind us," Solomon breathed.

Constance, who had heard something altogether different, veered across the lane, dragging Solomon with her, to a rather run-down building. She put her ear to the door. Unmistakably, a donkey brayed within.

She grinned. "I'll bet any of the servants could have broken in here and borrowed the donk—"

He stepped closer, placing his fingers urgently against her lips. She stared up at him in startlement. But he really had heard something else. And it was behind them. Someone's stealthy footsteps.

Her blood chilled. Had someone noticed her leaving the kitchen and followed her? A burly man moved among the shadows of the lane. He was not exactly subtle. More of a brute than a spy. Surely one of Lambert's bodyguards…

And she had to have a reason for being here with Solomon that was not searching for donkeys or comparing notes on Lambert's villainy. She slid her arms around Solomon's neck and tugged him closer.

He came easily, co-operating at once, not only bending his head to hers, but covering her mouth with his as though it were the most natural thing in the world.

*It is. Oh God, it is…*

While the footman's casual footsteps grew nearer, Solomon

seemed to be entirely focused on kissing her. The thoroughness of his acting was totally unexpected. He pressed her closer into the doorway, caressing the sides of her breasts, her waist, her hips, while he kissed her on and on, deeper and deeper.

This was what she had wanted that last night of their last case when she had lain in his arms, so dreadfully aware of her own desire and his. And it was…

She had no words. Instead of trying to find them, she opened her eyes, peering at the footman—surely it was Pat—as he sauntered down the lane, hands in pockets, whistling in a manner that somehow told her he was vastly entertained. He turned the corner of the lane.

"He's gone," she muttered against Solomon's lips.

One of his hands stilled, the other came up and touched her cheek, the corner of her mouth, but he did not stop kissing her. Even though he no longer needed to touch her. Bemused by this stunning fact, she forgot to hold her own feelings in check, and they washed over her in a tidal wave of sweet awareness and heavy desire.

*Oh, Solomon, Solomon, I can never come back from this…*

Some remnant of sanity must have remained hanging by a thread, for somehow she was able to drag her mouth free. "You can stop pretending now."

She drawled the words, meaning them to be light, but her voice shook damnably. She could not give him this advantage over her, betray this weakness that would appall them both just as soon as he stood a few more inches away from her.

"I stopped pretending a long time ago," he said huskily. He cleared his throat and stood back. "Although I admit this is neither the time nor the place." He tucked an escaped lock of hair behind her ear and straightened her shawl before drawing her hand through the crook of his arm. "Let us walk more sedately and make our plans for the morrow."

She resented that he could even think at that moment, but she walked blindly forward, one foot in front of the other, and wondered how she would ever live with this.

With an effort, she said, "Angela believes the ghost won't come without the fog. It never has before."

"And what do you believe?" he asked.

"That she comes every Thursday and Saturday without fail, but when it's misty, she changes her routine, coming and going earlier. She probably has the non-foggy days timed to perfection, so that she avoids the garden patrols and walks boldly through the garden to the cellar while everyone else is busy around the dining room and can't see her. On foggy days, she takes longer because she can't see so well, and probably comes earlier or later. The house staff probably do things out of time too, so everything is just very slightly out of schedule, and mistakes are made."

She'd grasped on to this explanation, stumbled over it by accident with some desperation, though as she blurted it out, it made a kind of sense. Which was a huge relief. It meant she could escape this unbearable moment, hide what Solomon had done to her, what she had done to herself by caring, by wanting more than she could ever have. He had always got through her guard, ever since he had crashed into her, saving her life by his lightning-swift reaction. Now she had to rebuild her armor, and she couldn't do it with him anywhere near.

"Maybe," he said thoughtfully.

"Good," she said, slipping her hand free of his arm. "Tomorrow, then. Come earlier. Goodnight."

She sensed his surprise as she turned and fled. "Constance—"

She flapped one dismissive hand and kept going.

# CHAPTER THIRTEEN

W AS THERE EVER a more maddening woman than Constance Silver?

Solomon moved after her along the lane, keeping to the shadows in case the footman came back. He watched as she entered the garden and listened with some difficulty to the sounds of her return to the house.

The footman following her had not been one of the regular patrols. Somebody was suspicious of her, which, to Solomon, made it more imperative than ever that she did not stay there. Even though they seemed to have allayed that suspicion for now, by giving her a sweetheart.

And he wasn't. She had made that abundantly clear.

He lurked outside the gate, straining his ears for any sounds of anger within, while his mind and his body wrestled with what had just happened between him and Constance.

The embrace had been her idea, although the kiss had been his—that amazing, blinding, overwhelming kiss…

*"I stopped pretending a long time ago."* It was true—with the first touch of his mouth on hers, in fact.

She hadn't fought him off. She hadn't even started. She had accepted the pretense. And he had made several startling discoveries, not least of which was the sheer bliss of kissing Constance Silver. Even though—and this was another discovery—the courtesan did not know how to kiss as lovers did.

That pained him, and yet filled him with wonder and hope.

Kissing her was an exquisite pleasure that he could not bring himself to end. How could he when she began to kiss him back, to melt into his arms, accepting the urgency of his body and his lips? And he had known with terrifying clarity that this was *right*.

This love that he had not wanted was right. Constance, his friend, his partner in all things…

What had Juliet said? *"She* would *leave it for you. To be* with *you."* To be with Constance was all he wanted, and the knowledge that she was his as he was hers overwhelmed him.

He had made an attempt to bring back sanity, to give them a moment to adjust, to talk of the case they were working on, though it was so much less important than what he really wanted to say…

Although she had tried to play along in her flippant way, she was shaken. He had even been foolishly pleased by that—after all, so was he—only she had bolted so quickly and so determinedly that he had the appalling fear he was wrong.

He had overstepped, insulted her with the kind of passion she had stepped away from years ago. How could he have been so blind to her true feelings? To have initiated this at such a time when there was no time or place to explain, to talk. He had just grabbed the moment.

And lost it.

Lost her?

He should have spoken of his feelings, asked about hers… Now the moment had gone, and he had upset them both.

He had never been good at romantic relationships. In truth, he had never tried much because he had never truly cared. A little affection, a little physical pleasure… Nothing had ever compared to this feeling for Constance.

Since he could hear nothing untoward coming from the house, he walked away. By the time he found a hackney, he knew he would not give up. Not just for his own sake but for hers.

HE FOUND JANEY in her hat and coat, about to leave the office.

"Mrs. Silver's taken her stuff," she greeted him. "A gentleman came to see you with a view to employing your services. I made an appointment for him tomorrow at ten. And there's two letters of inquiry on your desk. G'night!"

Solomon blinked. "Hold on! Where has Mrs. Silver gone with her things?"

"Covent Garden. Above the shop your man showed her this afternoon. Said she'd drop in tomorrow."

So she was safe, at least. He relaxed. "Thank you," he said. "Goodnight."

Grateful for the prospect of another client—and something else to focus his mind on—he walked into his office and read the letters of inquiry. Smiling, he sat down and wrote replies, suggesting appointments next week, by which time he hoped to be free of Angela Lambert, who, however, might not speak to them again once they went after her husband.

He looked forward to telling Constance about the prospective new clients. At last, things seemed to be moving forward for their business. At the very least, surely it would mean he still saw her every day.

Unless she no longer wanted to.

PAT HAD CLEARLY blabbed about what he had seen in the mews, for Constance was teased mercilessly from the moment she stepped back into the kitchen that evening. She turned it all off with jokes and laughter, a rather professional performance accomplished without the necessity of thought.

She couldn't think because her mind was in such turmoil. And that, in her position, was dangerous. She received a sharp reminder when she walked upstairs and, her mind still busy with Solomon and her reactions to his touch, into the main bedchamber.

She knew Angela was in her parlor, for she had rung for tea there. But she had, unforgivably, forgotten about Lambert.

By the light of one pale lamp, he stood by the bedroom window, one curtain drawn back just enough for him to see onto the street below. He didn't immediately notice her entrance, which at least gave her a moment to hide her shock and to observe him while he was unaware.

He wasn't what she expected.

In that first moment, there was no sign of the entitled, brutal man who had fought, stolen, and murdered his way out of the gutter, who had caused the death and injury of his tenants and stood by in the shadows while his partner was vilified for it. To say nothing of murdering that partner.

If she hadn't been so sure he had murdered Gregg, she could almost have imagined he had just learned of the body's discovery and was grieving.

She could not stand gawking at him. Nor could she bolt back out again without being obvious. So, without closing the door, she merely carried her bundle of Angela's freshly laundered underclothes and put them quietly away in their correct drawers.

Was that *sorrow* she had glimpsed in his face? Certainly, it was something softer than she had ever seen or expected. For the first time, she had an inkling why Angela remained with him, and for his sake strove to better herself. It was not simply his power over her, or the convenience of his wealth.

Constance knew what it was like, to be so desperate to escape that one would do anything. And then the path was set and you couldn't stop. You were afraid to stop in case you went back there.

"Silver," he said from the window, as though both recalling her name from a thousand others and relishing the sound of it on his tongue. "Are you settling into your new position?"

"Yes, sir," she replied, remembering to curtsey as she closed the drawer and turned to face him. She should say, *Excuse me*, and leave, but this unexpectedly human side of Lambert was a rare opportunity, fascinating in its way. "Everyone is very kind and helpful."

"I understand you are, too. My wife likes you. That is rarer than you might think. And she finds you useful."

"A basic requirement of servants, sir."

His lip twitched upward. "I suppose so. Tell me, where did you learn all your ladylike speech and manners?"

"Observation. And mimicry."

There was a hint of derision in his smile now. "Work for many noble ladies, did you?"

"I have served my share of the nobility," Constance said with perfect truth, and then wanted to laugh, because it was the sort of remark that had always amused and shocked Solomon.

But she should not have let down her guard. Lambert had crossed the room and stood closer to her now, and there was no softness in his eyes, only sharp observation, a sheer distance that caused her stomach to plummet. This man *used* people for his own ends. Beyond that, they had no value to him. A moment's sadness did not make him a kind or sensitive man. Her skin prickled with alarm.

"Fall from grace, did you?" he asked, his lip curling.

"You've no cause to think that, sir," she said, allowing self-righteousness into her voice.

"Why else'd you be slumming it with the likes of us?"

"Your coin's as good as anyone else's, sir. Better than some of them noble households." She hoped he noted her grammatical slip, that it would put him at his ease.

Amusement sparked in his eyes. "Are you saving up for a reason? Got a young man who wants to marry you?"

She dropped her eyes. Had word got back to him already about her meeting with Solomon? Inevitably. Very little would be allowed to happen in this household without his knowledge.

"Maybe, sir," she said coyly, "though that's a long time away."

"Doesn't have to be," he said. "It you're loyal. Might even find a place for your man, if he fits. What does he do?"

"He's a clerk, sir. For a shipping company." *Sort of, in a very senior capacity...*

"Is he?" Lambert's gaze was speculative, though whether he was considering the shipping clerk or Constance was impossible to tell.

He didn't come any closer, but neither did he show any signs of either leaving or dismissing her. Her flesh began to crawl. She had no idea what he was thinking, and that was unusual enough to be frightening.

"We'll see," he murmured, moving away from her at last.

She breathed an inward sigh of relief, but to her alarm he was tugging off his necktie. She had to get out. Now.

Casually—and yet she was sure it was not casual at all—he dropped the tie on the bed and kept walking toward his open dressing room door. Constance was afraid to breathe. *Don't dare lock it and turn back to me...*

He walked on through the door, closed it, and locked it from the other side.

Constance exhaled in a rush and sank down on the nearest chair. Just like after their last encounter, she was shaking.

Only a few moments later, she sprang up again as the door to the passage opened.

Angela whisked inside and closed the door. "Ah, you're here already. Good." Her gaze fixed on the necktie lying across the bed. "When was he here?"

"Just a few minutes ago."

For the first time, there was suspicion in Angela's eyes when they met Constance's, veiled yet unmistakable. "Did he speak to you?"

"Just to ask how I was settling in. He went into the dressing room."

Did she imagine Constance was casting out lures to Lambert? Or did she not trust him to keep his hands off any woman? Had he left the tie deliberately to sow doubt in his wife's mind? Or was it some kind of signal to Angela? That her husband would be joining her for his marital rights?

"Unhook me," Angela said abruptly. "And then you may go to bed."

Constance was no prude, of necessity. But she did wonder how to fashion earplugs for the night.

JULIET SILVER CALLED at the office the following morning to thank Solomon and give him a note of her address. "To pass on to Connie."

"Of course. I'm glad you found something suitable," he said.

"Oh, it's more than suitable. It's got a shop window. Never thought I'd be able to have such a place for my little curiosities."

"Some of your curiosities are worth a fair bit of money."

"I know, and now I can get what they're worth—which I'll need to, to pay that rent. In the meantime, I could do with some shelving in the shop and the storeroom. You don't happen to know an honest carpenter, do you?"

"Funnily enough, I do," Solomon said, thinking of Lenny Knox. "I'll send him along later today."

Juliet smiled and hefted herself to her feet. "My Connie's done well for herself to find you. Don't give up on her."

Solomon, vaguely irritated, said nothing, merely rose politely to see her off the premises before his ten o'clock appointment turned up.

At the front door, she paused. "You said something about buying my old place. You still interested? What would you give me for it? I could always sell it to Boggie for a pretty decent price, but I hate to think what he'd do with the place. Come to that, what would *you* do?"

"I'm not sure yet," Solomon said. "I have a few people to see. I suppose you've no running water in the building or proper sewer outside?"

"Don't be daft."

"I'll send someone round today or tomorrow, but if Boggie tracks you down, tell him we already have a deal. Don't give him this address," he added, thinking of Janey on her own. "Send him to my office at St. Catherine's." He gave her one of the older cards with his main company address.

"Damn, I wish I'd met you when I was young and beautiful," Juliet said.

ANGELA HAD BEEN glad to spend last night in her husband's arms. Quite apart from the physical pleasures to be found there, it reaffirmed that she always won. His affairs never mattered. He always came back to her. It did Silver no harm to see that either, just in case she was getting ideas.

Not for the first time, as Silver fastened her dress and brushed her hair and chatted of nothing by way of speech lessons, Angela wondered about the extent of the woman's relationship with Mr. Grey. He was an impressive specimen, and he certainly carried himself like a king, but he undoubtedly possessed nothing like Caleb's wealth. If he did, neither of them would be scratching around to make a living from other people's squalid problems.

Angela wondered idly what it would take to bring Silver permanently into the fold. She would have to be more than a lady's maid. A secretary, perhaps. Or a companion to accompany her to the great houses Caleb was conquering…

Too soon to suggest such a thing.

"Well?" she asked. "Do you know who the ghost is?"

Rather to Angela's surprise, Silver said, "Yes, I think we do, though we don't yet know her purpose. I propose to find that out today."

"She won't come today," Angela said impatiently. "There's no fog,"

"She might. If she does, then you will have your answers. If she doesn't, we'll have them later. But my theory is she comes every Thursday and Saturday, at fixed times that are thrown off kilter in storms or fogs, when traveling is difficult."

"And goes into my cellar? Why? We saw no sign of her on Thursday."

"No, but we were somewhat distracted by a dead body on Thursday."

"So what do you mean to do?"

"Follow her into the cellar."

"If she comes," Angela said. She met Silver's eyes in the mirror and held them. "Who do you think she is?"

"It is only a theory, so you must not act on it. But I think it's the wife of Frank Fraser, the rent collector in St. Giles."

Angela was startled. How did Silver even know about the rent collector in St. Giles? "Iris Fraser?" she said in astonishment. "Why on earth would *she* creep into my cellar?"

"Perhaps she is conducting some kind of liaison with one of your servants."

*Not the servants. Caleb, Caleb, have you no standards?* Angela curled her lip. "I don't see Duggin standing for that."

"On the contrary, I doubt Duggin is interested how your servants conduct themselves so long as they do their jobs and do not endanger you or Mr. Lambert."

Angela laughed and pushed back her chair to stand. "Well, I can't imagine Iris Fraser—who's a silly bit of fluff if ever I met one—being a danger to anyone."

She went down to breakfast. Caleb had already gone, so she didn't linger. Instead, she visited the kitchen to confer with Ida Feathers, who was alone with a cup of tea, though it smelled more like gin.

"That girl of yours is stepping out," Ida said slyly. "With the bloke who came here with her on Thursday night, I reckon. Very intimate, they was, according to Bert. The fine ladies would kick her out without a character."

"Then it's fortunate I'm not a fine lady."

"Yes, you are," Ida said. "You've just more sense. And more heart. I think Silver knows when she's well off."

"I hope so. When does she usually go to meet him?"

"Around seven each evening, when we're all busy and she's got nothing to do."

"That's what I thought." For a moment, Angela almost asked her about Iris Fraser. But no, she would not betray such ugly suspicion, even to Ida. She, Angela, was his wife, his support.

"What are your thoughts about dinner this evening?" she asked, as though she cared.

CONSTANCE HAD LEARNED long ago that very few men, whatever awful things they had done, were completely beyond redemption. She had supposed Lambert to be one of those rare exceptions, and was as happy as Solomon to bring him down if she could. Her only concern had been for Angela, who, like other women before her, loved an evil man and would always stand by him.

But as she went about her duties that day, tidying and caring for Angela's clothes as she had once done for her own in the early days of her ambitions, she realized she was regarding him differently since last night.

Like herself, like Solomon, Lambert was a driven man. Determined to rise as high as he could above the grinding poverty he must have been born into, he had followed a cruel, merciless path, and succeeded, however many people suffered and died for it. But he was not unaware of that awfulness. He did not like it.

That was what she had glimpsed in him last night.

He still repelled her, but few people were *all* bad; he was not unsavable. Maybe she and Solomon should not be trying so hard to ruin him. They should be finding a way to redeem him, for Angela, for all the poor devils who depended on him. After all, who was she to judge anyone for breaking the law? She did it all the time.

Surely Angela was already trying to mitigate the worst of his neglect and exploitation? That was why Cathy Knox had spoken to her, why she spent her days visiting Lambert's various properties and businesses, trying to ensure there was no repeat of the St. Giles disaster.

No one had employed Silver and Grey to bring Lambert to justice; that was their own self-righteous quest.

She wanted Solomon's perspective on the matter.

Her heart gave a little skip. Meeting Solomon again as though nothing had happened between them—as though she, the notorious courtesan, had not been devastated by a mere kiss— filled her with dread as well as longing. She was behaving like a very young girl in the throes of early besottedness. But then, she had missed that stage in her life. She had never been *besotted*. Until now. And it had to be with him, the upright man who did not care to pay for his pleasures. He would never love a prostitute, a woman who sold other women. Whatever their personal friendship, he would never see beyond that.

And yet he had kissed her like *that*. He desired her. She had always known it, though he had never given in to it, even for a moment, until last night. And now he must know how he moved her, and she could not live with that. She had to pretend it didn't matter, that it meant nothing to her.

Only, why had he done it?

Had he just given in to loneliness? Why should he not take the comfort of a woman who was happy to oblige? He had disdained the services of her establishment. Because it was Constance he wanted? Was he about to propose some kind of arrangement to her, despite his misgivings over her profession? After all, he understood better now the purposes of her establishment…

Her heart beat thunderously in her breast. Was this not what she wanted? The most she could ever have?

Of course, he did not know she had no professional skills. All her talents lay in enticement, in matching her clients to other women.

As she hung Angela's cleaned walking dress from yesterday back in the wardrobe, a wave of desolation swept over her. She closed the wardrobe and sank into the armchair, staring at nothing as realization hit her.

She could not bear that kind of relationship, not with him. It was too soulless to make him happy. And it would destroy her. She had to be more than her profession. She was Solomon's partner, not his whore.

She jumped up again, lashing herself with the word until the pain around her heart began to ease.

She did what she always did, concentrated on the business in hand. Not Lambert, not Solomon, except in so far as he was involved in the capture of their garden ghost. Those butterflies in her stomach were all for that moment, not the moment she next saw Solomon. And that she could live with.

She drew out her watch. Only a few hours to go.

# CHAPTER FOURTEEN

L ENNY KNOX HAD found his first peace since the accident in the simplicity of hard work. Mrs. Silver—the elder Mrs. Silver— was a pleasant old bird, brought him lots of tea, and admired his work.

Once he would have valued that more than he did now. He had no one to work for without Cathy and little Kitty. But he wouldn't think of that. Work had got him through the day. And the day before, the odd business of following Lambert's wife with the friendly Janey had helped too.

He knew he should stop for the evening and go home, only home was that room full of people, half of them bereaved or injured or dying. At least the anger had come back. For the first couple of weeks after the accident there had only been shock, numbness alternating with the sheer impossibility of going on without his wife and daughter.

And then there had been Solomon Grey asking questions, and a spurt of anger had come back, along with curiosity. The man was actually trying to do something to make Lambert pay…

"Here, love, ain't you worked enough for the day?" Mrs. Silver said, coming into the shop from the back. "You want to go home and get some dinner."

He smiled perfunctorily. "Suppose I do. I can come back tomorrow, if you don't mind me working on the sabbath."

"I think I *need* you working on the sabbath, if it don't offend you."

She probably thought he needed to get the job finished in

order to eat. In fact he didn't, since Mr. Grey had paid him for following Lambert.

"Tell you what, duck, you go round to the Crown and bring back some hot dinner for us both. I could use the company."

So could Lenny. It was an excuse not to go back for another hour.

He walked along to the Crown eagerly enough. He even had a quick pint first, which was when the anger surged back.

Vengeance was all he had left. He gazed at the public house door and imagined racing through it and running all the way to Lambert's house. The bastard wouldn't be expecting it there, not with Gregg already dead. He began to smile, flexing his fingers.

SOLOMON REACHED THE lane behind the Lamberts' house even earlier than usual. As before, he hid in a disused shed that smelled of things he didn't want to think about, while the usual patrols of Lambert's men passed him by, not even glancing in the cracked window.

They were not much use as watchmen. Which made him wonder again what their purpose was. Was it just Lambert's warning to the criminal rivals of his past? Or did he really fear some kind of threat? If so, his men had grown lax. The ghost was not the only one who could get into Lambert's garden. Or Lambert's house.

After last night, and the way Constance had fled, Solomon would not have been surprised if she had waited until the last moment to let him into the garden. But oddly enough, shortly after the patrol of the footmen, he heard the sound of the gate opening once more and risked a glance out of the window.

A Constance-shaped figure emerged from the darkness. He eased out of the shed door. Its hinges *did* creak, and she swung to face him.

"Solomon," she said lightly. She even took his arm immediately, and, warmed, he began to hope that he not made an irremediable misstep after all. "What news?"

"We have a new case, a gentleman whose jewels have been stolen. And the prospect of two other clients whom I have invited to call on us next week."

"Well, that is good!" She was so clearly pleased that he knew she would not end their partnership. Not for the first time, he was overthinking personal matters. What had happened last night was not the huge anxiety he had made it into. Just a moment that got a little out of hand. Human nature. She understood that.

"And in the house?"

"In the house… I'm wondering if, perhaps, he is not quite as awful as we think. He might be more ignorant and struggling than totally evil. But that doesn't really affect the matter in hand. Angela doesn't think our ghost will show itself, but she accepts that we have to look. The trouble is, she doesn't have cellar keys, and I'm not sure I can pick that lock so that we can lie in wait there for her."

"Then we hide in the garden," Solomon said, "and rush her as soon as she unlocks the door."

"That's what I was thinking. If we fail, and she leaves the key in the inside of the cellar door again, I can probably turn it again from the outside. But we should be able to hide easily enough in the shadows at that side of the house. There's the boundary wall and bushes too. We'll just have to be quick—and quiet, so we don't attract the attention of the servants."

"Or her ally or lover or whoever it is she meets there. Perhaps she's just stealing Lambert's wine, a couple of bottles at a time."

"It takes her an awfully long time to select them, then. Shall we go?"

"Yes. Constance?" Perhaps he should leave it alone, since she so clearly had chosen to do so. But she was just a little too airy in her manner, and if he had learned anything in life, it was that one could never go back, only forward.

"Yes?" She increased her pace, already reaching for the garden door.

He caught her hand. "We will talk. When the case is done."

"Of course we will. Hush."

That was why she was in such a hurry. In the garden they could not talk in more than faint breaths for fear of being overheard. She did not want to talk.

Maddening woman. Was it not she who had first spoken to him of friendship and happiness?

They slipped into the garden, keeping to the shadows of trees and walls until they found the corner of the house. From there, in the darkness, it was almost impossible to tell where the cellar door was, still perfectly covered by its disguising tangle of ivy and creepers.

They stood side by side, close to the boundary wall, Constance almost squashed into the narrow space between it and the house. The light from the kitchen windows did not penetrate here, although as Solomon's eyes grew used to this particular gloom, he began to make out the more worn and ravaged area of ivy covering the door. He suspected it had been knotted together several times, and thickened with bits of new growth from elsewhere. Someone had taken a lot of care to keep it hidden. And yet the ghost knew exactly how to find it.

One footman alone came out with his lantern and did another patrol around the garden. Solomon closed his fingers around Constance's hand, and she did not pull away. But again, it was a cursory inspection, concentrated mainly on the fact that the garden door was still locked. The biggest danger was the light from the guard's swinging lantern catching them by accident. In fact, it did sweep over them once, in a blinding flash, but the man did not notice. He was intent on returning to the warmth of the kitchen.

And two minutes after the kitchen door closed behind him, just as Constance had suspected, the garden door opened silently once more. Solomon almost missed it. The ghost did indeed wait for a patrol to pass before she entered. She used a key, and she locked the door behind her again before flitting across the garden. Veiled, slender, and graceful, she followed almost exactly the route he and Constance had taken.

Without the fog, there was little ghostly about her. Although she made no sound, she was quick and confident in her movements. Anyone glimpsing her would assume she had every right to be there.

Apart from the veil.

Only when out of sight of the kitchen window did the "ghost" veer away from the wall—and those hiding against it— and walk straight to the hidden cellar door.

She took another key from her coat. Constance tensed, releasing his hand.

The ghost was alarmingly quick. She had the door uncovered, unlocked, and open almost before they had begun to move. Solomon lengthened his stride, reaching her just as the door began to close.

He wrenched it from her hold, flinging it wide and catching it in his other hand. Constance ducked beneath his arm and strode inside before him.

Following, he could barely make out the ghost's shape, falling back before Constance with a gasp of shock.

"C-Caleb?" she whispered.

Solomon remembered the barrel by the door and found the candle and matches by feel. He struck a match and lit the waiting candle, before turning and facing their ghost.

Iris Fraser stared back, white and frightened. "Who are you? Where is Caleb?"

"Eating his dinner, I should think," Constance replied. "I'm afraid we work for Mrs. Lambert."

A faint moaning sound issued from her. "It isn't what you think. It's over. I won't ever see him again. I came to tell him. *Please* go away!"

"You're frightened of him," Constance said. "I think you'd better tell us everything, so we can decide how to protect you."

"You don't understand! My best—my *only*—protection is for you to bugger off. This'll be hard enough without him finding you here. He'll think I blabbed!"

"Then talk quickly," Constance said. "You must know he has a house full of thugs."

She moaned again. "At least they can't come down here unless he calls 'em. Here, let me lock that door. You were too rough, you'll have torn all the ivy…"

Brushing past both Constance and Solomon, she opened the door enough to reach her arm around it. Leaves rustled and the door closed silently. She locked it, leaving the key in the door.

*Habit*, thought Solomon. This was how Constance had got in before, turning the key from the other side of the lock. "What do you do here?"

She gave him an incredulous look, the candlelight exaggerating her expression almost grotesquely. "What d'you think? We have an arrangement. Twice a week. He gives me presents and Frank sells them."

"Your husband *knows* about this arrangement?" Solomon said with distaste.

"It's the only way to escape," Iris said defensively.

"And one gets used to little bits of luxury," Constance said. Unlike Solomon, she wasn't judging. She understood desperation, the doubtful pleasure of having more than your neighbors did. And yet she could never be Iris. "So you're his lover and he gives you presents. Every Thursday and Saturday."

"It's a secret," Iris said, her eyes darting about. "Don't tell her nibs, or she'll have a go at him and he'll blame me."

"He doesn't want her to know," Solomon said impatiently. Most men would keep such arrangements from their wives.

"She loves him."

"And he loves her," Constance murmured.

"Maybe." Iris's voice was less certain now. "Not sure he's

capable of that, but she means more than anyone else. If he can love anyone, it's her. He relies on her. And she on him."

"The perfect marriage," Solomon said wryly. "Does she not forgive his peccadillos? Forgive me, but you can't imagine you're the first or the last."

"She forgives *mostly*," Iris said.

Solomon lifted the candle high. "What happened to Huxley Gregg?"

"Got done in in Devil's Acre, didn't he?"

"Actually, he got done in here," Constance said, pointing to the door on the left, now closed. "Through there, in fact. Why would Lambert kill Gregg?"

"Christ, I don't know. Why does he do anything? Maybe Gregg made a pass at his wife. Maybe he looked at him wrong. Maybe he was stealing. How would I know?"

"Aren't you afraid of your arrangement with such a man?" Constance asked.

"Yes," Iris said. "Not that he ever hurt me, mind, and the presents were nice. But I don't want people to find out. I want to be a respectable woman, a proper wife."

Constance's breath caught. It might have been laughter, though Solomon couldn't tell for sure. "It's not exactly a cozy love nest, is it? Couldn't he do better than a grimy cellar? Or is that what arouses him?"

"You've got a filthy mind, you have," Iris said contemptuously.

"It takes all sorts to make a world," Constance replied. "Which room did you use? Why did you not hear us blundering about in here on Thursday night when we found Gregg's body? Or were you just hiding?"

"Thursday? I never heard anything. You don't in there. It's like a bloody great quilt around the walls."

"Show us," Solomon said.

Fear widened Iris's eyes once more. "I can't! He could come down any moment!"

"Not for another half-hour," Constance said. "At the least, you've still time to make yourself beautiful for him."

"I've come to end it," Iris repeated. "Which'll be hard enough without you two nosing about. What'd she send you after me for?"

"To find out if you were a ghost."

Unexpectedly, Iris grinned. "He thought that were funny. Even when Mrs. Lambert saw me and she thought the same thing. Look, if I show you, will you go away and not tell Mrs. Lambert who I am?"

"We might leave it to Caleb to tell her that," Constance said.

Iris hesitated only a moment more before turning and walking deeper into the cellar. Solomon held his candle higher to light the way. His skin prickled at the thought of Lambert's thugs bursting out from behind all those closed doors.

Iris walked up the steps toward the main part of the house. A door stood closed at the top, and another to the right. She opened the one on the right—more smooth, well-oiled hinges—and walked in.

They followed her into a medium-sized chamber. The walls could indeed be described as quilted, like the padded cells of Bedlam, only more luxurious. Perhaps it had once been used for a similar purpose, to keep some poor soul safe and secure. Now it contained a framed bed, a luxurious carpet, and a wardrobe.

Just another love nest for another man who always wanted more than he had.

That was the trouble with striving, Solomon knew. One always wanted more. As he wanted more than Constance's friendship. But this was entirely *not* the place to even think of such things.

Having swept the candle around the walls, ceiling, and floor, he brought it back to the bed and walked past the headboard. And that was when they all saw him.

A man's head lay on the red-stained pillow, the covers drawn up to his chin. His eyes were open and staring, but he would never see anything again.

Iris let out a howl of pure fear that curdled the blood.

CALEB LAMBERT HAD been murdered. Blood sang in Constance's ears at the enormity. She and Solomon had got everything wrong somehow and a man had died. Another man had died while they danced after ghosts and spoke self-righteously about bringing him to justice.

Well, it was God's justice he faced now.

The three people staring at him in terrible fascination, however, would be facing justice of a different sort if Lambert's thugs found them here, bending over the body. Constance swung fiercely on Iris, and the weird noise she was making cut off like a tap.

"Don't touch anything," Solomon said—quite unnecessarily. "Back out the way we came."

Constance forced her mind to work again. "I have to tell Angela."

"We have to tell the police," Solomon retorted.

"Yes, but Angela will send someone. They won't go if *we* tell them."

"The police," Iris squeaked with horror. "I'm not having anything to do with them! What would Frank say?"

"No one cares," Solomon said brutally. "Go home, by all means, but the police may well want to speak to you."

"Look on the bright side," Constance said as flippancy reasserted itself. "You're one of the three people in the world who couldn't possibly have done it." Who could have?

Giving up entirely on stealth, Iris flew across the cellar, out of the door, and down the garden path. By the time Constance and Solomon arrived at the kitchen, the garden door was already blowing open in the wind and there was no sign of Iris at all.

Goldie let them in, smirking. "Going to introduce us to your young man, Miss Silver?"

"It's not a social call," Constance said. "Where is Mrs. Lambert?"

Everyone was seated around the table, gawping at them.

"In the dining room, of course," Goldie said. "She's had her first course, but she's waiting for his nibs before she wants the second. Gawd knows where he is."

"And it's none of your business," Duggin growled.

Duggin, the only person apart from Lambert himself to have a key to the wine cellar and that padded room…

With difficulty, Constance prevented herself from grabbing Solomon's hand as she hurried across the kitchen to the stairs. She was shaking, and every hair on the back of her neck stood up. But no one stopped them going.

"None of them look worried," Solomon muttered when the baize door swung shut behind them. "They don't know he's dead."

"Which leaves Angela, who doesn't have a key."

"Could she have followed him in? Like we did to Iris? Could anyone else?"

Constance didn't answer. She knocked and walked into the dining room, where Angela sat alone at the table, somehow bereft in her splendid evening gown and pearls. There was not a mark on her, though her face was rigid, her lips compressed—whether with annoyance at her husband or with Constance and Solomon was not clear.

"Mrs. Lambert, we have terrible news," Constance said in a rush. "Mr. Lambert is dead."

"Nonsense. He's fetching a bottle of wine that Duggin couldn't find. And for want of it, the whole dinner is spoiling."

"Oh, he's in the cellar," Solomon said. "In a room at the top of the stairs there, and he is quite, quite dead."

Angela stared at him, the blood draining out of her face. Abruptly, she rose and reached behind her to pull the bell. She tugged it sharply three times.

"You saw him?" she flung at Solomon. "How did you get in?"

"Behind your ghost, who has a key to the outside cellar door."

Angela blinked rapidly, perhaps to adjust from the huge fact of her husband's death to the trivia of the ghost. "She's here?"

The door opened and Duggin strode in, panting as though he had run all the way, and glaring at Solomon. "Wanting rid of anyone, ma'am?"

"No. Let me into the cellar."

He blinked. "Ma'am, I really don't advise—"

"*Now*," she snapped.

Duggin inhaled sharply, turned on his heel, and stalked out. Angela followed, Constance and Solomon at her heels.

Pat and Robin stood either side of the baize door.

"Shift," Duggin barked, and they did. Constance would not have been surprised if he'd simply marched back down to the kitchen, but he didn't. He took the keys from his pocket, inserted one into the cellar door, and went in.

The padded room was open and visible from the stair light.

"Don't come in!" Duggin shouted at Angela, but he was too late. She was in, and she saw. She fell to her knees with an inhuman cry, not entirely unlike Iris's.

Duggin shut the door in their faces.

Constance's heart ached. Not for Lambert, though he was beyond saving now, but for Angela, whose world, whose entire reason for living, was crumbling to nothing. She turned back to the baize door and walked out into the hall, Solomon silent beside her.

Pat and Robin were scowling at her. "What the hell's going on?" Robin demanded.

Constance drew in her breath. "I'm afraid Mr. Lambert is dead."

"Dead?" There was disbelief, almost incomprehension. If they were acting, it was very good. But then, they didn't have the key to cellar either. Only Duggin had, and they had left him alone with Angela.

Constance clutched hard at Solomon's arm. He glanced at her, but before they could speak, the baize door swung open again and Angela herself came through, white and stunned.

"Pat, go and fetch a policeman," she said.

"A *policeman*?" Pat repeated, as if she had asked him to fetch in the plague.

She nodded. "Go now."

Pat closed his mouth and ran off to obey.

For a moment, Angela stood very still. Her face was rigid with some superhuman self-control. Constance focused on her hands, which grasped the folds of her elegant gown. They were trembling with shock. Much like her own.

"Go back to the kitchen with Duggin," Angela said to Pat. "We'll search the house, but not until the police have gone."

Pat and Duggin vanished through the baize door in silence, and at last Angela regarded Constance, though her gaze flickered once to Solomon and back.

"Come with me," she said abruptly.

# CHAPTER FIFTEEN

ANGELA LED THEM to her parlor, which was in semidarkness. She did not appear to notice, merely sat down. Solomon turned up the lamp and lit a few candles. Light flared across the severe bones of Angela's face, and it struck Constance irrelevantly how beautiful she was, especially with this new vulnerability softening her usual appearance.

"How could this have happened?" Angela said hoarsely, although it was obvious she was not yet ready to listen to answers.

By way of silent comfort, which was all she could offer, Constance sat down close to her. Angela was not a woman who would appreciate being touched. Solomon took the stopper from a decanter and sniffed it, before pouring amber liquid into a glass and bringing it to Angela.

She took it mechanically, gazing into the glass. "Brandy. I kept it here for Caleb, for when he joined me here to talk." Her lips twisted. "I prefer gin, myself—it's low and common like me, eh, Mrs. Silver? Do I tell the policeman who you really are?"

"Yes, but not in front of your staff if you don't want them to know."

"A lot of things will come out now…things I would rather keep private."

The humiliation of her beloved husband's faithlessness, for one thing. There could be no misunderstanding that padded bedchamber.

Or did she mean Lambert's connection to Gregg? Or evidence

of other crimes that might be found at the house? Constance doubted the latter—apart from the blood on the cellar floor where Gregg had died.

Another shiver of acute discomfort shook her. Why would Lambert leave such evidence of that worst of all crimes, amongst all his efforts to keep the house and his future respectable? Or at least legal.

"Just tell the police the truth, Mrs. Lambert," Solomon advised.

Angela swallowed some brandy. "I hired you for a quite different investigation. You found my answer, but just too late…"

Constance exchanged a quick, puzzled glance with Solomon.

"You don't have to stay," Angela said listlessly.

"We will," Solomon said. "At least until the police have gone."

Angela seemed both surprised and relieved by the speed with which she appeared to be about to get rid of the uniformed police constable whom Pat brought to the parlor. This individual stood to attention, his tall hat clutched under his arm. He had already been shown the body, and merely took a note of everyone's name before warning severely that no one was to leave the house for the time being, and that his colleague would be guarding the dwelling.

"Is that it?" Angela said, incredulous and yet relieved. "You're going now?"

"Not until the detectives get here, ma'am," the constable said woodenly.

Angela's gaze flew in alarm to Constance and Solomon. "Detectives?"

"They're trained to find the evidence that will lead them to the culprit," Constance said.

Angela swore beneath her breath, muttering, "I could tell them that."

It was another long hour before the detective turned up in the shape of Inspector Harris and his sergeant, Flynn, whom

Constance remembered well from the murder at Greenforth Manor in the summer.

Flynn cast them a surprised grin and took out his notebook, while Harris merely scowled at them before sitting down opposite the widow.

"My sincere condolences, Mrs. Lambert," he said. "I'm sorry to annoy you at such a time, but I'm afraid there are some upsetting questions I must ask you."

"Ask," Angela said indifferently.

"Thank you. When did you last see your husband alive?"

"We'd just gone into the dining room, so I suppose it was about seven o'clock."

"But he did not dine?"

Angela shook her head. "The servants had already served the first course, and we were about to sit down when Duggin said there was some difficulty with the wine my husband had chosen."

A faint spasm crossed Harris's face, perhaps at the idea of someone like Lambert possessing enough knowledge to choose wine. Or even, knowing the man's criminal background, sheer annoyance that he could afford it.

"What difficulty?" he asked mildly.

Angela shrugged. "Duggin couldn't find it, though Caleb swore it was there. He went to fetch it."

"Did Duggin go with him?"

"No, he waited in the dining room to open the wine. Neither of us expected my husband to be more than a moment or two."

"But he was."

Angela nodded. "I presumed he'd been distracted by some matter of business, which happened quite often. So after about five minutes, I dismissed Duggin to warn the kitchen to hold back the next courses, and ate my soup."

"So when did you suspect something was wrong?"

"When my maid came and told me." Angela flicked one hand toward Constance.

Sergeant Flynn cast her a startled glance.

Harris sighed. "And what exactly did she tell you?"

"That Caleb was dead," Angela whispered, covering her eyes with her hand. "In the wine cellar."

"What did you do then?"

"I sent for Duggin—apart from my husband, only he has the keys to the cellar—and told him to let me in."

Harris leaned forward in his chair. "Then Mr. Lambert had locked the door behind him again? Even though he only went in to collect a bottle of wine?"

It was a good point, and Constance could see it register on Angela's face.

She blinked rapidly. "I suppose he must have, for Duggin had to unlock the door."

"It's a large cellar," Harris observed. "With several rooms. How did you know he was in that particular room at the top of the cellar stairs?"

"The door to it was open," Angela said, rubbing her forehead hard, as though to dislodge the memory of what she had seen.

"Did you know about that room?" Harris asked.

"No. I never went into the cellar. That was Caleb's business, as the kitchen was mine."

"I see." Harris turned his gaze on Constance. "I hesitate to ask, but how did you know that Mr. Lambert was dead?"

"We found him," Constance said. "You know Mrs. Lambert employed us to find out about the ghostly figure seen in the mist by herself and several of the servants. We had worked out that she came on regular days, so we lay in wait for her this evening, to confirm her identity and discover what she was doing here. We followed her into the cellar from the garden."

"When, precisely?"

"About seven. Just after Bert the footman checked that the door to the mews at the bottom of the garden was locked."

Harris frowned. "The same time Mr. Lambert went into the cellar. Did you see him? Hear him?"

"No," Constance said. But Harris was right. They should have heard Lambert. Especially if he come for a bottle of wine—he would have come all the way down the cellar steps to where the racks of wine bottles stood, and where they had confronted Iris Fraser. They must have missed the murder by mere *seconds*.

"And how did she get into the cellar?" Harris demanded.

"With a key. She had it with her."

Angela threw back her head and opened her suddenly burning eyes wide, glaring at Harris. "She had a key! She murdered my husband."

Harris blinked. "I don't see how or when. Who is this woman?"

"Iris Fraser," Solomon said. "Her husband collected the rents at the tenement that collapsed in St. Giles."

"Did he, by God?" Harris said.

"She was my husband's mistress," Angela said, a weird mixture of humiliation and triumph echoing through her voice. "He was done with her and she murdered him!"

Constance stared at the woman. The certainty in Angela's voice was so convincing that, just for a moment, she believed her. Silence pressed around them.

"That isn't actually possible," Solomon said. "We watched her come through the door from the mews, and we followed her straight into the cellar, where she was never out of our sight, even for an instant."

Angela turned away. "It was her," she said stubbornly. "She had a key. She could have come in at any time. And out again. She could even have run out the front door and round to the mews just to fool you."

"How would she even know to do that?" Solomon asked gently.

"Well, you'd questioned her already, hadn't you?" Angela retorted. "She knew who you were. She fooled you into giving her an alibi."

Harris said firmly, "You have to leave such deductions to us, ma'am. We'll get to the truth of the matter, from the evidence.

You won't mind my speaking to your servants?"

Angela raised a weary hand. "Do what you must."

Harris rose to his feet. "Thank you, ma'am. I won't detain you any longer this evening."

Angela, already lost in her own thoughts, seemed barely to hear him. He turned away, then abruptly spun back to face her.

"How long have you known about your husband's affair with this Iris Fraser?"

"For sure? Only since he told me last night."

"And what makes you think your husband ended the affair? Did he tell you that too?"

"Yes, he did." Sudden color swept through her white face, but she looked Harris in the eye. "We were intimate last night. For the first time in many weeks. Believe me, I *know* it was over." She jerked her head very slightly toward Constance. "*She* knows it, too."

To her annoyance, heat seeped into Constance's face. The men in the room were all looking at her.

She lifted her chin. "I slept in the dressing room off Mrs. Lambert's bedroom. I heard Mr. Lambert's voice, so I know he was there last night. I have no idea what they talked about."

They had most certainly made love, but she had no intention of confirming that, and she was fairly sure Inspector Harris would not ask her.

She was right.

Harris nodded curtly, said goodnight, and departed, Flynn at his heels.

"You can go," Angela flung at her. "I don't need you any-more."

The suspicion that Constance was being manipulated surged forward and would have stuck, except there was something very like disappointment, even hurt, in Angela's eyes. She had expected Constance to back up her accusation against Iris. Instead, Constance had let Solomon disprove it.

Solomon was already on his feet. Constance rose more slowly.

"Will you manage?" she asked Angela. "I can stay."

Solomon's arm twitched, but he said nothing. Was that a faint softening in Angela's face?

"I know. But I need to be alone."

Constance swallowed and nodded once before she walked toward the door.

"Come back tomorrow," Angela said from her chair. "If you want to."

"Goodnight," Solomon said. Constance was not capable of speech.

They walked into the empty hall and across toward the front door, which she had never used before.

"Do you want to get your things?" Solomon murmured.

"Tomorrow will do." Suddenly, she just wanted out of there. The whole building and everyone in it oppressed her. Though Solomon stopped to speak to the constable at the door, she kept on walking and let herself out.

The cold air was a relief. She lifted her face into it, and a moment later, Solomon swung his overcoat around her shoulders.

"Thank you," she whispered, taking his arm. "Let's find a hackney."

"This is wrong," Solomon said abruptly. "All wrong."

"It's certainly not what we expected when we set out so smugly to catch our ghost. Do you think Iris could have done it, Solomon? In the way Angela suggested?"

"It's possible, I suppose, but I don't believe it."

"Why not?" she asked, because she really wanted to know.

He shrugged. "It's just about possible for her to have entered the house before we started watching, and then run out again in time to come back in while we were watching. I just don't see why she *would* go back in."

"So that we would give her an alibi. Which we did."

"And Angela didn't like it," Solomon pointed out.

"She wants it to be Iris. That's jealousy and grief talking. A desire for revenge. When she thinks about it, I'm sure she'd rather know who really killed him."

"And it might even be Iris."

"In a fit of pique because her stream of presents had ended?" Constance said doubtfully.

"It must have been powerful pique." He glanced down at her. "I just asked the constable how Lambert died. An axe through his head."

"Jesus," she whispered. "Just like Gregg. *Could* she have killed them both?"

"I don't think she could have killed either of them, physically speaking. She's agile, but she's not strong—never had to do the kind of work that gives you the muscle to swing an axe with such force."

Constance caught her breath. "No, but *Frank* Fraser could. He knows about the affair. The key's been in Iris's possession for weeks. He could have taken it at any time and had it copied. He can't have liked the arrangement."

"Or its ending?" Solomon said thoughtfully. "Well, if he did it, I expect he's already scarpered."

"But we have the same problem. We didn't see him go in or out."

"The police might yet find him hiding in one of the cellar rooms."

She shivered. "I hope they do, and then this whole case will be over. But I'm not convinced, are you? But it seems to me the only other person who could have done it is Duggin, and he's devoted to Lambert. *Was* devoted to Lambert."

Solomon considered. "He was the one who sent Lambert to the wine cellar in search of the missing bottle. He waited a few minutes with Angela and then she dismissed him with a message for the kitchen. He could have gone into the cellar then, whacked his master, and emerged again, locking the door behind him and meaning, presumably, to get rid of the body at some later date."

"It works, except… Wouldn't we have heard him? If by some miracle we just missed Lambert coming into the cellar from the house, surely we weren't late enough to have missed Duggin murdering him? Everything was quiet, and we can't have been *that* distracted by Iris's sordid little tale."

"It makes no sense," Solomon agreed. "Though I suppose Duggin might have killed Gregg for Lambert's sake, only without telling him? It would explain why the body wasn't moved immediately."

"But not why Duggin would have killed Gregg without Lambert's specific instructions. Maybe Gregg assaulted his daughter?"

"Guesswork, with absolutely no evidence," Solomon said dismissively. "Could one of the other servants have stolen Duggin's cellar key temporarily and copied it?"

"I suppose so, though I don't see why. Or how, to be honest. They're pretty much in awe of him. And Lambert."

"And Mrs. Lambert?"

Constance thought about it. "I thought at first they didn't respect her. The day I arrived, Bert took me to her parlor without even knocking. But they're just not proper servants. They don't know how to behave. I think they do respect her, though they're not scared of her the way they are of Lambert and Duggin. In fact, they like her. Mrs. Feathers, the cook, will do anything for her."

"Even kill her husband?"

"Oh yes," Constance said. "But she'd poison his food, not hit him with an axe. She wouldn't have the…" She trailed off, then drew in a breath. "Wouldn't have the strength? She took Gregg's body on a donkey through the streets at some speed and dumped it in Devil's Acre. Maybe she *does* have the strength."

"Or maybe someone helped her get Gregg onto the donkey and she really doesn't have the strength. Hopefully the police will be able to get the truth out of the servants."

"They're not the sort of people who'll ever talk to the police."

Solomon grimaced. "And if they do, it will only be exactly

what Angela told them to say. Would they tell you the truth?"

"I doubt it. I'm still the outsider. But I'll try. If they think Angela trusts me, they might talk to me." She glanced up at Solomon, who was waving down a hackney. "Do you think she does trust me?"

The hackney stopped behind them.

"Grosvenor Square, please," Solomon told the jarvey, before opening the door and handing her inside. He climbed up and sat beside her. "The question is, really, do *you* trust *her?*"

# CHAPTER SIXTEEN

I T WAS A spectacularly good question. Did Constance trust Angela Lambert?

The hackney jolted its way onward among the sea of costermongers and criers still lurking around Westminster.

"I don't know," she said. "Something has changed and I can't put my finger on what it is."

"Something in you?" Solomon asked. "Or in her?"

"In my perception of her. I feel for her. I always did. I thought she was like me, but she isn't. I feel for her losing her husband—she genuinely loved him, I'm sure of that—but I don't trust her not to use me or anyone else to get her revenge. Does that make sense?"

"Then you don't think she did it?" Solomon asked.

"She doesn't have a key."

"More than anyone else, she had opportunity to take it and copy it. You say Bert is always with her, but he isn't. She came to see us without him, remember?"

Constance, who had, in fact, forgotten that, nodded slowly. "And if she didn't have her own key, Duggin opened the cellar door for her quickly enough when she told him to." She didn't want it to be Angela, but she forced herself to consider the possibility.

"She couldn't have done it herself," she continued. "She was in the dining room at least until Duggin left her. And we found her there surely a bare ten minutes later. She was wearing the same clothes and there was not a mark on her, not a drop of blood."

"Nor on anyone else, so far as I could see," Solomon said. "Would that even be possible? We need to ask the police surgeon."

"I'm sure Harris has already done so. No, I don't think Angela can have done it herself, but she could have ordered someone else to do it. Perhaps she didn't really think they'd go through with it. She did seem genuinely shocked."

"Whom would she have ordered?"

"Bert?" She shook her head. "I don't know. Their first loyalty always seemed to be to Lambert, not Angela. We need to get times from the kitchen staff."

"And not neglect other possibilities," Solomon said. "Such as Frank Fraser. Who will pretty much do anything for money."

Constance sat up straight. "Including lend his wife's key, or another copy of it, to whoever wished Lambert and Gregg ill! Which must be just about everyone in that tenement, even the ones who didn't start off in the collapsed building next door..."

"I don't know about *everyone*," Solomon argued. "You'd need to be pretty brave to set foot in Lambert's territory, extremely determined. And patient enough to find out everything about the servants' movements and the Lamberts' habits. To say nothing of knowing when Gregg would visit them."

He didn't look happy about it, and she soon worked out why. "You are thinking of Lenny Knox."

"I am," Solomon said, "and I don't want to be. I like him. And I don't believe he's a violent man."

"Everyone has a breaking point. What happened to his wife and child could easily be his."

"I know," Solomon said. "And he was more than happy to help me try to prove Lambert's responsibility for the disaster."

Constance thought about this for a while. "He's all in favor of responsibility, isn't he? For factory owners and landlords and the government. I'm not sure he would murder in secret and run.

Wouldn't he take responsibility for his crimes and make the point of why he'd committed them very loudly indeed?"

"In his right mind, I think he would." He shook his head, as if trying to clear it of annoying suspicions. Constance knew how he felt. "We have quite an array of suspects now."

"And no one to pay us for finding out the truth. It's quite…liberating, isn't it?"

A smile flickered across his face. "It is."

They were in Grosvenor Square already. The time always passed too quickly with Solomon.

He was gazing out of the window. "I can stop for a while, if you like, while we talk about it."

Her eyes widened. "You would come into my establishment in the hours of darkness? Knowing what bacchanals go on there?"

He smiled lazily. "I am wise to your ways, Constance Silver. I am sure there are routes in that avoid your guests."

There were, and she intended to use them, even if she made an appearance in the salon later on. He had never asked her where she wanted the hackney to take her. She was just glad he understood that she needed this night in her own place, sur-rounded by the familiar.

For the first time, she wondered if he had a different motive. He had offered to come in. With no other man would she have assumed it was from kindness, from knowledge that Lambert's murder all but under their noses had thrown her utterly.

"I am far too honorable to thus ruin your reputation," she said lightly. "I will see you at the office tomorrow."

She rapped on the ceiling, and the carriage drew to a halt. Not at her front door, but just around the corner. Once, it had been amusing to see if Solomon would ever enter her house of ill repute that she knew he disdained. He had, in broad delight, when he first proposed their investigation partnership. But something had changed, and she was too tired, too confused, to work out what it was.

Solomon in her sitting room, where no man had ever set

foot. Exciting thought, tempting and sweet and utterly wrong.

*"We'll talk later, when the case is over,"* he had said last night. Technically, it was over now. They had uncovered the ghost. In normal circumstances, she would be delighted by his company, by the opportunity to relax and talk about something, anything. But not this.

He sat very still in the stationary carriage, watching her, the glow from the street lamp casting a shadow over one side of his face. Even weary, she felt the familiar thrill of butterflies in her stomach, the jolt of attraction that had always been there.

Normally, he treated her with courtesy, as though she were a lady. He alighted from the carriage to hand her down. Tonight, he was not moving. So she did, almost in panic, reaching for the door.

And he was before her, forcing her to fall back while he opened the door and kicked down the steps. From the street he held out his hand, as he always did, yet it seemed such a huge matter to place her hers upon it as she stepped down.

His fingers curled around hers. "Constance. Will you not let me talk to you? To ask you—"

"Not tonight, Solomon," she interrupted, keeping her voice light and careless. "Like Angela, it seems I need to be alone. Goodnight."

He released her at once. Perversely, she was disappointed. Relief rolled off her, leaving only loneliness, as old and familiar as breathing. She walked away from him, around the corner. She might have imagined the soft "Goodnight" that followed her.

She wanted to cry.

"THE STRAND, PLEASE," Solomon said bleakly to the jarvey, and climbed back into the hackney.

Slumped back against the bench, he missed the warmth of

Constance's nearness and cursed himself for a fool.

The end of a case had always been difficult for them. At Greenforth, he had bolted from his own growing feelings. At the Maules' house, he had held her in the glow of comfort and so much more, and she was the one who fled. He'd salvaged that with his proposal of partnership, which she had jumped at. This time…

He just had to be patient, to meet at the office when she was ready. For they both knew the case was not truly over.

It hurt that Constance did not need him as he needed her. He would have battered his own hopes into nothing and withdrawn from the lists for good had it not been for the way she'd kissed him. And the warmth of her eyes, her easy friendship and the occasional, betraying catch of her breath. And her mother's pronouncement: *"She* would *leave it for you. To be* with *you."*

Not tonight she wouldn't. Something was wrong, and she would not talk to him. That hurt too, for they had both told each other things that no one else knew. About her secret longing for true family, for the identity a father might bring her. About David, whose loss was always with him, a black hole of grief and guilt.

Whatever troubled her did not need to be about him. It could be the Lamberts. It could be her mother, her own business, her own friends. Whatever, he just had to step back and be there if and when she needed him. He was used to his own corroding loneliness.

A light shone in the window above his front door. When he let himself in, his butler Jenks came to greet him—his expression, as always, one of welcome indifference—and took Solomon's hat and coat.

"Have you dined, sir? Would you care for a bite of supper?"

"I would," Solomon replied, surprising himself with the truth.

Mounting the stairs to his sitting room, he lit the lamps and candles, poured himself a small brandy, and sat down by the fire.

When had it become not enough to enjoy a solitary drink, a

solitary meal, the warmth of his own fireside?

When Constance Silver had exploded into his life. Disruptive, intriguing, funny, unafraid, rabidly curious, and entirely unashamed. And why should she be? It was he who felt ashamed of once disdaining her as less than him. He had been fighting against such disdain all his life, even as he climbed into the ranks of the wealthy and internationally respected. Sought after, he kept his social distance. And yet he would be proud to walk into a dinner party or a ball or Lady Swan's charity evening with Constance Silver on his arm.

He wanted to dance with her. Court her. Win her.

He gazed into the flames, giving his imagination free rein, while around him, Jenks set the table with one place and brought in a light supper and a bottle of wine, from which he would drink only one glass.

He rose and sat at the table. Jenks bowed and withdrew. And Solomon imagined Constance sitting opposite him, laughing, teasing, talking. Could she want those things too? With him? He ached with not having them, with not knowing. And yet not knowing was better than being rejected.

Tonight, he would think of her. Tomorrow, he would return to Lambert's murder.

"THEY'VE MISSED YOU," Janey said as Constance drank her first coffee of the morning.

"Who?" Constance asked distractedly.

"The girls. The guests. It all livened up last night when you made your appearance downstairs. It was a good night."

Constance forced herself to smile. Although she had been tired to the bone, she had forced herself to change and pamper her hair and skin, then go down to the salon, just to prove she still could, just to make sure standards had not slipped in her absence.

She knew from the reactions of the men, and the smiles of the girls, that she sparkled. But only on the outside. It was a professional sparkle she had learned long ago how to achieve because it was better for business. She had even sung for them, but that made her want to weep, because Solomon had not heard her as he had at the Maules' house.

What was the matter with her? She had to find some equilibrium, some way to deal with the new turbulence she felt around him. Perhaps Lady Griz or someone else would introduce him to a kind, beautiful woman who would be his forever. It would break Constance's heart, but it was better than the proposition he was surely about to make to her.

*Why?*

At the beginning, had she not wanted that proposition? As something so much better than the blatant transactions of her establishment? A secret yearning that had only grown with their friendship until it was unbearable. And she didn't even know why.

"What d'you think?" Janey said.

Constance blinked, aware she had missed something. "About what?"

"About me working at Silver and Grey rather than being a maid—don't think I'm cut out for that, but I like being at the office, and finding out about people. Mr. Grey said I was good at it."

"But you were so eager to be a lady's maid," Constance reminded her.

Janey grimaced. "I was eager to be respectable, and I wanted to be the best, but I can't even stop swearing. How would that go down with some hoity-toity mistress? To say nothing of a stuck-up butler and all the other servants?"

"Not well," Constance agreed. "Which is why I'm trying to cure you of the habit. But, you know, you can't swear at our clients either."

"Don't have to, do I? Got set things to say to them, then smile and show them out."

Constance regarded her doubtfully. She had spent so little time in the office with Janey that she could not judge. "I'll speak to Mr. Grey and we'll think about it. You've certainly been invaluable this week."

Janey grinned. "I have, haven't I? You wanting a bath? And what you going to wear?"

What with bathing and dealing with a few housekeeping matters before she left the house, it was after eleven o'clock before Constance let herself into the Silver and Grey offices.

She knew at once that Solomon was there. She could smell him, *feel* him. Though her heart beat too loudly, she kept to the ritual they had formed in the first, un-busy days of opening.

She stuck her head into his office, uttering a cheerful "Good morning."

He rose from behind his desk. "Good morning. Angela has paid."

Contance raised her eyebrows and walked across to him. "In full?"

"Including your wages for four days' work as her maid."

"She's paying us off," Constance said slowly. "Does that mean she doesn't want to see me today after all?"

"I think we should go."

"So do I. The house is likely to be swarming with police, after all. Cup of tea before we go?"

"Why not?"

She smiled to see that the stove was lit in the kitchen. Perhaps nothing had changed after all. She would keep their conversation impersonal.

"How is Janey managing in the office?" she asked as she brought in the tray and set it on the low table between the armchair.

"Well. She takes in the post, notes appointments, and, so far as I know, hasn't put any clients off. Someone knocked in passing yesterday, so we now have three appointments next week, and some jewels to find. She and Lenny Knox did a good job between them of following Angela Lambert."

"Knox," Constance repeated, pouring a splash of milk into the cups. "Is he still in St. Giles?"

"Actually, we can probably find him at your mother's new shop in Covent Garden."

Constance blinked and set down the jug.

"He's building her some shelves," Solomon said gravely.

"You're not paying for this, are you? I don't see how she can afford the rent, never mind refitting the entire premises."

"With the sale of her old place to me. I have plans for it, particularly if I can persuade a few people to invest in running water, underground sewers, and the development of the building into decent flats."

"Solomon, no one can afford decent flats round there. And those who can wouldn't be seen dead in St. Giles."

"The point is, they *will* be able to afford them."

"They'll sublet every space and you'll be back to an over-crowded slum in no time."

"Not necessarily. The rents will be reasonable, and subletting will not be allowed."

"If they're that reasonable, you'll lose money."

"I know. I plan to raise funds at Lady Swan's charity ball. I've spoken to Sir Nicholas about it already. It's an experiment, though a drop in the ocean of what is needed. But I digress. I propose we seek out Angela and the servants first, and then your mother and Knox."

Since Constance had much the same thoughts, she saw no reason to argue.

She had no idea how she would be greeted at the Lambert house, so she made no effort to throw off Solomon's company. Angela's payment clearly ended their old association, and the entire household was likely to be suspicious of the newcomer who had decamped in her mistress's time of trouble.

However, it was Bert who opened the front door to them,

and he actually looked relieved to see Constance. He threw the door open wide. "Just the person she needs. The police are here again, and she won't come out the parlor."

At least she'd got out of her bed.

"Just go in," Bert said carelessly, though he looked Solomon up and down as he laid his hat on the table. "I'll tell Mr. Duggin." This may or may not have been a warning shot across Solomon's bow.

Solomon said nothing. Constance walked down the hall to the back parlor and knocked.

"Come in," Angela commanded with impatience.

Exchanging a quick glance, they entered and found the widow at her desk. She stood abruptly at the sight of them. "Mrs. Silver. I hoped you'd come. Those bloody peelers are here again, poking around, asking questions."

"It's their job," Constance replied.

"Well, they're upsetting my people, and *they* have jobs to do. I'd help if I could—for once—but I don't know what they want or why."

"Is Inspector Harris here?" Constance asked.

"The governor? Oh yes, he's there, going through Caleb's office, cheeky bas—"

"If you like," Solomon interrupted mildly, "I'll go and talk to him."

"Good idea," Constance agreed, for they needed to talk to Harris. And Angela seemed to want to speak to her.

"Directly across the hall," Angela said.

Solomon bowed slightly and left the room.

"How are you?" Constance asked quietly when the door had closed behind him.

"I'm holding together by a thread. I feel if I sit down without doing something, I'll shatter. I don't want to think."

"Do you have family who can come and be with you?"

Angela looked at Constance as though she'd grown horns. "They're no use to me. You are."

"We received your payment," Constance said. "In the circumstances, you didn't have to be quite so prompt, but thank you."

"I wanted an end to it—your investigation for me, and your maid pretense. I'd like to offer you a different position."

Constance blinked. "You would?" Was she asking Silver and Grey to investigate her husband's death? Should they accept payment for something they fully intended to do anyway? Although not necessarily to Angela's benefit.

Angela's eyes were shrewd, a businesswoman's eyes, not those of a just-bereaved widow. "You've been useful to me. Even in the few days you've been here. I've come to rely on you. You're a clever woman, Mrs. Silver, and there ain't so many of us about."

"*Are not* so many of us about," Constance corrected her.

Angela's lips twitched in response. "You see? But that's a side benefit. If that was all you did, you'd be bored in a week. Less. I want you to learn my business, help me expand it, be my lieutenant, if you like. As I was Caleb's."

It was odd, but even while everything in her revolted against subservience to anyone, let alone to the woman who inherited Lambert's gruesome businesses, Constance felt a spark of pride to be asked.

"You've taken me by surprise," she said honestly. "I don't know what to say."

"Think about it. After all, we can't even move here with the peelers strutting about." Angela rose abruptly and picked an invitation card off the desk. "Caleb was very proud of this," she said, showing the card to Constance. "Lady Swan invited both of us to her charity ball. Her husband's the sort of business associate he always wanted, and I was to go with him."

Perhaps that explained the odd urgency of Angela's desire to speak better. And the new gown, of course, which would now have to be sacrificed for mourning black. "I'm sorry."

Angela shook her head. "Don't be. I'm going to go anyway,

in Caleb's honor, make the large donation he meant to, and it will be twice as touching now I'm so newly widowed."

Constane blinked. "It will also be twice as shocking. In their world, you would barely leave the house for a year."

"They won't accept me anyway, though they'll grab my money quick enough. I might as well make an impression. And that impression will be better if you come with me to keep me right on manners. It could be your first duty in your new position."

Constance almost laughed. The idea of her, the notorious courtesan, guiding the steps of the plebian, if not downright underworld, widow through the Society of well-born, rich, and respectable people…

But Angela had no idea how Constance's presence would embarrass at least some of the gentlemen and outrage all of their wives. She swallowed back her mirth and considered Angela's whole proposal.

The temptation to string her along was strong—to learn about Lambert's business while she pretended to think about the offer. But Constance did not have the luxury of time to win the amount of trust that would surely be necessary. Nor did it seem terribly fair play. The woman was at a low ebb, and Constance owed her honesty.

"I don't need to think about your offer, Mrs. Lambert. I'm grateful and flattered, but I have my own business."

Angela cast a quick, derisive glance at the door. "You mean *he* does."

"We are partners."

"More than that, from what I hear."

Constance hoped the sudden heat did not show in her face. "A certain amount of subterfuge is necessary in our business."

Angela waved that aside. "I don't care about your personal life. I'm talking about my business."

"And I about mine. I can't do both, Mrs. Lambert, though I thank you for the offer."

"I'm disappointed," Angela said after a moment. She leaned back in her chair. "And yet you came back."

"I said I would."

"And there's your things in my dressing room. I had Goldie pack them up."

She'd had Goldie go through them. Thank God Constance had kept nothing she'd written down. "Thank you. Mrs. Lambert… You don't really think Iris Fraser murdered your husband, do you?"

Angela's face changed. She was no longer the hard-eyed businesswoman but a wrathful goddess. "I know she did. And she'll pay."

"You must leave it to the law," Constance said urgently.

Angela looked away. "I know that. But even they can't miss. They got an intruder with a motive."

"And an alibi."

"Not necessarily," Angela replied. "But everyone else in the house has got one. You sneaking off into the garden early nearly lost yours, but at least you were with *him*. And you know the inspector, don't you?"

"Harris? Yes, slightly."

"How'd that come about, then?"

"Accident. He was investigating another crime."

"Did he solve it?"

Constance met her gaze. "Yes. Don't underestimate him."

In fact, he had only *nearly* solved it. It had been Constance and Solomon who found the missing piece of the puzzle via a very risky maneuver. But she needed to warn Angela, who had probably seen her husband run rings around lesser policemen for years.

"I won't," Angela said. "Nor you, neither."

SOLOMON FOUND INSPECTOR Harris in the pantry, interviewing Duggin the butler, who had *thug* written all over him, and was not remotely intimidated. Of the two of them, it was Harris who looked more harassed. As Solomon stuck his head around the door, the inspector waved a frustrated hand.

"You can go, for now. I want a word with this gentleman, too."

"Don't we all," Duggin murmured on his insolent way past Solomon. He left the door open.

Solomon closed it.

"Was that a threat?" Harris asked.

"I rather think it was." And Duggin didn't care who heard it. "He's not afraid in the slightest."

"Which probably means he didn't do it. I can't dispute his story, and the other so-called servants tell the same one. Ghostly sightings and all."

"Iris was undoubtedly our ghost. She's been coming here for weeks, if not months."

"Duggin claims to know his master had thrown her over. Same story as Mrs. Lambert."

"Do you believe them?" Solomon asked.

"Do *you*?" Harris countered.

"I believe he might have meant to. He seems to have relied on his wife, so if it came down to a choice, Angela would win, hands down. But I would doubt Iris cared enough to take an axe to him. She claims *she* had come to end it, and there was certainly no blood on her."

"A jury would likely still convict her," Harris said. "Adulteress. Scorned, deprived of funds, intruding where she had no decent business to be. Conceivably, she could have croaked him the moment he entered the cellar and bolted out the front in time for you to see her coming back in from the garden. I just can't see why she'd bother. A jury might care about that. There's probably enough to hang her. Especially when everyone else in the premises, including you and Mrs. Silver, can account for each other during the five minutes or so in which he must have died."

"Duggin can't. He could easily have gone into the wine cellar on his way from the dining room to the kitchen."

"Not according to the other servants, who claim they heard him enter by the baize door and come straight downstairs into the kitchen."

"The baize door doesn't make a noise. I've never encountered such well-oiled hinges as there are in this house. And garden."

"Maybe. But they'd hear his feet on the steps. He lumbers."

"True."

"Are they scared enough to lie for him? Loyal enough?"

"I suppose his daughter is, at least. But someone's lying. If it isn't Iris, it's everyone else." A suspicion, not entirely new, flared in Solomon's mind.

Who would everyone in the house lie for?

# CHAPTER SEVENTEEN

"Learn anything?" Solomon asked as they settled into the hackney he had hailed in Victoria Street.

"Nothing I'm sure is any use." Constance met his gaze. "She offered me a position as her lieutenant."

"Did she indeed?" Solomon said, his eyes widening. "I wonder why?"

For an instant, she looked annoyed, then laughter sprang into her eyes, catching at his breath. "It's as well I have you to depress any delusions I might have of my own worth!"

"I'm not sure it's just your worth she's recognizing," Solomon said. "She's securing your loyalty. Or trying to."

"It crossed my mind," Constance admitted. "But she's like Lambert in one way—one of these people you cannot ignore."

"What did you say?"

She stared at him. "I said I'd start tomorrow. What do you think I said?"

He sighed. "I wondered if you couldn't string her along for a little and learn what we need to know."

"I thought about it. But Lambert's dead. We can't punish him again for the disaster in St. Giles, or for Gregg's murder."

"Then you have lost interest in discovering the truth?"

She shifted position on the hard bench. "Of course not. But even I have some standards. I couldn't lie to her. I told her Silver and Grey was all I had time for. She thinks I work for you."

"How ironic, when it is the other way around," Solomon murmured.

"What?"

"Nothing. Did she mind that you turned her down?"

"I don't think she has given up hope of changing my mind. Did you learn anything?"

"Harris doesn't believe Iris did it, but he's afraid lack of evidence against anyone else will pressure him into arresting her. He has superiors who like results more than truth."

Constance gazed beyond him out of the window. "Someone is lying."

"I rather think they're *all* lying. We need to speak to the Frasers again."

"After Lenny Knox."

CONSTANCE WAS BOTH impressed and alarmed by her mother's new shop. Although not huge, it was in a good location for passing customers and had a decent window for displays. Some elegant curios had already been placed there, along with a sign that read, *Opening Soon*. A curtain hid the rest of the shop from view.

Solomon led her through a narrow close to the back door of the building, which boasted a large brass knocker in the shape of a gargoyle. His brief rap was answered by Juliet herself, beaming and pleased with herself.

"Come in, come in! What do you think, Connie?"

"A long step up from Seven Dials."

They stood in a cozy room behind the shop. It had a stove, a desk and chair, and an easy chair. The window was barred, though it had a pretty curtain. It had two internal doors, one half open to a staircase.

"Lenny's working behind the door to the shop," Juliet said, "so I'll show you upstairs first. Got a proper kitchen up there."

She didn't puff as she used to on her way upstairs. It came to

Constance that her mother was happier than she had been for years. It seemed to make a difference to her health. *Thank you, Solomon.*

It was undoubtedly a pleasant place to live, and Juliet clearly took great pride in it. She parked Solomon in a bright, as-yet-uncluttered sitting room, saying to Constance, "Come and I'll show you the rest. He's seen it already."

The twinge in Constance's stomach was not jealousy. Of course it was not. And yet it was something to do with her mother closing in on *her* friend. When had she become so small-minded? Perhaps it was indeed jealousy. Or the realization that she and her mother were not so different and never had been.

Politely, she admired her mother's new bedroom, the spare bedroom—currently used as a storage room for the things that would go in the shop—and a very decent kitchen, where a kettle was coming to the boil.

"Got running water," Juliet boasted, turning on the tap just to show her.

"It's a good place," Constance said. "But seriously, can you afford it?"

"If the shop does well."

"And in the meantime?"

"Your Mr. Grey has bought my old place. Ain't worth much, but it'll keep me going for a while, buy me new stock—"

"Not stolen, Ma," Constance said firmly.

Juliet looked at her irritably. "We all do what we have to in order to get by. You know that. What makes you so sure I'd never even try for respectability?"

"Because you've never known it," Constance said bluntly. God knew that was not her mother's fault, but though it hadn't been meant unkindly, Juliet was frowning, the light of pride dying in her eyes. Her lips thinned.

"And you have? You run a brothel, Constance. The title of abbess is mockery and it sure as hell isn't respectable. And you needn't imagine you're some high lord's bastard, raising you above the rest of us, because you aren't, and even if you were, it'd change nothing."

Constance gripped the back of the nearest chair. Her knuckles were white. She didn't even know what to be angry about first.

"Then whose child am I?" The words almost burst out of her.

"You're mine," Juliet snapped, glaring back at her. "There's no bolt of thunder, no god-in-the-machine that will win your Mr. Grey for you. He'll always be above our touch."

Sometimes Constance forgot her mother had some smattering of education. She had taught Constance to read and write, after all. She had taught her so many things among all the confusion of drink and loneliness and despair. In spite of everything, Juliet had made her daughter's rise possible. That made Constance ashamed of both of them, and yet it should make her proud.

Emotion clogged her throat. Maybe she *was* proud. Either way, she couldn't bear any more of this.

"Where's the tea?" she asked aggressively.

SOLOMON SENSED SOME kind of atmosphere between the mother and daughter as they brought in tea. They didn't speak to each other, although there was no overt hostility between them.

"One reason we came was to talk to Lenny," Solomon said, setting down his cup.

A cynical smile flickered on Juliet's lips. "What d'you want with him?"

"Was he working here yesterday?" Constance asked.

"He came round in the evening. Why?"

"What time?"

"Gawd, I don't know. Six? Just before?"

"And when did he leave?"

"After eight, by the time we had supper. He needs feeding up, poor devil."

"And you were with him all that time?" Solomon asked.

"Pretty much. Had a lot to talk about. He made me some drawings. Clever bloke, your Lenny. I'm grateful. Now, why do you care where he was?"

"'Pretty much' isn't an answer," Constance said. "Did he go out in that time?"

"He went and got us some supper from the Crown, but he was only gone half an hour or so."

"Could you be more exact?" Solomon pressed.

"Maybe an hour," Juliet said grudgingly. "And the food was hot!"

Solomon exchanged glances with Constance. An hour would have given him just enough time, but he would have had to know the habits of the household.

He'd already proved adept at watching and following...

"Shall we take him a cup of tea?" Constance suggested.

"No point if you can't get in the shop door," Juliet pointed out, though she did pour a third cup with a spoonful of sugar, which she handed to Constance without comment.

Knox himself opened the shop door when Solomon called to him. He gave his shy, distracted smile and motioned them to enter. "Mind the mess, though!"

It was a useful warning, for tools and pieces of wood of many sizes littered the floor. He had begun constructing shelving along all the available back wall.

"It will go around the sides as well, and we'll have a couple of central cabinets, too," he said.

Solomon was inspecting the frame nearest the door. "You do good work."

"I do. I won't overcharge her."

"I never supposed you would," Solomon said, amused. "I would not have recommended you if I had. Actually, we came to pick your brains about Caleb Lambert."

Constance sat down on a clear patch of floor and set Knox's tea down. They all sat like children.

"What about Lambert?" Knox asked coldly. His eyes were like flint.

"Did you know he was dead?" Solomon said.

The hard eyes widened and blinked. Some emotion sparked there, though Solomon couldn't read it. It was almost disappointment, not quite relief.

"Good," he said. "Saves some poor bastard—begging your pardon, ma'am—from hanging for murder."

"Actually, it probably doesn't," Constance said. "Some bastard, poor or otherwise, *did* murder him."

He stared at her, transferred his gaze to Solomon as though for confirmation, then exhaled slowly. "Forgive me if I hope they never catch him."

"Then you think it was someone affected by the collapse of the tenement?" Solomon asked.

"Seems reasonable, considering both he and Gregg have been murdered now."

"Do you know who did it?" Constance asked bluntly.

"No. Though I'm not sure I'd tell you if I did."

"Can you tell us anything about Lambert's household? Who lives there, when they come and go?"

Knox's lips curled back, making his pleasant face ugly. "No. I know where it is, because Miss Janey and me went there and followed his wife from there and back again. On your instructions. Nice, big place," he added bitterly.

"You didn't by any chance happen to go there again for any reason? For instance, did you see who went in and out of the grounds yesterday evening?"

"I'd go mad doing that." There was desolation in Knox's voice, though he kept his gaze on his hands in his lap. "I couldn't allow myself near him. I don't know that would ever have changed."

"Then you weren't there?" Solomon persisted, although he tried to infuse disappointment into his voice. Constance had taken great care with the phrasing of her questions, and Solomon had no desire to upset Knox with suspicion on top of what the poor man was already suffering.

"No." Knox raised his eyes to Solomon's somewhat defiantly. "But I'm glad he's dead. Never thought I'd think that about anyone, but I do."

"HE DIDN'T DO it," Constance said with certainty as they walked through the flower market close to her mother's house. "It's not in his nature."

"The trouble is," Solomon replied, "his nature is not quite stable right now. I could almost believe he did it and lost the memory of it in his own overwhelming grief."

Constance frowned at him. "Is that even possible? Supposing it is, you have absolutely no evidence of it."

Solomon was quiet for a moment. "There is violence in him. Behind his eyes. I feel it when he speaks of Lambert. Don't you? He's hiding something."

"Yet you sent him to my *mother*?"

"He's not a madman. I'm merely considering possibilities. But if the same person murdered both Gregg and Lambert, I would seriously doubt Lenny is our man. When I first saw him, he seemed…comatose."

"But Gregg would already have been dead by then. Maybe his state was due less to grief than to shock at committing murder. Solomon, I don't like that idea at all."

"Well, as you say, there's absolutely no evidence of it. We need to find out what the Frasers did with their keys."

Constance hesitated, glancing over her shoulder as though she could thus make sure of her mother's safety. Distant, half-forgotten childhood memories prickled, times when her mother hadn't come home, when other women had taken Constance in, fed her the odd scrap and not let her see her mother for several days. She had come to understand that her mother had been hurt or sick in those times. The awfulness of that was still unbearable. It was surely the root of everything she had done since…

"Constance. He won't hurt her." Solomon's familiar, soft voice penetrated the sudden bleakness. "I don't truly believe he killed Gregg or Lambert."

"Then why mention it?" she snapped. She knew why. It was how they reached the truth, throwing possibilities around to discard or disprove or investigate further.

"Do you want to go back?" he asked patiently.

She focused on him once more, on the concern in his face, and somehow it soothed her, warmed her. She drew in a breath. "No. No, I'm being silly. Let's beard the Frasers in their den."

The Frasers, however, did not at first answer their door. Constance could hear them arguing as soon as she stepped into the passage from the street, even over the noise of the women fighting in the muddy street outside and the thundering feet of filthy, ragged children playing on the stairs out of the rain. She had had to stop Solomon from interfering in the women's fight— they would only have turned on him—by dragging him inside.

"It's all noise, no claws," she told him, having learned the difference long ago.

He looked doubtful, but appeared to bow to her greater knowledge. The raised voices in the Frasers' room cut off instantly at his first knock. On the other side of the door, nothing moved. At least they weren't climbing out of the window.

On the stairs, a male voice swore at the children, who paid it no heed whatsoever. They thundered back down the stairs, the tiny boy at the front clutching a large key in his grubby little fist.

On impulse, Constance strode to the foot of the stairs and caught him. They others piled into his back, swearing as fluently as the man who'd just told them off, and trying to wrestle the key from the boy at the front, who held on grimly.

Constance solved that argument by plucking it from him herself and holding it too high for any of them to reach. It felt rather like the garden door key to the Lamberts' property.

"Oi!" said the largest child, who might have been all of seven. "That's his! Give it back!"

"It's treasure," said the tiny boy earnestly. "They're trying to get it off me. Pretend, like."

"So give him it back," the biggest commanded.

"Not until you tell me where you got it," Constance said. "In fact, I'll give you all a penny each if you tell me truth."

The children exchanged glances. "Found it," muttered the largest boy.

"I thought you did. Where?"

"Out the back." He jerked his head toward the door at the other end of the passage. One of the planks was missing. From the stink that drifted in, a sewer ran right through the backyard.

"When?"

"This morning."

"Good for you." She doubted many of the miserable rooms here had keys, apart from the Frasers'. Delving into her reticule, she retrieved a handful of pennies and gave one to each child. They snatched the coins with awe. "See if you can find any more out there, and I'll pay you again."

They looked at her, their eyes suddenly old and hard, well beyond their years. She could see they were considering rushing her and just snatching her reticule and all its contents.

"Really?" she said, gazing back.

Solomon materialized beside her, large and solid.

The biggest boy shrugged philosophically. "All right. We'll look. Cost you twopence, though. Each!"

"Done," Constance said. "Wait for us here if you find anything."

They dashed off again toward the back door, children once more. Constance met Solomon's gaze.

"They threw the keys out the window?" he suggested.

"Wouldn't you if the police were coming? At least they decided to brazen it out rather than bolt."

They returned to the Frasers' door, and Solomon knocked again. A faint rustling could be heard, the ghost of a whisper, and then nothing.

"We're not the peelers," Constance said, getting her lips as close to the crack in the door as she dared.

A hectic whispering ensued. Solomon raised his eyebrows and then his hand to knock somewhat more forcefully, but before he could, the door opened a crack and Frank Fraser's nose appeared.

"You again?" he snarled at Solomon. "What d'you want now?"

"Do you want me to tell you out here?" Solomon asked. "The police won't be so accommodating, you know."

The door opened another inch, then a foot. Solomon did the rest by simply pushing the door and, for once, walking in ahead of Constance.

The room was warm enough for Fraser to be in his shirt sleeves. Iris wore a pretty pink dress with a modest crinoline. She seemed to have no concept of being out of place in the neighborhood—or perhaps she enjoyed being the *grande dame* of the tenement.

"Well?" Fraser asked aggressively, while Iris looked Constance's rather drab gray dress up and down and all but preened.

"We need to see your keys to Lambert's property," Solomon said.

"You ain't even got the authority to ask," Fraser sneered.

"True. But the police do, and I suspect they're already on their way. There's a possibility we can save them the trouble, but you need to answer our questions and do as we ask. The keys, if you please."

"Haven't got any keys," Iris said loudly. "We don't know what you're talking about."

Solomon sighed. "We saw you using at least two keys last night. The police already know about them."

"You can't prove it," Fraser said. "Neither can they."

Constance held up the key. "The children found it under your window," she said, exaggerating the nearness for effect. "They're now hunting for the rest. How many are they going to find?"

The couple exchanged glances.

"It proves nothing!" Fraser said.

"Along with our testimony, it proves a likelihood," Solomon said. "Look, we just want the truth. If neither of you killed Gregg or Lambert, I don't care if you've a key to every room in his house. We know about the garden door and the cellar."

"That's all I had, sir," Iris said earnestly. "Truth, sir. Just enough to let me in without his wife knowing."

"Did you ever use those keys?" Solomon asked, swinging suddenly on Fraser.

"Course I bloody didn't!" Fraser exploded. "What d'you take me for?"

"Leaving that aside," Solomon said smoothly, "did you ever lend those keys to anyone else? Between Mrs. Fraser's visits, perhaps?"

"And have everyone know we had them?" Iris said. "Not a chance!"

"Perhaps you copied them and sold them to one of Lambert's many enemies," Constance suggested. "After the collapse next door, for example."

"After that," Fraser said forcefully, "we had to be more careful than ever. Everyone knew Lambert was the real landlord, and anyone to do with him had a target on their back. It was hard enough for us without being accused of visiting the bastard."

"And yet Mrs. Fraser continued to do so," Constance pointed out, catching Iris's gaze. "When did Lambert break it off between you?"

Iris blinked. "I wish he bloody had."

Constance believed her. Which meant Angela had lied. Constance had already been fairly sure of that, though she could understand the pride behind the untruth.

"So whom did you sell those copies to?" Solomon asked.

Fraser clawed one hand through his hair. "What copies? I told you, I wouldn't risk it!"

"Don't want word to get around that you sold your wife to Lambert for a few dresses?" Solomon asked.

Fraser flushed angrily and took a hasty step forward. Solomon raised one eyebrow, and Fraser's fist unclenched. He knew exactly what he had done, whether through greed or complaisance.

"Iris went last night to end it," he said urgently. "Neither of us could take it anymore. We're looking for a new place, as proper caretakers. I'd have thrown those keys away as soon as she got home, whether or not Lambert turned up his toes."

"Could anyone have broken in here and taken the keys without your knowledge?" Constance asked.

"I don't see how," Fraser said, tugging at his hair again. "One of us is usually here."

"Did anyone ask to borrow the keys? Offer to buy them?"

"No," Fraser said bitterly. "I wish they had. Then I wouldn't have had to throw them out the bleeding window."

"IT HAS TO be someone in the Lamberts' house," Constance said discontentedly. She now had both keys in her reticule and several fewer coins. "Which means someone is lying."

"It means they're all lying," Solomon corrected her.

Her stomach twisted. She knew it was true. The question was, were they covering for themselves or Angela? Were they even lying on her instructions? Was she trying to protect one of them? Unlikely, if they had murdered her beloved husband.

The carriage stopped at Scotland Yard, and Solomon instructed it to wait. Inside, they were told Inspector Harris was not in the station. Constance was about to hand over the keys with a message when Sergeant Flynn appeared, escorting a man handcuffed to a uniformed police officer.

"Hello!" he said, looking startled to see them. "Are you waiting for the inspector?"

"Or you, if you have a moment," Solomon said.

"I do. Just finished a different murder case."

Constance glanced after the handcuffed man, who seemed to have put up no kind of fight. His shoulders were slumped, not defeated so much as…lost.

"A difficult one?" Solomon asked.

Flynn sighed. "No. If it's not rot for robbery, it's nearly always the husband. What can I do for you?"

As Constance blindly handed over the keys and Solomon explained their significance, the sergeant's words echoed in her head.

*"It's nearly always the husband."*

The very intimacy of marriage intensified every emotion, every rage or sense of injustice. Had she been trying not to see it all along? Angela had been alone in the dining room when Lambert went in search of the wine. They only had Duggin's word that he had lingered with her at all…

*It's nearly always the husband.*

*Or the wife.*

## CHAPTER EIGHTEEN

"To the office?" Solomon suggested.

"No." Constance marched toward the hackney stand. "Back to the Lamberts'. And this time by the back door. You're right. The servants are all lying to the police, but they might not lie to me. Not if Harris has left, at any rate."

"Then let's go and see."

Though his words agreed, his tone was wary, and she knew he would insist on coming with her. In truth, though she might despise herself for it, she felt safer with him there. After all, she had no idea how far Angela had taken the others into her confidence. And Constance had refused a well-paid position with her. Did that make her suspicious?

Alighting from the hackney, they walked in at the front gates and around the side of the house to the back door.

Duggin opened it and stared at them without blinking. "Well, well, look what the cat's dragged in."

"Good day to you, too," Constance murmured.

At least he stood back and let them enter, before turning back to the large table, where he appeared, incongruously, to be polishing silver cutlery.

"Thought you were leaving her in the lurch," Duggin said, sitting down.

"We understand each other," Constance said vaguely. "Where is everyone else?"

"About their own duties. Apart from Mrs. Feathers, who's

having a lie-down."

Presumably the gin had got the better of her, which was unusual. Although she tippled all the time, she had never appeared to be drunk. Well, the situation in the house was considerably more stressful than usual.

"Is she well?" Constance asked.

Duggin grunted.

"How is Mrs. Lambert?" she asked brightly.

"Better since the peelers decamped."

"Are they going to pin it on Iris Fraser?" Solomon asked.

Duggin sneered. "If the cap fits her."

"I don't think it does," Constance argued, "and the inspector will know that too. He's not a fool. Help me here, Mr. Duggin, so we can clear everything up quickly. When you went down to the cellar in the first place, looking for the wine Mr. Lambert had ordered, was anyone else in there?"

He shrugged. "Didn't see anyone. But then, I didn't look. My attention was all on bottles. She could have been there."

"Was the key in the cellar door out to the garden?" Solomon asked.

"I didn't notice."

"Did you look inside that padded room?" Constance asked. There was no point in asking if he'd known about the room. Of course he had. He'd been covering for Lambert with his wife for months, if not years.

"It was closed," Duggin said. "I went straight down the steps to the cellar."

"How long were you there?"

"I don't know. Five minutes? Ten? What does it matter?"

"It matters when you came back up," Constance said mildly, "when you announced dinner and when Mr. Lambert went to look for the missing bottle."

"Christ, I've been telling this to the police all bloody morning. I must've gone down to the cellar about half past six to look for the wine, come back about twenty minutes to seven, then seen to the places in the dining room. Dinner was at seven o'clock. It's always at seven o'clock. So it must have been two minutes past when his nibs went down."

"Then Iris can't have done it, because at two minutes past she was with us."

"Then she must have done it between twenty to seven and seven, mustn't she? While you two lovebirds were otherwise engaged."

Constance felt heat rise into her face, but Solomon leaned forward in his chair, saying, "Whom are you protecting? Why are you so determined to attribute this to Iris? How long have you known about her affair with Lambert?"

Duggin only smiled. It wasn't pleasant, but Constance pursued the issue.

"You've always known, haven't you? Nothing much happens in this house without your knowledge. You've got the key to the cellar. You can tell Mrs. Lambert, as I'm sure you have, that her husband is in his study when he's actually trysting in his padded room."

Duggin didn't so much as glance at her.

"When did she find out?" Solomon asked conversationally.

Duggin actually laughed. "How would I know? She's mistress of the house, isn't she?"

Constance pounced. "Meaning that nothing much happens in this house without *her* knowledge either?"

That got Duggin's attention, and his eyes were murderous. "*You* are accusing *her*?"

Of course. It had to be Angela he was protecting. She had always known that. So, it seemed, had Solomon.

"You think she isn't capable of killing?" he asked. "Or of jealousy?"

Duggin had himself in hand again. "She knew her place was safe. She was his wife, had all his respect."

"Not sure tumbling his mistress beneath his wife's roof shows a lot of respect."

Duggin turned his villain's glare on Solomon this time. "Really? Not sure you're going to fit in here, Mr. Lovebird."

"I don't intend to, Mr. Duggin."

"Then you'd better stay away, hadn't you?"

"You're protecting her," Constance said. "Everyone is, or trying to. But the thing is, you can't protect her with lies. We need to know the truth to get justice for Mr. Lambert."

Something flickered in his eyes then. Guilt? Shame? Acknowledgment that he'd almost forgotten his master in support of his mistress? "That needn't trouble you or the peelers."

"It's a new world, Mr. Duggin. The peelers are everywhere. You know that, or you wouldn't be setting Iris up for them."

"I ain't setting anyone up. If you can't see the truth—which is none of your concern anyway—that ain't my problem. That inspector's round there now arresting Iris Fraser."

Constance doubted that. Sergeant Flynn had said nothing about it. But either way, she would never budge Duggin from his story. He had been too well primed, and only one person could have done that. The woman who commanded his loyalty, even above what he had always owed her husband.

Or…who else could matter more to Duggin more than either of the Lamberts? His own flesh and blood.

Goldie.

Why on earth would Goldie have killed Lambert? Had he been having an affair with her too? More to the point, had Duggin found out and taken an axe to his master?

Melodrama. Speculation without any evidence whatsoever… No, Constance was clutching at straws, because she still didn't want it to be Angela…

Duggin's transfer of loyalty had more likely happened over years, without his daughter's involvement, probably without any of them noticing. The staff were all afraid of Lambert, but Angela had their love. And she knew her husband's business inside out. She had been grooming herself to take over, though no doubt her discovery of Lambert's betrayal with Iris had been the last straw, determining the timing and the ruthlessness of his removal.

Lambert had been a frightening man with an unexpectedly vulnerable edge. Constance had caught a glimpse of that the night she walked in on him in Angela's bedroom. Angela, on the other hand, was a vulnerable woman, bound in steel…and the fire of revenge.

Duggin had either murdered Lambert on her orders, or he had let her into the cellar to do it herself.

*No blood on her clothes*, she reminded herself. And none on Duggin's. And yet they had to be in league. One of them had done it. She knew it but would never get Duggin to admit it. She needed to persuade or even trick one of the other servants into giving something away. The truth was so close that she could touch it…

She stood abruptly, blinking at the chair where Ida Feathers always sat. A cold dread twisted in her stomach.

"Why is Mrs. Feathers not cooking?" she asked.

Duggin gestured with his curled hand toward his mouth in the universal sign for drinking.

"And you're allowing it?" Constance said in disbelief. "Now?"

"She'll still rustle up something tasty in time," Duggin said. "You'll see."

Ida knew everything, all her mistress's business. And she was a drunk who talked too much. Though she'd never dropped any incriminating remarks in Constance's hearing, she had been quite open with her, a stranger, over her gin-spiked tea… In her moment of triumph, would Angela allow that risk to continue? With policemen all over the house?

"I'd better make sure she is well," Constance said firmly.

Duggin watched her as she walked toward Ida's door, but he made no effort to stop her, only shrugged and turned to Solomon.

"So why don't you think Iris did it, then?"

Oh yes, he was complacent, imagining he was toying with Solomon, who had seen the truth long before Constance had allowed herself to. No wonder he had tried to ger her to leave the house…

Her heart in her mouth, she knocked on the cook's door. And heard nothing. She steeled herself, opened the door, and walked in.

The room was gloomy, but not dark, since a modicum of daylight drifted from a barred window that looked only onto the close-by boundary wall at the side of the house. It stank of old gin and new.

For an instant, Constance imagined she was gazing at pile of bedclothes. But she wasn't.

Ida sat on the bed, her legs crossed like a child, a bottle half-way to her mouth—a moment frozen in time like a painting or a photograph.

When she lowered the bottle, Constance felt her breath rush out in relief. Had she really imagined the woman was dead in *that* position? A most unlikely rigor mortis.

"Hallo, my love," Ida said in a surprised tone.

"I came to see if you were well," Constance managed. "You're usually cooking at this time of day."

"She don't have much appetite right now," Ida said dreamily. "Truth to tell, ain't got much meself. But there, life goes on, and you're probably right." She took a last swig of gin and shoved in the stopper she held clutched in her other hand. "You staying on with her, then?"

"Probably not," Constance said. "But I wanted to help sort out the mess."

"You leave it to her. She can sort out anything." Ida smiled at nothing in particular and distractedly pulled the stopper out of her bottle again. Generously, she offered it to Constance, who sank down on the edge of the bed to take it from her.

"She is a strong woman," Constance said. "One needs to be in this world."

"You're not wrong. It's a blow, though. She loved him very hard, you know."

"And yet she killed him in the end."

Ida didn't even look surprised. She just smiled and held out her hand for the bottle. Constance hung on to it.

"I just don't understand the timing," she said. "There were so few minutes she could have done it, and there was no blood on her clothes."

"Oh, time's whatever you want it to be. Some people call midday dinnertime. I was one of 'em till we had to learn nob ways. So seven o'clock is dinnertime now. No one even looks at the clock."

Constance's breath caught. "You made it early."

"First course on the table by quarter to the hour."

"And he was in the cellar two minutes later…" Then Duggin and Angela had both lied. They hadn't lingered in the dining room together. One—or both—had followed Lambert into the cellar, distracted him into the padded room, and killed him. While Constance and Solomon had been talking, watching in the garden, at least ten minutes before Iris had arrived.

"Apron," Constance blurted. "There must be a bloody apron or something in the laundry…"

"Don't be daft," Ida said. As if she couldn't help it, her eyes strayed to the floor at the far side of the bed.

*She's got the bloodstained apron!*

Her heart thundering, Constance held out the bottle to Ida, who took it. Hopefully it would distract her…

Constance rose, and those bright, red-tinged eyes followed her.

Ida smiled winningly. "Don't be daft, girl. I'm just helping you understand, because I like you. She likes you. But it won't do you no good to betray us. I'll just deny it, and you can't prove nothing without my testimony."

"And a bloodstained apron," Constance said. She could see it now, stained dark in streaks and crumpled into a ball, half under the bed.

"I'm the cook. I get animal blood on me all the time. That's why I wear an apron. Leave it, love. You know he had it coming."

Constance caught her gaze and held it fiercely. "You are covering up a *murder!*"

"So I am, dear, so I am," Ida said comfortably.

And that was when Constance realized she had seen more than the apron on the floor. She glanced down again to be sure. A corked and labeled bottle of wine, still dusty from its stay in the cellar.

Her mind reeled. For the barest instant, she grasped blindly for the significance, and finally caught it. Ida wasn't covering for Angela. She had taken the bottle and hidden it to trick Duggin and Lambert, and very probably Angela too. Constance couldn't take her eyes off it.

"And Gregg?" she managed. "Why did Gregg have to die?"

"He knew too much. He threatened Angela as well as Lambert when he decided to spill his guts to the inquiry. He came round here specially to tell them that. Couldn't let him do it. So I had a quick word when he was leaving."

And now Constance knew too much too. That Solomon was only a few yards away on the other side of that door was not the comfort it should have been. She had to grab the evidence and get out of here…

Ida was edging toward the door side of the bed, stretching her feet toward the floor.

"It was you with Gregg's body that we chased to the edge of Devil's Acre," Constance blurted. "How on earth did you get it from the cellar and onto the donkey's back?"

"Angela helped me, of course. She knew what I'd done and why. We're used to working quick, her and me. And you were obliging enough, you and your lovely man, to wait where she'd put you."

"Did she always know the body was in the cellar?"

"Not till you told her." Feet on the floor, Ida bent as though to tie her flapping shoelaces.

"Did she know about Caleb, too? Is she covering for you, or

did you plan it tog—"

Contance ducked down and swiped up the bottle and the apron. In the same movement, she began to sprint back around the bed—and then skidded to a halt, for Ida lunged right at her, a bloody axe in both hands, wielded high above her head.

SOLOMON WAS NOT unaware of Duggin's hostility. In truth, he returned it. He was just better at keeping his distaste in check. He wished Constance better luck with the cook. Mostly, he was relieved that she had opened her mind to the possibility that Angela was the guilty party. Guilty of more than reluctant complicity with her husband.

He knew it hurt Constance. She had felt some kind of bond with the woman, an understanding that may have been sincere on one level but not on any others. A shared background of crime and squalor, followed by a climb to riches, did not make them sisters. But Constance liked to see the best in people, and where Angela was concerned, the scales seemed to fall from her eyes very slowly.

They needed the servants' testimony to get to Angela. The police would never get it from them, and clearly Constance carried no weight with Duggin, to whom she was still an outsider.

Solomon tried a different tactic.

"So is this it?"

"What?" Duggin asked.

"The rest of your life. From Lambert's strongman to Mrs. Lambert's butler. Is that really enough?"

Duggin smirked. "You really don't know what you're talking about. Mr. Lambert was a good man, a successful man, every-thing strictly legal."

"Is that why he was betrayed?"

"Ask the stupid little cow he was f—"

"Don't bother," Solomon said wearily. "Everyone knows Iris Fraser didn't do it."

Duggin regarded him with his pale, oddly inhuman eyes. "What's it to you, anyway? Why d'you care? No one thinks it was you or your girl."

"How do you know it wasn't?" Solomon asked softly.

Duggin's expression never changed. "How do you know what happens to people who ask too many questions?"

"Is that a threat, Mr. Duggin?"

"More questions," Duggin mocked.

"The thing is," Solomon taunted him, "you can't expect me to be afraid of such threats, can you? Not when you couldn't even protect the man who paid your wages."

That got a reaction, at least, a tightening of the face but no more. Upstairs, someone knocked loudly on the front door. Duggin didn't break eye contact.

"Which is oddest of all," Solomon said. "All the elaborate security in this house. Patrolling the grounds as though it's a royal palace, bodyguards for the master and mistress wherever they go, all under your supervision. And yet the master of the house is axed to death under his own roof, only a few feet away from you. What sort of message does that send to the denizens of your world?"

Duggin sprang to his feet, fists clenched, face ugly. Solomon, poised for possible attack, held his gaze without troubling to stand. At last, the man's pride was rattled, though to Solomon's annoyance, the timing was wrong.

Footsteps clattered down the stairs. One of the footmen, looking irritated, came first. Young and burly, he was a reinforcement for the enemy that Solomon could have done without. But ignoring Solomon, he addressed Duggin.

"Rozzers again, Mr. D."

Duggin released Solomon's gaze reluctantly and turned to face the footman and Sergeant Flynn. "Anyone'd think you worked here," he sneered.

"Right now I do," Flynn retorted. "Where's Inspector Harris?"

"How would I know? He left here an hour ago."

A frown of annoyance crossed Flynn's face. "I don't suppose he left a message for me or said where he was going?"

"To arrest Iris Fraser," Duggin replied with a sly glance at Solomon.

Flynn swore under his breath, then frowned, appearing to become aware of Solomon's presence for the first time. He opened his mouth, but Solomon never knew what he meant to say, for a sudden crash exploded across the kitchen.

Solomon sprang to his feet, shoving Duggin out of the way. The alarming noise had come from the cook's bedroom on the other side of the kitchen, and it was quickly followed by a furious groan of pain.

Solomon, in sheer terror for Constance's life, burst into the room with Flynn, Duggin, and the footman close on his heels.

The frail, gin-soaked old cook was wrestling an axe out of the wall with a cry of rage. A huge lump of plaster came with it as she staggered back with the force. Constance, who had clearly ducked out of the axe's path, sprang upright once more, a dusty wine bottle and bundle of stained white calico clutched to her chest.

Ida, her back to the newcomers and apparently oblivious to their entrance, hefted the axe with both hands. Solomon lunged forward and wrenched it from her astonishingly powerful grip. She spun around to face him, her empty fingers reaching for his face like claws.

With a complete lack of chivalry, Solomon knocked her aside into Flynn's hold so that he could get to Constance.

Wide-eyed and breathing rapidly, she didn't waste time by collapsing onto his willing chest. Instead, she grasped his arm in a grip that hurt.

"Mrs. Feathers killed them both!" she gasped. "She hid the wine bottle to get Lambert into the cellar at the right time. Her apron's covered in blood. So is the axe—I'm sure it's the same one that killed Gregg."

"Ida Feathers," said Flynn, grasping the old woman's suddenly limp arm, "I am arresting you for the attempted murder of Constance Silver. And on suspicion of the murder of Caleb Lambert."

"And Huxley Gregg," Constance insisted.

"I'm sure we'll get to that," Flynn said hastily.

"No, you won't," Duggin growled, advancing with menace, the footman poised at his side. "Let the poor old woman go." He fixed Flynn with his basilisk stare. "Trust me, peeler, it ain't worth it."

Flynn, who was made of sterner stuff than Duggin imagined, merely stared back.

But they could not afford a fight in this constricting space, not with thugs who were probably armed, and certainly not with Constance in the room, clutching her bottled evidence like a swaddled baby.

*Oh well.*

Solomon shook off Constance's hand and, uttering a wordless battle cry that could have come from any of his ancestors, charged past Flynn and Ida, wielding the axe before him.

# CHAPTER NINETEEN

HER JAW DROPPING at Solomon's bizarre behavior, Constance still followed him blindly. So did Flynn with the now-cowering Ida in his grasp. Duggin and Bert, taken by equal surprise, fell back before the onslaught, falling over each other to spill back into the kitchen.

"The back door!" Duggin yelled at Bert, who immediately ran there, snatching something out of his pocket that sprang open into a wicked-looking knife.

But Solomon, who'd stopped his bloodcurdling yell, clearly had no intention of leaving by the back door. After all, they had no key to escape by the garden door. Having driven Duggin in that direction, he said, "Constance. Up."

She tugged Flynn's sleeve with her free hand and obeyed, speeding up the stairs to the baize door. Anxiously, she glanced back at the kitchen. Duggin, armed with a carving knife, was circling Solomon. Bert moved toward him from the back door.

With startling suddenness, Solomon turned tail and ran, and abruptly, Constance wanted to laugh. The mirth bubbled up, joyous and no doubt hysterical as she burst through the baize door. She led the charge down the hall toward the front door, knowing Solomon was at her heels, and the evidence with them—the bottle, the apron, the axe, Ida, and Flynn, the policeman, the reliable witness to all. It was exhilarating, wonderful, the culminating triumph of Silver and Grey's first case…

Until two men emerged from doors on opposite sides of the hall. Pat and Robin. And Robin held a large black pistol, which he cocked and aimed at Constance's heart.

She stopped so fast, the carpet slid beneath her feet and she struggled for balance. She lowered the bottle, gripping it at her side instead. The apron was crushed under the same arm.

The pistol remained steady. Robin was not interested in the evidence. He neither knew nor cared what it was.

"Yes, far enough I think," came Duggin's sneering voice as he and Bert caught up behind them. "Now, we'll be having that stolen axe, and our cook."

"Your cook murdered your master," Constance said loudly. "She'll face justice."

"We got our own justice," Duggin said. "Drop the axe."

"Come and take it," Solomon invited him.

"I don't need to. How about Robin there takes your girl's face with a single shot?"

"In front of the police?" Solomon sounded amused, though Constance heard the tension behind it. He would give up the axe, force her to give up the evidence… And then they'd be murdered anyway, for police and the law mattered nothing to these people. No doubt their bodies would vanish into the swamp of the Devil's Acre. The murderers could lose themselves there too if necessary.

"No one's taking off anyone's face in this house," said Angela Lambert, her voice sharp with authority, causing all heads to snap around toward the staircase, which she descended dressed in deep mourning, all black bombazine and lace. Widowhood seemed to have lent her physical grace, for she all but glided down. "Put the gun away, Robin, before the police come in force and arrest us all."

Very reluctantly—and slowly—Robin lowered the pistol. Constance was afraid to breathe in case his finger twitched on the trigger and he fired in apparent "mistake."

"What *is* all this?" Angela asked.

Had she always possessed this tone of command? Had Constance just been deaf to it? Or had Lambert's death drawn it to the fore?

"Ida Feathers is under arrest for the murder of your husband, ma'am," Flynn announced, at his most wooden.

Growling and derisive hoots immediately issued from the servants. Angela stilled them with one raised hand, which then closed over the newel post at the foot of the stairs.

"Look at her," she snapped. "Have you ever met my late husband, sergeant? He was tall and strong, and yet you believe a little old woman addicted to her gin murdered him with an axe?" Her gaze swept from Flynn to Solomon to Constance. "Why are you letting this nonsense stand?"

Because it was true. The only question left was how much Angela had known, how much had been under her orders.

Constance raised the bottle. "Is this not the wine your husband went to look for in the cellar, minutes before he was killed? I've got her blood-soaked apron. The axe was under her bed! Are you telling us someone else just put those things in her room? They weren't even hidden."

"Is it not possible?" Angela said steadily. "Lots of people pass through the kitchen. And you know the woman drinks. Someone has taken advantage."

"There is also the small matter of her attacking Mrs. Silver with said axe," Flynn said dryly.

Angela's gaze flew back to Constance, who met it steadily.

"She knew exactly where it was," Constance said. "She told me everything."

Angela's eyes did not waver. But Constance could almost see the calculation going on behind them. Angela had a choice to make that would affect all her people and her own future. One word, one gesture from her would see violence done and her devoted cook probably freed, at least for now.

But Angela would never go back, only forward.

"It will prove to be a mistake," she said dismissively. "A

laughable one. But if you're so determined, take her. For now."

Her own people were staring at her, baffled, suspicious, and not best pleased.

Solomon walked forward and opened the front door. Flynn backed out of it, still grasping Ida by her arm. She went willingly, almost trustingly now, no doubt because Angela had promised it was temporary.

Solomon took Constance by the hand, urging her to the front door, putting himself between her and Lambert's men. Angela's men.

Angela's voice stayed her. "You've made your choice, then?"

"So have you." Constance walked out of the house, every hair on the back of her neck standing up in dread. They left utter silence behind them.

IT WAS A long two hours later before they had each made their statements to the police. They emerged slightly numb, though Solomon was aware of a certain satisfaction. The end of their first case.

But as the hackney rattled across cobbles, he was aware Constance did not appear to share his feelings. She was quiet, distracted, gazing out of each window in turn, shifting restlessly on the bench beside him.

"What is it?" he asked.

She shook her head. "It doesn't feel…finished. We've always known before—the murderer is revealed, we emerge safely from the fire in the nick of time, and the mystery is over."

He raised his brows. "You are complaining about the lack of fire? We found the murderer, though to be honest, right up until I saw Mrs. Feathers with the axe, my money was on Angela."

"So was mine." She focused her gaze on his face. "Do you think she did it too? Were they in league?"

It was a thought that had crossed his mind more than once. "Ida never told you they were, though she seems to have admitted everything else to you, despite her denials to the police. Besides, why would Ida need to steal the wine if they were allies? Together, they could have found a simpler way to entice him into the cellar. Duggin certainly wasn't in on it. I doubt Angela was, though she may have guessed. After all, she helped Ida get rid of Gregg's body."

Constance moved her hip, her skirts brushing against him. "Then why do I feel it isn't over?"

"Because this mystery has never been entirely about ghosts, or even Gregg's murder. There's the negligence that led to the collapse of the tenement. Angela now owns both buildings in St. Giles and many others elsewhere. Perhaps she will be a better landlord."

"And perhaps she won't."

"I thought you liked her."

"I did. Part of me still does. I understand her, or think I do, but...but she is not a good woman, Solomon."

He groped toward understanding and found something astonishing. "She is not like you, Constance. She was never like you."

"There are parallels."

He reached out and covered the hand in her lap. "No," he said gently. "There are not."

"You don't know, Sol," she said, a curious desperation in her voice. Her hand twisted and clung to his. "You don't know the things I've done."

"Then you can tell me one day, if you like. Or not. Our pasts change nothing between us now."

Her dubious glance made him scowl.

"I am not ashamed of you, Constance Silver," he said roughly. "Did you really think I was? I thought we accepted each other."

"Acceptance," she said. "That is what Angela's looking for. I wanted it too. Oh, not from Society—I am realistic enough to know I will never have that. But from certain people."

"Me?"

She nodded and met his gaze with defiance. "I never apologize for being a whore. Do you close your eyes to what I am?"

"You cannot be labeled, Constance. I won't try." Frustration shook him, for yet again they were in the wrong place and the wrong time to say what he needed to. He tightened his fingers around hers, let his thumb caress her palm, heard the catch of her breath. "Come with me to the Swans' charity ball."

She blinked once, then broke into a peal of genuine laughter that was both infectious and arousing. "Can you imagine me hobnobbing with the philanthropic righteous? The wealthy Christian ladies and the respectable gentlemen who secretly frequent my establishment? I've never met Lady Swan—or her husband, come to that—but I would most certainly not do that to her."

"And yet you are one of the major contributors to her charity. I think you'll find you are invited already. Brazen it out, Constance. She has invited you to do so. I shall escort you if you'll let me, and dance with you. So will Dragan Tizsa and Lord James."

"They will be there?" she said uncertainly.

"I believe so."

For a moment he thought she was actually considering it, maybe even that she would enjoy dancing with him…

"Angela Lambert asked me to go with her and keep her right in Polite Society."

Unreasonably annoyed by the reintroduction of that name, he retorted, "And yet *you* are not worthy to attend? Constance—"

She raised her arm, rapping sharply on the ceiling to instruct the jarvey to stop. "I need fresh air, Solomon. I'll walk home from here. I'll see you in the office on Monday when we move on to our next case."

He knew better than to try to stop her. One of them always ran away at the end of a case, as if afraid of having nothing but mystery between them. Or afraid of admitting to anything else.

She was gone in a flash. He reinstructed the coachman to take him home and sat back on the hard bench. He couldn't even see her through the window.

Bleakly, he forced himself to acknowledge the other possible reason for this particular bolt. She didn't want any personal relationship with him, only their business partnership. Whatever the attraction between them—and it had always been there—it was not strong enough for her to pursue it. And she didn't want him to. That was why she ran away. Or was it?

*Maddening woman.* Maddening, wretched, awkward, *beloved* woman.

THEIR NEW CASE, the search for stolen jewels, began the following day, and Constance was glad of it. It kept her from thinking of Solomon and his offer to escort her to Lady Swan's party. In fact, since they divided all the pawnshops and jeweler's in London between then, it kept them physically apart too.

She returned to the office briefly at midday as she realized she had failed to make use of her mother's valuable resources. She scribbled a note, asking Juliet the best places to look for stolen diamonds, inviting her to drop into the office with any ideas or to leave a message with Janey. She then went off to find a likely messenger, paid the boy, and went back to her own search.

Since she more than half expected Juliet to either ignore the message or forget to answer, she wasn't entirely surprised to find no reply at the office at six o'clock that evening. Nor was there any sign of Solomon, so she and Janey closed up and left together. Janey introduced her to the omnibus, for which Constance was grateful after an unsuccessful day's trudging up and down city streets and questioning both respectable jewelers and wary pawnshop proprietors.

At home, the main surprise awaited her in the receiving salon.

"A Mrs. Jules, ma'am," the footman told her from his stance opposite the salon door.

"Really?" Her mother had never once set foot in any of her establishments before. It made Constance extremely suspicious as she peeled off her gloves, untied her hat, and left them over the banister in her haste.

Juliet had been made comfortable. An empty cup and saucer had been abandoned at her elbow, and a glass containing the indifferent sherry was clutched in her plump right hand.

"Wotcha, Con," she said amiably. "Just admiring your fine room. Guaranteed to cool the ardor with relentless subtlety."

"That's the plan. I meet visitors here and decide whether or not to give them a chance."

"Your haughty servants expect me to run away with the silver," Juliet said. Loudly enough for Anthony, the footman in the hall, to hear.

"Only because they don't know you're my mother," Constance said, gratified to see Juliet's eyebrows fly up in astonishment. "I'm not ashamed of you, Ma. What are you doing here? I can't imagine it's idle curiosity."

"Hardly," her mother said. Opening her reticule, she emptied the contents into her lap, where they glittered like ice. She removed a handkerchief and a few coins from the pile and held up a shining diamond necklace. A matching bracelet, earrings, and a brooch remained in her lap. "These what you're looking for?"

Constance closed her mouth and swallowed. And swallowed again before she risked trying to speak. "They could be. I hesitate to ask where you got them."

"Good. 'Cause I won't tell you. One of the last lots I bought to fence. Got it all for a song, for obvious reasons. It's got to be recognizable to somebody. I could never have sold it without breaking it all up, and that seemed a shame. Besides, I's already decided to go straight, so I never did anything with it."

"That," Constance said slowly, "has to be the most stupendous trick of fate, or luck, or whatever you call it, ever."

"Maybe you're due some luck."

Constance gave a crooked smile and waved around her. "This is all luck."

"No, it's hard work and good sense."

Constance blinked at this unprecedented praise.

"You think I don't know? Was never proud? I don't want you in this game, but if you have to be, you couldn't do better. And before you spin me some more tales, I know what else you do."

Girls still talked on the streets, and Juliet still knew them. Constance's haven was not unknown.

"I'll show these to my client tomorrow," she managed. "What do you want for them?"

"If he's paying, I'll take what I spent. Otherwise you can just have 'em. To be honest, I don't want them in my house, since the rozzers are likely to poke around at first."

Constance took the jewels from her, dropping them into her own reticule. "This might just be the easiest fee we'll ever earn. Whether or not they're my client's, thank you."

"Don't thank me. You're helping me out." Juliet struggled out of the too-comfortable chair, and Constance knew an echo of the old panic she had felt as a child whenever her mother left her.

"Do you want a bite to eat?" she blurted. "We'll have no guests before eight, so there's plenty of time."

"Not today," Juliet said, as Constance knew she would. Though her mother could still surprise her. "Got things to do if I'm to open this week. But I'll come another day. If you like."

"I *would* like," Constance said, and meant it.

Her mother nodded, then turned away as though to hide her own pleasure. Her breath caught. "Con?"

"Yes?"

"I don't know who your father is. Never did, never cared, because whoever he was, he didn't matter. You were always enough."

Emotion swept up, contradictory and confused. Constance's

throat tightened unbearably.

Juliet grasped the door handle, then glanced over her shoulder. "I'm sorry I wasn't." She tugged open the door and stomped off, leaving Constance staring after her.

A second later, she gasped and hurried after her mother, brushing past Anthony at the door. Juliet was halfway down the steps.

"You're daft," Constance called after her, and her voice barely broke at all. "And still *much* more than enough!"

Juliet laughed, lifted an airy hand, and fled. But Constance could tell, just from her jaunty wobble, that she was glad.

And so was Constance.

THE FOLLOWING DAY, Constance and Solomon called upon their client, who was overjoyed to identify Juliet's jewels as his. He immediately gave them a banker's draft for the rest of their fee and sent them away with effusive thanks, just in time to meet their next client, who had a very interesting problem of his own.

Even so, Constance found it hard to think about the new case. Her mind kept straying back to the Lamberts, to the dead, the injured, and the bereaved, and to the vileness of exploitative slum landlords.

Eventually, as she should have done from the beginning, she went into Solomon's office and talked to him about it. After that, the decision about Lady Swan's party was easy.

# CHAPTER TWENTY

ANGELA'S NERVES WERE jumping as she journeyed from her own house to the Swans'. She would have preferred to do this in the calming company of Mrs. Silver, who would have removed any accidental hint of vulgarity from her dress and made those minor changes that made all the difference to a person's confidence.

It was incredibly difficult to step into this superior world of wealth and respectability alone. She wasn't sure she could have done it had not the even larger matter of grief hung over her. Walking alone into a party of hostile humans was nothing beside the hugeness of widowhood, of sole responsibility for the organization.

She forced her tense shoulders to relax and lifted her chin with pride. If she had learned anything over the last two or three years, it was that, alone, she could do anything she wished.

This was to have been Caleb's big moment. When he, born with nothing in the lawless filth of the Devil's Acre, stepped into the world of the truly powerful. He had paid a fortune for these tickets, and Angela was determined to put them to good purpose.

Sir Nicholas Swan's house was nothing great. It was not in a fashionably gracious Mayfair Square but on the edges of the river, a large, old building with a kind of brooding beauty. Not so very different from her own, she told herself as she alighted and walked boldly up to the front steps in the extravagant glow of many lamps.

A liveried footman took her invitation card with a bow. Another took her wrap and she was free to follow the bright, sparkling people in front of her up a polished but not-too-grand staircase, and into a large drawing room full of people.

Angela's heart thudded as she realized the couple just inside the door must be Sir Nicholas Swan and his wife. She had found out what she could about them, of course, and she knew Lady Swan had once been a governess. To Angela, that put them on a more even footing. She was able to look the younger woman in the eye and say, "Good evening. I know we have not met. I am Mrs. Lambert, Caleb Lambert's widow."

Lady Swan had already stretched out her hand in greeting, and she did not withdraw it, though her eyes widened slightly— no doubt at Angela's black silk ensemble with a solitary jet necklace at her throat.

"Mrs. Lambert! Thank you so much for coming at this distressing time. Our condolences upon your tragic loss. This is my husband, Sir Nicholas."

Swan was more of a shock. He had one of those dark, brooding faces with a haughty, aristocratic nose and extraordinarily sharp eyes that served as a warning against complaisance. However, he was politeness itself, bowing over her black-gloved hand and murmuring his own words of sympathy.

Angela, aware that in this world, one did not discuss business upon arrival, merely inclined her head and passed on into the room.

In the sea of bright colors and glittering jewels, she must have stood out like a sore thumb, a specter at the feast. She meant to. A lackey offered her a glass of fizzing wine, which she took and then moved among the rich and the privileged, all here to flaunt their charitable credentials. Well, she could and would out-flaunt them there, too.

She encountered a few surprised glances, as Silver had warned her she would. Widows still in the full black of recent mourning did not attend large or frivolous events. Well, she would not stay for the frivolity. It might have been fun to dance with Caleb here, sharing the wonder of what they had achieved.

But Ida had removed all chance of that. Gin must finally have addled the woman's brain. Angela's planned takeover of the organization would have been much subtler, leaving her husband as the figurehead to trot out at parties like this one. Instead, with her house crawling with peelers and her cook under arrest for two murders, she would have to let Ida swing, and face these kinds of affairs quite alone.

But instead of feeling daunted, she discovered a sense of elation. These powerful people were wondering who she was, admiring her courage—or her eccentricity—in attending this charitable evening alone.

Since she knew no one, she had no need to speak to any of them, merely drifted among them. Music began, gentle and exquisite, and she followed it to the far end of the room, where a slightly raised platform had been set up by an area of uncarpeted, polished floor that was clearly meant for dancing. At the moment, people merely milled across it, greeting each other in the plummy accents Caleb had aspired to.

The musicians played various stringed instruments. Angela was surprised to see a young woman among them. She wore spectacles and a simple evening gown that was not new, and she played the violin. She drew Angela's attention, not because she was particularly beautiful but because she was lost in the music she played, caring nothing for the wealth and chatter around her.

Angela's gaze lingered.

"You are admiring the violinist, ma'am?"

Angela turned quickly, because she recognized the deep, soft voice. Mr. Solomon Grey, austerely handsome in strict evening dress, looked back at her with a faint smile. He did not seem remotely surprised to see her, but then, he wouldn't. She had told Silver she meant to attend, and Silver had turned down the opportunity to work for her. A mistake the girl might yet learn to regret.

"Mr. Grey. Yes, there is something most appealing about her. I must ask Lady Swan for her name."

"I can tell you that. She is Lady Grizelda Tizsa, a daughter of the Duke of Kelburn."

It all proved how right she was to have encouraged Caleb to involve himself in carefully chosen charities. It really was the route to aristocratic associations.

"Perhaps you might introduce me later," she said, more to depress Grey's pretensions than because she actually thought he could truly perform such an introduction.

"I might," Grey said, turning to the man approaching on his left. "In fact, here is her brother-in-law, Lord Trent. My lord, Mrs. Lambert."

The lord inclined his fair, haughty head to her and clapped Grey on the shoulder in a familiar kind of way. Which was odd, considering Grey's lowly living as an investigator. Though not quite so odd as the catch in Trent's breath as Constance Silver materialized on Grey's other side.

"Mrs. Silver, what an unexpected pleasure," he said, his voice rich with some amusement Angela could not account for. Nor could she account for the gorgeous gown and jewels worn by the lowly investigator's partner. Silver was, in fact, breathtakingly beautiful, which might have accounted for the male stares around her.

Angela was piqued to have been upstaged. No matter—this was her evening, and she would complete it with grace. She inclined her head to Silver, who returned the gesture. The faint smile on her lips was merely social and aimed at no one.

Unease seeped through Angela. She had the feeling she was missing something. Something she should have known or troubled to find out.

The music reached its close and was rewarded with enthusiastic applause. The violinist bowed with unexpected shyness and not a great deal of grace. But her moment in the limelight was short-lived. She moved over to make way for Sir Nicholas and

Lady Swan.

"Our first thanks of the evening have to go to our distinguished musicians," Sir Nicholas stated. "And I promise you will hear more of them later, including a duet my wife will perform with Lady Grizelda. But before we reach the fun part of the evening, my wife and I are most grateful that you have joined us in the much more serious purpose of raising money for the rehousing of London's poorest.

"You are all aware of the horrific existence of slum dwellings and the vile conditions in which we, the richest country in the world, expect other human beings to live. The links between such places and disease and crime are too well known. As are other tragedies such as the recent collapse of a neglected building in St. Giles that killed and injured so many. The funds you have donated this evening, together with what we have already raised, will now make it possible to clear part of St. Giles of dangerous buildings and open sewers and build decent homes where people can live, rather than merely exist on the verge of early death for themselves and their children.

"Without being too somber, I am delighted to announce that our project begins next week with the best engineers and builders, closely supervised and overseen by our own board, headed by our kind patrons, His Grace of Kelburn and Lord Trent."

He smiled. "And that, I think, is enough of announcements! Please—"

*This* was Angela's moment.

She stepped forward and said clearly, "Your pardon, sir, but might I make a short announcement, too?"

She had practiced that line and a few others in front of the mirror. She knew her accent was not perfect, but neither did it shriek Devil's Acre. Following Silver's advice, she did not try to impersonate the nobs. And she had everyone's attention, even their respect for her widowhood.

Swan barely hesitated before he extended his hand to help her onto the platform. Then she stood before a sea of wealthy, pampered, expectant faces.

"I shall not keep you, and I shall not stay. It is not a week since my husband's untimely passing, so my only purpose here is to announce what he intended to, and what I, as his widow and heir, will honor." From her reticule, she took the folded banker's draft and handed it to Sir Nicholas. "In memory of my beloved husband."

She was gratified to see Sir Nicholas's eyes widen.

"Mrs. Lambert! This is a considerable sum of money..." he said, clearly awed.

"It is," she agreed. "And what is more, I will personally supply a company of builders and materials—"

"That, though generous, is out of the question," Sir Nicholas said.

Taken by surprise, Angela took a moment to understand him. "I beg your pardon?" she said frigidly.

"You are of course welcome to submit the names of your company and the sources of your material, but obviously they will be subjected to the same rigorous inspections as everyone else."

"Inspections?" It felt like swearing in church.

"That is the system we have agreed," Grey said quietly from the floor below her. "To prevent the fraud and waste of previous projects of building and repair that either don't happen or are undertaken with cheap, unreliable materials and shoddy workmanship. Everyone involved must sign up to this system of inspections. Which, of course, you are invited to do." His lips curved as he held her gaze. "If you still wish to."

For the first time, it entered her head that Grey was rather more than the grubby little investigator who presumed on the brains and the body of his partner. His evening clothes were exquisitely made from the finest cloth. He looked far too aloof to be a friend of these important men, and yet they all seemed to know him...

"Mr. Grey," she said, clinging to politeness, "you speak for—"

"For the board," Sir Nicholas said, "of which he is the new chairman and a longstanding member."

"It is not pleasant," said the violinist unexpectedly from Lady Swan's side, "to have one's donations and offers hemmed in by conditions and boundaries, but sadly, we have found it necessary. Although the inquiry into the St. Giles disaster has been shut down upon the deaths of both landlords concerned, it did manage to point out several of the landlords' failings—repairs either ignored or carried out with cheap materials by men without skill or knowledge."

Angela stared at her. "You are accusing me of offering cheap material and unskilled workmen?"

"We are making sure you don't," Grey said. "Since your late husband had a poor record in such matters."

Heat burned in Angela's face from humiliation and anger. "How dare you?"

"Eighteen people died, Mrs. Lambert. Countless more cannot work through injury. Some don't even have a roof over their heads anymore."

"If you're talking about that building that collapsed in St, Giles, the landlord was not my husband but Huxley Gregg!"

"They were in partnership," Silver said. "Gregg's was the name used, but Lambert was the man who collected. There may not be documents to that effect, but there are several witness statements and the cooperation of banks that do prove the connection."

Angela stared at her. *Bloody little traitress.* No wonder she would not be brought in to the fold... And she wasn't remotely intimidated. If anything, the Devil's Acre stared out of her lovely eyes.

"You are hurling vile accusations at a widow," Angela said hoarsely, shading her eyes.

"It is a vile situation," Constance agreed. "And you are, of course, at perfect liberty to withdraw what I'm sure is a most generous donation."

It was only then that Angela began to realize the full scale of her defeat. She could snatch back the draft and save herself some money, but either way, this Society and their wealthy business was closed to her for good. It wasn't just that an opportunity to make a lot of money had been shut down, but she had been exposed along with Caleb. Rightly so, for she was complicit in it all. But now, even without legal inquiries or prosecutions, her wings were clipped. The business she had fought to control would grow no further, and instead would shrink. The horror of slipping back into the kind of life she inflicted on her sick, overcrowded tenants chilled her blood.

It was true what she had said to Silver. She really should have listened to Cathy Knox and seen to those repairs. A few pounds was all it would have cost them…

The silence in the room was deafening. Sir Nicholas held out the banker's draft out to her.

She stared at it. She could snatch it back and stalk out. It was a lot of money. But this was to have been her night, watched from on high by a proud, if dead, Caleb. And a gesture was clearly called for.

"Keep it," she said grandly. "For your worthy work. Despite your calumny against my late husband, I wish you well in the project. Good evening, Lady Swan."

She stepped down unaided and walked, head high, through the crowd, which parted for her.

She had just given away a horrendous amount of money and gained nothing in return. Nothing.

She was at the foot of the stairs before she realized Silver and Grey were following her.

"Seeing me off the premises?" she said bitterly.

"Making sure you get there in one piece," Silver said. "Only fair when you did the same for us. There's a lot of ill feeling over what happened in St. Giles. Some will regard your donation as blood money."

"That lot ain't innocent," Angela said with contempt.

"Some of them are undoubtedly two-faced, as no one knows better than I, but they don't get to dictate the building work either."

Angela regarded her with growing rancor. "I trusted you, and you stabbed me in the back."

"I almost trusted *you*," Silver said sadly. "But you were manipulating us all the time. You wanted to lower Caleb's hold over his people and gain their support for your leadership with the discovery of his sneaking, squalid affair with Iris under your roof, despite his show of respect to you. You might even have had your own *will no one rid me of this turbulent priest?* moment. Did you hint to Ida Feathers?"

It was the only way to hurt her. "You'll never know, will you? Enjoy your respectability, Silver. It'll drown you in the end."

As a closing line, Angela rather liked it, but Silver ruined it with a spurt of laughter. "Respectability? Angela, I am the madam of a very fine brothel."

*Constance Silver…* At last Angela recognized the name. Without meaning to, she swiveled her gaze to Solomon Grey.

"Oh, he is respectable," Silver assured her. "One of the richest men you'll ever meet, but he can't resist a puzzle."

"Or a dance," Grey said, as the footman opened the front door. "Goodbye, Mrs. Lambert."

CONSTANCE DID NOT turn away until the door clicked shut behind Angela Lambert.

"I suppose you are sorry for her," Solomon said quietly, without accusation.

"Actually, I'm not. She didn't take the money back. It *is* blood money, and you can't buy redemption, but in her mind, I think it's as close as she'll come. She knows the doors are closed to her and she'll probably turn her attention now to Caleb's other businesses."

"And she knows she is under scrutiny for the things she doesn't want to be remembered for."

*A bit like my mother!* Laughter caught in her throat. "Oh, the devil. Solomon, dance with me since I'm here, just once, and then I shall unburden poor Lady Swan of my embarrassing presence."

"Actually, people seem more intrigued than embarrassed by you. You might be the most spectacular of the charity's supporters, but you are far from the only oddity present."

"*Oddity?*" she repeated. "I have a good mind to take my womanly wiles elsewhere."

"You can't," he said. "I've invited you and you're mine."

Stupidly, her heart gave a wild little bound, preventing the smart riposte that hovered on her lips.

In the drawing room, though the walls were lined with people gossiping over the exciting encounter with Lambert's wife, the first waltz was already underway. Lady Griz was sawing away at her violin, and the dance floor whirled with color and glitter.

A few men whispered and giggled behind their hands at the sight of Constance, but not too loudly, for their wives and mothers were present too. No one stalked out at seeing her, no doubt because they would then have to explain to said wives and mothers precisely how they knew who she was. The same kind of reasoning kept the respectable but knowing ladies in the room.

It amused Constance, but it didn't matter to her, not when she strolled at *his* side.

*For this dance, I am his.*

And God help her, it was sweet to be taken in his strong arms, to be held and twirled in the exhilarating Viennese manner. The man had grace and charisma and a light, guiding touch. She felt as if she were spinning off the tension of the case, which was closed, at last, as successfully as they could do within the law. They had solved another case by an incredible piece of good fortune, and were embarking upon two more. Everything was right with the world, and she gave herself leave to enjoy these moments in Solomon's arms. He would never know how intensely.

They waltzed without words, letting their bodies speak. Solomon's beautiful, dark eyes never left her. *My friend, my partner...*

Because she was so absorbed in her own foolish bliss, it was some time before she realized the most astounding thing of all.

Solomon was happy.

She had accused him once of being a stranger to happiness, to those moments of pure joy that made life so precious. She had vowed to find happiness for him, and yet never imagined it would be in a mere dance.

And somehow that was perfection. In wonder, she danced on, utterly lost in the moment that should never end.

It did, of course, as the dance came to a close, and she no longer had the excuse to touch him, to hold his hand and gaze into his eyes like a moonling. But it seemed the communication remained, for as one, they walked out of the drawing room and back downstairs.

She would not draw attention to her presence by seeking out Lady Swan, although she would write her a polite note tomorrow. Solomon murmured something to the footman in the hall, and after only a moment, he placed her evening cloak about her shoulders. His touch made her shiver with awareness once more.

Solomon's carriage awaited them—when had he ordered it?—and he handed her inside. He sat down beside her, not touching, though as soon as the horses moved forward, he swiveled and took both her hands in his.

"Constance. I have something to ask you now."

Reality walloped her, almost like a physical blow. The warmth drained from her, leaving her suddenly anguished.

"Don't, Sol," she whispered. "Please don't."

"Why not?" he asked ruefully.

"Because I don't know if I'll have the strength... Hasn't it been a wonderful evening?"

"It has. Which is why I have to ask. I cannot go on like this,

Constance, with so much simmering beneath the surface. I need…" He caught his breath. "No. First, I want you to know that you are always my friend. Whatever you do or say tonight, whatever decisions we come to, you and I will always be friends. Yes?"

*Then don't speak, don't ask, because I'm not sure I can forgive…*

And yet why not? He was right. Even if she could never meet him or look at him again, even if there were no more mysteries together, on some level they would always be friends.

"Yes," she said shakily. "But please leave it there. Don't—"

"Will you marry me, Constance?" he said desperately.

Something thudded into her stomach, probably her heart. She could not have heard him aright. She only knew her jaw dropped when she tried to speak. Hastily, she closed her mouth, swallowed, and tried again.

"Wh-what did you say?"

A frown flickered across his brow. "I've taken you by surprise," he said slowly, searching her eyes. "What did you think I was going to ask you?"

What men always asked her. The transaction she could not bear with him. But that was not what he'd asked.

"I realize I am probably mad or deaf," she said shakily, "but what you just said sounded ridiculously like a proposal of marriage."

"Why ridiculous?"

"Because you're hugely wealthy and terribly respectable, and I'm the madam of a brothel!"

"We both know what you really are. And what the world says about me behind my back, if not to my face. None of that matters to us. Will you marry me?"

"But…but *why?*"

His Adam's apple jerked, but still he held her gaze. "Because I don't like being without you. Because you infuriate me and make me laugh and think and…you make me happy." His fingers tightened on hers. "And I love you, God help me. I love you. And if you don't yet love me, there is something…"

He trailed off, for without meaning to she had wriggled one hand free and reached up to touch his face with wonder. Annoyed by her gloves, she tugged them off and cupped his face in both trembling hands.

"You love me," she whispered in wonder. "*You* love *me*. In spite of everything…"

"*Because* of everything. It just is."

She trailed her fingers across his lips, which could kiss so fiendishly, so tenderly. "I never thought… I never imagined…"

"Will you risk it?" he asked. "With me? If not, we are still friends. There is still Silver and Grey. But this feeling, this need, is eating me up inside, *gnawing*…"

"Pain and joy and all shades in between," she said.

His shoulders relaxed. A smile tugged at the corners of his eyes. He caught her hand against his lips and kissed it. "You do understand."

"I always loved you. Though I never wanted to, never imagined, ne—"

"Hush," Solomon said hoarsely, and seized her mouth as though he were starving.

So lost was she in his astounding kisses that she didn't notice the carriage had stopped outside her establishment off Grosvenor Square, until he reluctantly raised his head.

The lights were on in the downstairs salons—and, no doubt in the first-floor bedrooms.

"Your house will be quieter," she said.

"Indubitably. But we are not married yet. I shall call tomorrow."

She blinked at him and drew back. "Solomon Grey, are you turning me down?"

He kissed her with an overt, exciting sensuality that left her breathless. "No. I'm courting you."

No one had ever courted her before. "Will I like it?"

His lips twitched. "I hope so. I suspect I will too."

Releasing her, he opened the carriage door and kicked down the steps before alighting and handing her down.

"Solomon?" she said breathlessly. "Are we engaged to be married?"

Somehow, his dark eyes blazed in the lamplight and his teeth shone white. "Oh yes."

She laughed with pure joy as she walked up to the front door. And best of all, she heard the echo of his own happiness behind her.

# About the Author

Mary Lancaster lives in Scotland with her husband, three mostly grown-up kids and a small, crazy dog.

Her first literary love was historical fiction, a genre which she relishes mixing up with romance and adventure in her own writing. Her most recent books are light, fun Regency romances written for Dragonblade Publishing: *The Imperial Season* series set at the Congress of Vienna; and the popular *Blackhaven Brides* series, which is set in a fashionable English spa town frequented by the great and the bad of Regency society.

Connect with Mary on-line – she loves to hear from readers:

Email Mary:
Mary@MaryLancaster.com

Website:
www.MaryLancaster.com

Newsletter sign-up:
http://eepurl.com/b4Xoif

Facebook:
facebook.com/mary.lancaster.1656

Facebook Author Page:
facebook.com/MaryLancasterNovelist

Twitter:
@MaryLancNovels

Amazon Author Page:
amazon.com/Mary-Lancaster/e/B00DJ5IACI

Bookbub:
bookbub.com/profile/mary-lancaster